She tur... she had... only the... day marry, but the hero of her heart.

Despite his years away from the reservation, Joe Ornelas looked every inch the proud Navajo. Just the sight of him created unwelcome quivers inside her. Leftover mementos of a time when she had thought herself falling in love with him. Wasn't it perfectly natural for her body to react in such a way?

Joe came toward her. Slowly. Hesitantly. She waited. Holding her breath. He was as handsome, as utterly masculine, as he had been the day they first met. Never before had she felt such an instant attraction to a man.

Never before did she have to fight so hard to deny it....

Dear Reader,

You've loved Beverly Barton's miniseries THE
PROTECTORS since it started, so I know you'll be
thrilled to find another installment leading off this month.
Navajo's Woman features a to-swoon-for Native American
hero, a heroine capable of standing up to this tough cop—
and enough steam to heat your house. Enjoy!

A YEAR OF LOVING DANGEROUSLY continues with
bestselling author Linda Turner's *The Enemy's Daughter.*
This story of subterfuge and irresistible passion—not to
mention heart-stopping suspense—is set in the Australian
outback, and I know you'll want to go along for the ride.
Ruth Langan completes her trilogy with *Seducing Celeste,*
the last of THE SULLIVAN SISTERS. Don't miss
this emotional read. Then check out Karen Templeton's
Runaway Bridesmaid, a reunion romance with a heroine
who's got quite a secret. Elane Osborn's *Which Twin?*
offers a new twist on the popular twins plotline, while
Linda Winstead Jones rounds out the month with
Madigan's Wife, a wonderful tale of an ex-couple who
truly belong together.

As always, we've got six exciting romances to tempt
you—and we'll be back next month with six more. Enjoy!

Leslie Wainger

Leslie J. Wainger
Executive Senior Editor

Please address questions and book requests to:
Silhouette Reader Service
U.S.: 3010 Walden Ave., P.O. Box 1325, Buffalo, NY 14269
Canadian: P.O. Box 609, Fort Erie, Ont. L2A 5X3

Navajo's Woman
BEVERLY BARTON

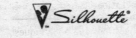

INTIMATE MOMENTS™

Published by Silhouette Books

America's Publisher of Contemporary Romance

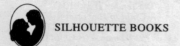 SILHOUETTE BOOKS

ISBN 0-373-27133-6

NAVAJO'S WOMAN

Books by Beverly Barton

Silhouette Intimate Moments

This Side of Heaven #453
Paladin's Woman #515
Lover and Deceiver #557
The Outcast #614
*Defending His Own #670
*Guarding Jeannie #688
*Blackwood's Woman #707
*Roarke's Wife #807
*A Man Like Morgan Kane #819
*Gabriel Hawk's Lady #830
Emily and the Stranger #860
Lone Wolf's Lady #877
*Keeping Annie Safe #937
*Murdock's Last Stand #979
*Egan Cassidy's Kid #1015
Her Secret Weapon #1034
*Navajo's Woman #1063

Silhouette Desire

Yankee Lover #580
Lucky in Love #628
Out of Danger #662
Sugar Hill #687
Talk of the Town #711
The Wanderer #766
Cameron #796
The Mother of My Child #831
Nothing But Trouble #881
The Tender Trap #1047
A Child of Her Own #1077
†His Secret Child #1203
†His Woman, His Child #1209
†Having His Baby #1216

*The Protectors
†3 Babies for 3 Brothers

Silhouette Books

36 Hours
Nine Months

The Fortunes of Texas
In the Arms of a Hero

3,2,1...Married!
"Getting Personal"

BEVERLY BARTON

has been in love with romance since her grandfather gave her an illustrated book of *Beauty and the Beast*. An avid reader since childhood, Beverly wrote her first book at the age of nine. After marriage to her own "hero" and the births of her daughter and son, Beverly chose to be a full-time homemaker, aka wife, mother, friend and volunteer. The author of over thirty-five books, Beverly is a member of Romance Writers of America and helped found the Heart of Dixie chapter in Alabama. She has won numerous awards and made the Waldenbooks and *USA Today* bestseller lists.

To some strong, brave ladies, who have recently gone through a trial of fire, each in her own way. My friends, Marilyn Elrod, Wendy Corsi Staub, Jan Powell and my dear sister-in-law, Winnie Bradford.

Prologue

Bobby Yazzi lay on the floor. Dead. Blood from two fatal bullet wounds covered his yellow shirt and stained the handwoven rug beneath him. Russ Lapahie stood frozen to the spot, his body partially blocking Jewel Begay, who waited in the shadows several feet behind him. If the killer could see her in the semidarkness, he probably wouldn't be able to tell anything except that she was female. With a backward wave of his hand, Russ warned her to escape while she could.

Suddenly he heard the sound of running feet and the outside door slamming shut. Momentary relief spread through him when he realized that she had understood his signal to get the hell out of there. But that relief was short-lived. Across the room, hovering like a fire-breathing dragon preparing to emerge from his den, Bobby's murderer narrowed his gaze and aimed his weapon once again. Light from the lone lamp shining in the living room of Bobby's apartment hit the metal of the gun, which glimmered like diamonds.

Russ had seen the killer's face and recognized him. He was a witness to the murder, and the killer couldn't allow him to live. If he moved, he'd be shot. But if he didn't move... Hell, he was damned no matter what he did.

"Russ, what's going on in here?" Eddie Whitehorn called out as he came barreling through the front door. "Jewel just came out, got in the car and she—" Eddie came to an abrupt halt at Russ's side when he saw the body lying in the middle of the living room floor.

The next thing Russ knew, the dragon emerged. A couple of shots rang out. He and Eddie hit the floor. Crawling. Then they jumped up and ran as fast as their legs would carry them. Breathless. The cool night breeze enveloped their warm, perspiring bodies. Air on dampness. Cold on hot.

"Where's the car?" Russ screamed, in order to hear his own voice over the drumbeat of his heart thundering inside his head.

"Jewel and Martina left us." Eddie ran to keep up with Russ.

Each trying to catch his breath, the two boys hid behind a car parked across the street. Porch lights began coming on. Window blinds and shades came up. A couple of doors opened and several brave residents emerged from their homes.

"We've got to keep running," Russ said. "We have to get out of here before he comes after us."

"We need to call the police," Eddie replied.

"Yeah, sure. And have them ask us what we were doing at Bobby Yazzi's. They'll think we went there for drugs. Man, they're liable to think we killed him!"

"But we didn't—"

"We can talk about this later." Russ grabbed Eddie's arm. "We have to go before he comes after us. I'm telling you, I'm in big trouble. The guy saw me. He knows I can identify him."

Sucking in air hurriedly, the boys eased out from behind the car and ran between a couple of houses. As they passed, Russ caught a glimpse of two men on the porch of the nearest house. The boys didn't linger, didn't slow their pace. Running faster and faster, Russ could think of nothing but getting away from the man who had killed Bobby. He had never seen a human being killed. Shot down. Never watched the blood drain quickly from a body until the heart stopped.

He couldn't let Bobby's murderer find him. And he couldn't call the police. With his reputation as a teenage delinquent, they'd probably lock him up and throw away the key. He had only one choice. Run and hide. And since those people back there had seen Eddie with him, had seen both of them running away from the scene of the crime, then his best friend was in almost as much trouble as he was. If they were going to stay one step ahead of the killer and the police, they'd have to stick together.

Chapter 1

Andi Stephens wandered about inside her house, meandering from room to room in search of something to do—something to occupy her mind. Maybe she should have stayed at the store and taken inventory or priced items for the upcoming sale, but her assistant Barbara Redhorse usually took care of those matters. When she had decided to remain in New Mexico after her initial visit over five years ago, she had needed something to do, something that would occupy her time and also involve her in learning more about her Navajo roots. Her good friend, Joanna Blackwood, had been the one to suggest opening a Native American Arts and Crafts store in Gallup. So, she had delved in to her sizable inheritance from her grandfather and invested in a local business, which actually turned a profit the very first year. But today even her flourishing store couldn't keep her focused. Having been restless and slightly on edge for the past hour, she couldn't seem to relax. She had taken a shower and changed into her soft cotton pajamas, hoping that would put her in the mood for sleep. But she was too wired. And the odd thing was, she wasn't quite sure why. It was as if something was wrong, but she didn't know what. She had been prone to having uneasy feelings ever since she'd been a child. Not that she possessed psychic abilities or anything like that. Not really. She just occasionally got a sense of foreboding. And nine times out of ten, she was right.

She was worried enough to have called to check on her mother, who lived in South Carolina. But Rosemary Stephens had been entertaining a group of society friends and hadn't had time to say more than hello and goodbye. Andi had been tempted to telephone her stepmother who lived on the nearby Navajo Reservation, to check on her and Russ. And she had even started dialing her friend Joanna Blackwood's number before common sense took over and she hung up the phone. Joanna was expecting her fourth child, and although the pregnancy had been perfectly normal, there was always the chance that—

Stop this! an inner voice ordered. *Do you hear me? Stop borrowing trouble. If something is wrong, you'll find out soon enough. No need to make yourself sick.*

Andi found herself in her small kitchen—a bright, light room, with oak cabinets, cream walls and uncurtained windows that overlooked an enclosed backyard. Tea. She'd make herself a cup of herbal tea.

Within minutes, she removed the cup of water she'd heated in the microwave, added a raspberry tea bag and dunked it several times. She preferred her tea mild and plain.

Now what? she asked herself. Try to read? Listen to music? Watch TV? Finding herself back in the living room, she sat in her favorite seat, an oversize, hunter-green leather chair. She stretched her legs out atop the matching ottoman, took a sip of tea and considered her choices. Glancing at the mantel clock, she decided to catch the late-night news and weather.

The remote lay under a couple of magazines on the side table at her right. After several clicks, she found the local channel. But while she drank her tea, her mind wandered, so she paid little attention to the series of commercials that flickered across the twenty-six-inch screen. Ever since she'd had lunch with Joanna this past week, she'd been thinking about Joe Ornelas. Joanna had casually mentioned that Joe, her husband J.T.'s cousin, had sent her a baby gift, with a sweet note attached.

"I can't believe he picked out that adorable little frilly dress himself," Joanna had said.

"Maybe his girlfriend chose it," Andi had replied.

"Maybe. But J.T. says that Joe doesn't have anyone special in his life these days."

Yeah, sure. Like she'd believe that. Joe Ornelas wasn't the type to live without a woman. Perhaps there was no one he considered special, but she'd bet every dime of her inheritance that living there in Atlanta, Georgia, Joe had women swarming around him like bees. She figured he probably had to beat them off with a stick. After all, Joe was a hunk. And a lot of women had a penchant for handsome Native Americans.

Oh, great! You're batting a thousand tonight, aren't you, she scolded herself. *You go from being disturbed by uneasy feelings to mooning over a man who walked out on you five years ago. Andi Stephens, you need to get a life!*

Suddenly the news story on the television caught Andi's attention. She thought she'd heard her brother's name mentioned. Surely, not. The newscaster was talking about a murder case.

After turning up the sound, she focused on the screen. The female news anchor switched over to a live report from the scene of a shooting in Castle Springs, a small town northeast of Gallup and situated within the boundaries of the Navajo Reservation.

"According to his neighbors, Bobby Yazzi, the murder victim, was believed to be involved in selling drugs," the male news reporter said, while the cameraman gave a wide-angle shot of the victim's apartment and of residents milling around on the street. "Although the police haven't released any information about the murder itself, our sources have told us that some neighbors saw two young men running out of the duplex-apartment and into the alley behind their houses. The police have not confirmed this, nor have they identified the young men, but we're told that the eyewitnesses know who the men are and identified them as Russell Lapahie, Jr. and Eddie White-horn, both Navajo youths."

Andi set her tea aside, then listened carefully, trying to absorb every tidbit of information. How was this possible? What were Russ and Eddie doing anywhere near a man like Bobby Yazzi? Russ might be a bit of a hell-raiser, but he really wasn't a bad kid. He was a boy without a father. At sixteen, he was rebelling against his mother, his Native American heritage and anything that even hinted of adult authority.

Five years ago, her half-brother's life had been vastly altered, just as hers had been, when their father committed suicide. Andi had suspected that Russ wanted to distance himself from what friends and family considered his father's shame. Now this had happened. What could it mean?

She had to contact Doli. If her stepmother didn't know about this, then Andi would have to be the one to break

the news to her. Poor Doli. She'd felt lost and confused
trying to raise a strong-willed boy without a man to guide
him. She would blame herself for any trouble Russ had
landed in this time, as she had numerous times in the past.

"This just in," the newscaster reported. "The police
have put out an APB on Russell Lapahie, Jr. and Eddie
Whitehorn. Both young men are wanted for questioning
in the shooting death of Bobby Yazzi."

Poor boys, Andi thought. They had to be frightened.
Scared out of their minds. If they had witnessed the murder, then whoever killed Bobby would know that her
brother and Eddie could identify him.

Just as Andi stood, the telephone rang. With an unsteady hand, she lifted the receiver.

"Hello."

"Andi, this is J.T. By any chance, have you been
watching TV or listening to the radio?"

"Yes, I heard. Russ and Eddie are wanted for questioning." Andi gripped the phone tightly. "What were
they doing at Bobby Yazzi's apartment? Neither of them
are into drugs."

"I have no idea," J.T. said. "Have you spoken with
Doli?"

"No, I was just going to call her, but— Have you spoken to Eddie's parents?"

"Yeah." J.T. paused, took a deep breath and continued.
"I'm on my way over to Castle Springs now to meet Ed
and Kate at the police station. Do you want me to contact
Doli?"

"No, I'll call her and then I'll drive over to the reservation and stay with her until we find out what's going
on."

Andi said goodbye, hung up the receiver and huffed
out a long, loud sigh. Her uneasy feeling had proven to

be right, once again. Her unerringly accurate premonition of trouble had been fulfilled. That sense of foreboding had, in the past, forecast sickness, death and accidents, usually involving someone close to her. She wished that just this once she could have been wrong.

Russ hot-wired the old truck, a rusty relic from the fifties, but one that purred like a kitten when the motor turned over.

"Damn it, Russ, this is stealing!" Eddie, who sat alongside his friend in the cab of the truck, looked from side to side out the windows, then glanced over his shoulder.

"Hey, we have to get some kind of transportation, don't we?" Russ shifted gears, eased the truck backward and quickly maneuvered it onto the road. "We can't get very far on foot and we can't keep hiding out here in town. We're taking Mr. Lovato's truck in order to save our lives."

"Yeah, well, the police will call what we're doing stealing."

"I call it borrowing," Russ reiterated.

On the road out of Castle Springs, they met several trucks and a couple of cars, but traffic was slow and no one followed them. Eddie rolled down a window and the cool night wind whipped his long hair into his face.

He didn't know what the heck he was doing here, on the run with Russ. Everything had happened so fast, too fast for him to think straight, to reason the right and wrong, the good and the bad. If he'd had any sense at all, he'd have vetoed the idea of going to Bobby Yazzi's to pick up some beer. Everybody knew that Bobby could provide not only the drug of your choice, but liquor of any kind to underage drinkers. When Russ's date, Jewel

Begay, had made the suggestion to pick up some beer and
Russ had agreed, Eddie hadn't wanted to come off sound-
ing like some scared little boy. After all, he'd had a date
to impress. If Jewel hadn't arranged the double date, he
wouldn't have had a prayer of going out with a girl like
Martina. Pretty and popular and from a good Navajo family.

When his parents found out he'd been at Bobby
Yazzi's, what would they think? God, he hated even
imagining their reaction. Their eldest son, of whom they
were so proud, involved in a murder!

Russ flipped on the radio and fiddled with the dials,
zipping from one station to another, finally settling on
one. A country hit whined down to the last stanza, then
news on the half hour began.

"There's an update on the murder case we told you
about at ten," the announcer said. "Two Navajo youths—
Russell Lapahie, Jr. and Eddie Whitehorn, are wanted for
questioning in regard to the Bobby Yazzi murder that occurred around eight o'clock tonight. Both Lapahie and
Whitehorn were seen running from the victim's apartment
shortly after neighbors heard several shots fired.

"Lapahie, the son of former Navajo police captain,
Russell Lapahie, Sr., is a resident of Castle Springs and
well known in town. The other youth, Whitehorn, lives
on a sheep ranch between Castle Springs and Trinidad.
Police aren't saying if the boys are suspects in the case,
but they have issued an APB on the two."

Russ shut off the radio and increased the speed of the
truck. "Hell! I knew the police would think I did it. With
my record of trouble making and my father's reputation
ruined because your uncle Joe ratted on him, I'm as good
as dead."

"The police just want us for questioning," Eddie said.

"I think we should go back, turn ourselves in and tell them what happened."

"Do you honestly think they're going to believe us?"

"They might."

"Yeah, well, even if they do—and I don't think they will—what about the guy who really killed Bobby? He won't have any trouble killing both of us to keep us quiet."

"Jewel can back up your story. She went in at Bobby's with you."

"Jewel was so scared that she ran, didn't she? She didn't hang around to see if we got out okay. She's not going to want to get involved. She could easily deny having seen or heard anything, just to cover her own butt."

As much as Eddie hated to admit that Russ was right, he nodded his head in agreement. Being on the run from the police and from a ruthless killer wasn't what Eddie wanted. But what choice did he have? He couldn't turn against his best friend, could he?

"We're in this together, right?" Russ cut Eddie a sideways glance.

"Yeah. Right."

Joe Ornelas popped the caps off six bottles, placed the open beer on a tray and carried the refreshments out from behind the bar that separated his compact kitchen from his combination dining and living room. Hunter Whitelaw and Jack Parker still sat at the table where they'd been playing cards. Matt O'Brien picked up the TV remote and said something about checking ball scores on ESPN. Wolfe stood by the windows, his back to the rest of the Dundee agents, as he stared out into the rainy Atlanta night. Ellen Denby, their boss lady, came toward Joe, smiling.

"Need some help?" she asked.

"Just help yourself," he replied, holding the tray out to her. "What's up with Wolfe?" Joe nodded toward the solitary figure by the double windows that overlooked Salle Street. "This is the first time he's taken me up on my offer to play cards. I had begun to think he was avoiding our company."

Ellen lifted a bottle from the tray. "He knows all of us a little better than he did a few months ago. I think working closely with you and Hunter on rescuing Egan Cassidy's kid might have helped." Ellen glanced over her shoulder at Wolfe, who seemed preoccupied with his own thoughts. "He's a loner if I ever saw one."

"Where's that beer?" Hunter threw up his hand and motioned to Joe to come to him. "While you're making brownie points with the boss, I'm dying of thirst." Hunter laughed. Long, low, deep, grunting chuckles.

As Joe passed the sofa where Matt sat engrossed in the sportscast, Joe handed him a beer, then headed toward the table. He placed the tray in the center, which only five minutes earlier had held the night's winnings. After Jack and Hunter grabbed their beverages, Joe picked up the two remaining bottles and walked toward the man who had separated himself from the others.

"Beer?" Joe held up a bottle in offering.

Wolfe turned slowly, nodded, accepted the beer and said, "Thanks."

"I'm glad you decided to join us tonight," Joe told him.

"I appreciate your asking me." Wolfe lifted the bottle to his lips and downed a hefty swig.

"Feel free to join us anytime. The players change, depending on who's in town, and we rotate apartments. Next week, it's Ellen's turn."

"Uh-huh."

Joe had thought himself a man of few words, but compared to Wolfe he was a regular chatterbox. The others had speculated about the reclusive agent, who'd been with Dundee's Private Security and Investigation less than a year. Unlike the rest of them, who'd been hired by Ellen, Wolfe held the distinction of having been chosen by the owner of the agency, Sam Dundee. No one knew anything about Wolfe—not even Ellen. But she had quickly ascertained that the man had undeniable abilities. He was not only an expert marksman, but he had a knowledge of every aspect of the business, from weapons to strategy, from equipment to psychology.

"Damn!" Matt jumped up from the sofa. "I just lost fifty bucks on the Braves game."

"That's what you get for gambling," Ellen said.

"Look who's talking," Matt told her. "You lost thirty dollars tonight playing cards. Hell, add the fifty I lost on the ball game to the forty-five I lost here and I'm nearly a hundred dollars poorer."

"We had no idea what an expert card player Wolfe was," Hunter said. "He took us all to the cleaners."

"Are you sure you've never been a professional?" Matt asked, looking directly at Wolfe.

Wolfe shook his head. "No."

"Ah, the guy's just good at cards, the way he is at everything else." Hunter rose from his chair to his full six-four height.

Joe noted a pained expression on Wolfe's face, as if Hunter's comment had somehow hurt him. But surely, no one would be hurt by a sincere compliment, would they?

"I should be going." Wolfe placed his half-empty bottle down on the tray atop the table.

"Yeah, me, too." Matt downed the last drops of his

beer, then tossed the empty bottle to Joe, who caught it
effortlessly in his left hand while continuing to hold his
own bottle in his right.

"Yeah, it's about time I called it a night," Jack Parker
said in his deep, Texas drawl, then scooted back his chair
and got up.

The telephone rang just as Wolfe opened the apartment
door. Not looking back, he made a hasty exit. Jack Parker
waved goodbye and followed Wolfe. Matt lingered in the
doorway.

"Need a ride home, Denby?" He smiled, showing a
set of movie-star teeth.

"You know Hunter's taking me home," she replied.

"Yeah, I know, but you can't shoot a guy for trying."

"Our Ellen can and *would* shoot you." Hunter chuckled.

"You guys hold it down," Joe told them as he lifted
the telephone receiver. "Yeah, Ornelas here."

"Matt, you can give up trying," Ellen said, smiling. "I
don't date Dundee employees."

"So how come Hunter can escort you around and I
can't?" Matt leaned against the door.

Joe covered the receiver with his hand, gave his com-
panions a stern look and repeated, "Hold it down. I can't
hear what my sister's saying."

"Because Hunter is a gentleman and you're not," Ellen
said softly, then nodded and waved to Joe, letting him
know that she'd heard him, understood and would be quiet
now.

Joe removed his hand from the mouthpiece. "Sorry
about that, Kate, but I've got a few friends over tonight."

"You must come home, Joseph." Kate's voice held an
edge of near hysteria and it wasn't normal for his sweet,
easygoing sister to be this upset.

"What's wrong?"

"It's Eddie. He's in big trouble. We need you very badly."

"What kind of trouble is Eddie in?"

"Trouble with the—" Kate's voice broke "—the police." She sighed. "He and Russ Lapahie are wanted for questioning in the murder of Bobby Yazzi, a man who is known for selling drugs to our children."

Joe's heartbeat accelerated. Eddie was in trouble with the police? He couldn't imagine anything so ridiculous. Not a good kid like his eldest nephew, who was a bright student, an obedient son and a hard worker, helping his father on the ranch since he'd been not much more than a toddler.

"You said that Eddie is wanted by the police. Where is he now? Why hasn't he turned himself in?"

"We don't know where he is. Eddie and Russ are both missing. They've run away—"

Kate whimpered, and Joe knew she was struggling with her emotions, trying to not break down and cry.

"Andi says that their running makes them look guilty," Kate said.

"Andi's good at finding people guilty." The mention of Andi's name struck a disharmonious chord in Joe. He had spent five years trying to forget about the past, trying to put Andrea Stephens out of his mind.

"No, you misunderstand," Kate told him. "Andi doesn't think the boys are guilty. She knows they aren't capable of murder. She simply pointed out what is so obvious—that by running, Eddie and Russ have only made matters worse for themselves."

Ellen laid a hand on Joe's shoulder and whispered, "Is there anything we can do?"

"Hold on, Kate." Joe turned to Ellen. "Yeah. I'm go-

ing to need some time off. I have to go home. My
nephew's in trouble.''

"Take all the time you need," Ellen said. "If I or the
agency can help, all you have to do is call me."

"Thanks."

"We'll let ourselves out." Hunter escorted Ellen to the
open door, and they and Matt waved good-night, then
closed the door behind them.

"I'll take the first flight I can get. The Dundee jet isn't
available right now. I'll call you back when I've made
arrangements."

"Ed and I will meet your plane."

"Be brave."

"Yes, I am trying."

Joe replaced the receiver when the dial tone hummed
in his ear. He and Kate had been as close as a brother
and sister could be. He was the younger sibling, but only
two years separated them in age. She had married Ed
Whitehorn when she was twenty and had given birth to
her first child at twenty-one. The entire family had adored
Eddie, such a beautiful, clever child. Until Joe had re-
signed from the Navajo Tribal police force and left his
home in New Mexico five years ago, he and his nephew
had been the best of buddies. And even now, the two
spoke often on the phone. He simply could not imagine
how a good boy like Eddie could be involved in anyone's
murder, even as a witness. Unless he'd been in the wrong
place at the wrong time. But why would Eddie have been
anywhere near a known drug dealer? And why had the
boy run away?

Russ Lapahie was the answer to all Joe's questions. J.T.
had told him that Russell's son had been in and out of
trouble ever since Russell's death. Trouble at school, trouble at home and trouble with the law.

"Doli can't do anything with him," J.T. had said. "And he won't listen to Andi, either. They're both 'just women,' as far as Russ is concerned."

Joe grunted. To think that he had been the one to advise Ed and Kate not to forbid Eddie to hang out with Russ. He had mistakenly hoped that his nephew would be a good influence on Andi's brother. Now, it looked as if he'd been wrong. The opposite had happened.

He couldn't deny that his bad advice had been prompted partly out of guilt. After all, if Joe had looked the other way and kept his mouth shut five years ago, when he had discovered Russell Sr. was covering up his brother-in-law's livestock smuggling ring, his former police captain would still be alive. And Russ and Andi would still have their father. The way Joe figured it, he not only had to go home to help Eddie, but to help Russell's son, too.

"I want those boys found!" The dark hand that slammed down on the desk bore several crisscrossed scars, reminders of a long-ago knife fight. A fight he had won. Three diamond rings sparkled on various fingers, each catching the light from the green-shaded lamp to his right.

LeCroy Lanza glowered at his subordinates, both men killers by instinct and training. In his line of work, it didn't pay to send out a boy to do a man's job. He wanted Russ Lapahie and Eddie Whitehorn found and taken care of so that neither boy could identify him. He'd seen Russ's face and had laughed silently at the boy's wide-eyed shock after he'd witnessed the murder. He had seen the shadow of another person behind Russ, but LeCroy hadn't been able to make out much. At the time, he'd thought the second kid was female. Apparently, it had been Eddie.

In retrospect, he realized that he should have sent someone else to take care of Bobby Yazzi, the two-timing little son of a bitch. But LeCroy Lanza had a reputation to uphold. He was known for taking care of his problems personally. And Bobby had become a major problem. Who had he thought he was—lying and cheating, stealing from the man who'd set him up in business? Nobody cheated LeCroy Lanza and lived.

"Charlie, you find out where those boys went. Hire some trackers, if necessary. I'll call in a few favors and see if I can get any information that might help us." LeCroy gripped Charlie Kirk's shoulder. "I want those boys dead before they have a chance to talk to the police."

Chapter 2

Joe hadn't been home in five years, although his job as a Dundee agent had brought him out west a couple of times. When he'd left the reservation three weeks after Russell Lapahie's suicide, he'd gone straight to Atlanta and had begun working for the Dundee agency. A couple of times his sister Kate and her family had come to Georgia to visit, and he kept in contact weekly by phone. And he and his cousin J. T. Blackwood e-mailed each other on a regular basis and spoke on the phone from time to time. Otherwise, he had cut himself off from his past, from his people and from his heritage.

Did he ever miss his old life? Did a part of him still long to truly be one of the *Dine?* Yeah, sure, in those dark, lonely moments when he had allowed himself to remember, he'd longed to see the *Dinehtah.* The land of the Navajo. He had been born here in New Mexico, on the reservation, and had grown to manhood within the closely knit family of his mother's clan, just outside the

town of Castle Springs. He had been proud of his heritage
and honored to become a member of the Navajo Tribal
Police. Once, Joe had thought of himself as a good guy,
a role model for other Navajo youths, and at times, even
a hero. But his days of being a hero, in anyone's eyes,
including his own, died along with Russell Lapahie.

His devotion to his family and his people had been the
driving factor in his life, but all of that had ended the day
Russell committed suicide. His friends, acquaintances and
fellow officers seemed to forget that Russell had been the
one who had betrayed his trusted position on the police
force. That Russell had been the one who had committed
a crime. During the worst of the maelstrom that infected
their lives from the moment he arrested his captain until
after Russell's funeral, Joe had begun to doubt himself.
Had he been wrong to reveal the crime and arrest the
culprit because that man had been his friend and a supe-
rior officer? A lot of people seemed to think so. Including
Andi, Russell's daughter. She had turned on Joe with a
vengeance.

If she had stood by him, supported him, believed in
him, would he have stayed in Castle Springs? Maybe.
After all these years, he wasn't sure anymore. Not about
himself. And certainly not about his feelings for Andi. All
he knew was that at some time during the past five years,
his guilt and remorse over Russell's death had turned to
anger. How could a man he had hero-worshiped have
acted so dishonorably? Russell's actions had not only destroyed his own life, but altered the course of other lives.
Joe's. Andi's. Russ, Jr.'s. Doli's. Everyone who had loved
and trusted Russell.

Joe could not help thinking how odd it was that he, a
Navajo born on the reservation, who spoke Saad and had
tried to follow the traditional ways, who had once worn

a medicine pouch inside his trousers and kept a feather attached to the rearview mirror of his truck to ward off evil spirits, who had attended the Navajo Community College in Tsaile, had been forced to leave all that he cherished. And Andi, born and reared as a *bilagaana,* had stayed on in New Mexico and embraced the heritage of a father she had barely known, of a people who had been strangers to her.

Whenever J.T. happened to mention Andi, Joe always managed to change the subject. He hadn't wanted to hear anything about her, hadn't wanted to know if she had married, if she'd had children. She was nothing to him. Less than nothing. But today he would have to see her again, come face-to-face with the woman who, if she had truly loved him, might now be his wife.

There was a stark, majestic beauty to his homeland. Mesas and canyons, wide valleys and narrow mountain ranges. On this drive from the police station to Kate's ranch outside Castle Springs, he felt more homesick than he had when he'd been far away in Georgia. In five years, he had almost forgotten what it meant to be a Navajo, even though by his appearance alone he proclaimed his Native American ancestry. In Atlanta, he had grown accustomed to living a white man's life, which in many ways he enjoyed. He had once thought he could never survive in the outside world, the world to which Andi had belonged. Strange that he now felt like an outsider in his own land. When they had been dating, Andi had told him that she wasn't sure she could live on the reservation and adapt to Navajo life. Back then, he had thought their lifestyles might be the only factor that could keep them apart.

The road leading from the highway to Kate and Ed's ranch lay just ahead on the right. They had lived in a trailer when he'd left the reservation, but three years ago

they'd built a house in the middle of their land. He and
Kate shared acres of land that comprised the sheep ranch,
and his own small house still stood several miles from his
sister's.

Kate had offered to meet him at the airport, but he'd
told her that he would just rent a car and drive out to their
place. His first stop after landing in Gallup had been the
police station in Castle Springs. He hadn't been sure what
to expect, since most of the people working there had
been his fellow officers five years ago. The reunion had
been surprisingly friendly. The new captain and an old
friend, Bill Cummings, had shared all the information they
had on the Bobby Yazzi murder case.

"Do you really think that Russ and Eddie might have
killed Bobby?" Joe had asked.

"I would like to believe that the boys only witnessed
the murder," Bill had said. "Sometimes the innocent run,
but... They are not helping themselves by trying to elude
us. If they didn't kill Bobby, they should not have run."

Joe eased the rental car off onto the long, narrow road
winding through the ranch land. He dreaded facing Kate,
seeing the fear and agony in her eyes. Her first born was
in danger, and she was powerless to help him. She was
counting on her brother to save her son. Joe only hoped
he could.

When Joe drew near the house—a clapboard painted
the color of golden sand—his sister and brother-in-law
came out onto the porch. Kate lifted her hand to shield
her eyes from the sun when she walked into the yard. She
was a lovely woman. Short, slightly plump and exotically
dark. A pair of faded jeans clung to her womanly curves.

The moment he parked, Kate ran toward him. He had
no more than slammed the door shut when she stopped

directly in front of him. Tears clouded her black eyes. He grasped her shoulders.

"You must find Eddie," she said.

The trembling in her body vibrated through his hands. "I will find him. I promise." *Let me be able to keep that vow,* he prayed silently.

In his peripheral vision, Joe saw his brother-in-law's short, barrel-chested, stocky frame shadowed by the edge of the porch roof. At his side stood six-year-old Joey, Joe's namesake. And there, hiding halfway behind her brother, was ten-year-old Summer.

Kate grabbed Joe's hand. "Come. You must be tired and hungry after your long flight. I have stew ready for lunch."

Kate was so much like their mother had been, a gracious hostess to family and friends. Always enough food to share. Always a warm smile and a generous heart.

His dark-eyed niece and nephew stared at Joe, as Kate twined her arm through his and led him toward the house. Smiling at Joey, he ruffled the boy's hair.

Joey smiled back at him and said, *"Ya'at'eeh."*

"Welcome, Joseph." Ed Whitehorn nodded his head in greeting.

"Thank you." Joe liked Ed, a quiet, soft-spoken man, a hard worker and a devoted husband and father. Joe turned his attention to his shy little niece, a carbon copy of her mother. "Aren't you going to say hello to me, Summer?"

Leaning her head to one side and smiling timidly, she fluttered her long black eyelashes and spoke softly. "Hello, Uncle Joe."

"You've certainly grown since the last time I saw you. And you're as pretty as your mother."

Summer awarded Joe with a broad smile. "'*Ahehee*','" she said, thanking him for the compliment.

Joe lifted Joey to his shoulders, much to the boy's delight, then grasped Summer's hand and tugged her closer to him. "Your mother has promised me lunch. Is anyone else hungry?"

The children giggled as they entered the house with their uncle. Side by side, touching only in spirit, their parents followed.

Just an inch shy of six feet, Joe had to duck down to enter through the front door, in order to make sure Joey's head didn't strike the door frame. Once inside the house, Joe came to an abrupt halt before he had taken more than two steps into the cosy, colorful family room.

Standing there in the archway between the family room and the dining area was a woman. Long, flowing, dark brown hair cascaded over her shoulders. Pale golden eyes gazed at him. Andrea Stephens was tall, slender and somehow elegant in her jeans, boots and bold red-and-blue plaid shirt. Tiny diamonds sparkled in her earlobes, a remnant of her wealthy South Carolina upbringing. And a wide band of turquoise-laden silver circled her right wrist. Joe's stomach knotted painfully. He had given her the bracelet, created by his silversmith great-grandfather and passed down to him by his mother. Why did she still wear the bracelet? Or had she simply put it on today, to taunt him?

Joe eased Joey from his shoulders and placed the boy on his feet. Both children stayed at his side as he stood frozen to the spot. He said nothing, only stared at Andi. Kate and Ed came inside, and within minutes Kate hurried toward her guest.

"Andi is going to have lunch with us," Kate said. "She asked to be here to meet with you. She is as anxious to find the boys as we are. She is going to represent the Lapahie family today.''

''Where is Doli Lapahie?'' Joe asked, without breaking eye contact with Andi.

''My stepmother has been distraught since she learned about Bobby Yazzi's murder and the possibility that Russ witnessed the crime,'' Andi said. ''Dr. Harvey gave her a sedative last night and left instructions with her sister to keep her medicated if necessary. Doli is not a strong woman. Not since...''

Joe felt the sting of accusation without Andi actually blasting him with the words. He knew what she'd been about to say. *Not since my father killed himself. Not since you betrayed a man who had treated you like a son.*

Averting his gaze from her face, Joe cleared his throat. ''I stopped by the police station in Castle Springs, and Bill Cummings filled me in on what happened. I can't understand why Eddie and Russ ran away. If they weren't involved—''

Kate and Andi cut him off simultaneously, saying, ''They weren't involved.''

''How can you think such a thing?'' Kate glowered at her brother.

''Did Captain Cummings say that he believes Russ and Eddie were involved in Bobby Yazzi's murder?'' Andi asked.

''He didn't come right out and say so, but he's puzzled by their running away. I'm sure he told you that he sees it as a possible sign of guilt.''

''I do not believe my son is capable of killing another human being, and I told this to Bill Cummings last night.'' Kate shook her head, regret in her voice and apparent in the desolation of her expression.

"I agree," Joe said. "I don't think Eddie would kill someone."

Andi lurched forward, as if shoved by an unseen hand. Her topaz eyes gleamed brightly when she confronted Joe. "But you think Russ might have killed Bobby, don't you. You are only too eager to believe that this is all my brother's fault, just as you once—" Andi broke off, then rushed past Joe and outside, crashing the storm door closed behind her.

"Damn it, I didn't accuse Russ of anything!" Joe hammered his fist against the nearby wall. Nothing had changed—not between Andi and him. Her distrust and hatred pulsated with energy. She had not forgiven him and probably never would.

"Do not curse in front of my children," Kate scolded.

"Sorry." Joe rubbed his knuckles.

"You must go after Andi and tell her that you—"

"I'm not going after her. I didn't invite her here. I didn't want to see her or talk to her. As far as I'm concerned, she can go back to wherever she came from and stay there." He couldn't say—wouldn't admit to his family—that just the sight of Andi Stephens brought back all the emotions he had tried so hard to forget. The love and passion. The anger, guilt and remorse. She would forever be a reminder of his own shortcomings, his failure to live up to the expectations of all who had known and admired him.

Ed laid his hand on Joe's shoulder, but looked at his wife. "Take the children into the kitchen and prepare our lunch." The moment Kate scurried Joey and Summer through the house and disappeared into the kitchen, Ed tightened his hold on Joe. "We are all very worried. Kate and I. Doli and Andi. We are concerned about Eddie and

Russ. They are both only sixteen. Young men now, but in many ways still boys. Boys who need our help.''

Joe realized that Ed had just chastised him in his own kind, subtle way. ''That's why I came home. To help Eddie. And to help Russ, too. I figure I owe it to Russell to do what I can for his son.''

Ed patted Joe on the back. ''You are a good man.''

Joe shrugged. ''I'm not so sure about that. Nobody around here thought I was much of a hero five years ago, did they.''

''When Russell died, feelings were running high among family and friends,'' Ed told him. ''You did not give anyone a chance to recover from the shock, before you ran away.''

Yeah, he'd run, all right. As far and as fast as he could. Back in the good old days, when he'd been a policeman, he had respected himself and enjoyed the admiration of others. He had prided himself on being a good Navajo and a good man. But for the past five years he had questioned himself, every choice, every decision he'd made. He had thought he was doing the right thing when he exposed Russell's duplicity. The man had been his captain, his friend, a father figure to him since he'd been a teenager. And at the same time Russell Lapahie had been a man torn between duty and family loyalty, between upholding the law and breaking the commandments he had revered all his life.

And Joe had faced his own moment of truth. He had done the legally correct thing. But had he been wrong to expose Russell's crime? Damn the man for having put him in such a position. A part of him could not forgive Russell for having placed him in such a no-win situation. And another part would never forgive himself.

''Go. Speak with Andi.'' Ed squeezed Joe's shoulder,

then released his gentle hold and joined his wife in the kitchen.

Joe didn't move for several minutes. Everything within him balked at the suggestion. He couldn't talk to Andi, couldn't make her see reason. He'd been in her presence only a few minutes, and already she had put words into his mouth, immediately assuming the worst about him.

How would it be possible for the two of them to act like normal, rational people when they distrusted each other so vehemently? The past lay between them, an old wound reopened, or perhaps never truly healed. He suspected that Andi had no more come to terms with Russell's death than he had. Five years and fifteen-hundred miles apart—and yet they shared a grief that would forever bind them, and just as surely keep them apart.

Shaded by the branches of a pair of scraggly pinyon pines, Andi breathed deeply, drawing huge gulps of air into her lungs as she struggled to regain control of her emotions. She had known this would happen and yet she'd been given little choice but to come here today and meet Joe again after all these years. He had no more than opened his mouth before he'd practically accused Russ of being a murderer. Oh, he hadn't come right out and put his feelings into words, not exactly. But his meaning had been clear. He thought the worst of her brother, just as he had of her father.

If Doli were capable of dealing with this horrendous situation, Andi might be spared seeing Joe again, spending time with him. But Doli was an emotionally and physically fragile woman, even more so since her husband's death. Her stepmother had held her hand last night and pleaded with her to help Russ.

"You will find him," Doli had said. "And prove that he is an innocent boy."

From the moment she learned what had happened with Russ and Eddie, Andi had known that Kate and Ed would notify Joe. Who in their family was better qualified to track down his nephew than Joe Ornelas, former Navajo Tribal police officer and now an agent with a prestigious protection and security firm? And there had been no question in her mind that *she* would be the one to protect her brother, to make sure no one—especially not Joe—would place all the blame on Russ's shoulders. Somehow she had to find a way to grow a tougher hide, and do it immediately. Their meeting didn't bode well for future cooperation. But cooperate she would, even if it killed her. Whatever Joe did, she would be looking over his shoulder. Wherever he went, she would be one step behind him. When he found the boys, she would be at his side. No way would she trust him to look out for Russ's best interests. Only she could do that.

Andi would never allow Joe to destroy her brother, defile his reputation and publicly crucify him. She had been unable to help her father, to prevent him from taking his own life. But by God, she could and would do everything in her power to save Russ. She owed him that much. Owed her father, too, to protect his only son, not only from the real killer and the Navajo police, but from Joe Ornelas.

"Andi."

She went rigid at the sound of Joe's voice. Only in her dreams, often nightmares, had she heard Joe call to her. *Go away. Leave me alone,* she wanted to shout. He was the last man on earth she wanted to see, to be with. But they shared a common goal—the rescue of two young boys, each a family member, each a beloved child of people for whom they cared deeply.

You can do this, she told herself. *Put aside whatever you feel for Joe and do what must be done in order to save Russ.*

She turned to face the man she had once believed to be not only the person she would one day marry, but the hero of her heart. But Joe Ornelas was no hero. Not in her eyes or the eyes of his people.

Just the sight of him created unwelcome quivers inside her. Leftover mementos of a time when she had thought herself falling in love with him. Wasn't it perfectly natural for her body to react in such a way? It *was* possible to intensely dislike someone and yet still find them devastatingly attractive.

Another uphill battle to fight, she surmised. Although she had stopped caring for Joe years ago, her body had not forgotten the pleasure of his touch. Her one regret had become her one comfort—that in the past, their relationship had not had time to reach the point of complete sexual intimacy, before he betrayed her.

Joe came toward her. Slowly. Hesitantly. She waited. Holding her breath. He was as handsome, as utterly masculine, as he had been the day they first met. She remembered so well when her father had introduced them—the young man he thought of as a son and the daughter he'd never known existed. Her heart had beaten a little faster. Her stomach had filled with dancing butterflies. Never before had she felt such an instant attraction to a man.

Don't let those old feelings confuse you now, she cautioned herself. *Joe isn't here to help Russ. He's come home to help Eddie.* She didn't dare trust him.

A warm August breeze caressed Joe's long black hair. Several silky locks fell across his face. He brushed them aside with a sweep of his large, wide hand. A gray, short-sleeved cotton sweater covered his broad, muscular upper body and a pair of black jeans clung to his lean hips and long legs. The turquoise-nugget necklace with a circular silver center that he had always worn shone brightly against the coppery tan of his neck. Despite his years away from the reservation, he looked every inch the proud Navajo.

But this man wasn't the Joe Ornelas she had known. He had gone out into the world, far from his roots, and experienced life as the white man lived it. He had become a part of the society into which she had been born and reared. There had been a time when he had thought he could never survive in the white man's world, and she had been certain that she could never live the Navajo life. When they had first begun dating that difference had been the only thing she'd thought would ever come between them.

Joe halted several feet away from her. "Kate has lunch ready. Won't you come back inside and eat with us?"

"Yes, of course, I will," Andi replied. "I would never do anything to offend Kate. I know she's as distraught over what has happened with Russ and Eddie as Doli and I are."

"If I need to apologize—"

"You don't!" Andi's gaze locked with Joe's, and for one timeless moment she felt light-headed. Breaking eye contact, she shifted her feet back and forth in the dry soil, sending tiny dust storms up and about her ankles.

"Both J.T. and Kate have mentioned several times over the past few years that Doli has been having problems with Russ." Joe stood rigid as a statue, his hands tense, his expression guarded. "But I didn't mean to imply that I thought he had killed Bobby Yazzi."

"There isn't much point in our having this conversation, is there? Even if you don't believe that Russ is a murderer, you are convinced that however Russ and Eddie are involved with Bobby, Russ is somehow the one to blame."

"Why must you put words in my mouth?"

"Are you denying that you think Russ somehow influenced Eddie, that he's the one who got the two of them into trouble?"

"No, I cannot deny that I don't think Eddie would be in this situation on his own. But that doesn't mean I—"

"Why is it that you can so easily be judge, jury and executioner, when you don't have all the facts?" Andi walked over and stood in front of him, then lifted her head and glared into his solemn eyes.

"Damn," Joe cursed under his breath.

Andi trembled from head to toe. She balled her hands into tight fists as she held them on either side of her hips. With only the slightest provocation, she could easily pummel that broad chest, venting years of anger and frustration on his hard body. Joe had discovered her father's crime, and without giving him the benefit of the doubt or trying to understand what had motivated Russell, he had arrested a good man for one forgivable error in judgment. Joe had judged Russell Lapahie guilty and unknowingly sentenced him to death. The fact that Joe had not been the one who pulled the trigger on the gun that killed her father did not make him any the less guilty of his execution.

And it didn't help any more now than it had been five years ago that Joe felt guilty, that he was filled with remorse. She understood that Joe never meant to harm her father, but all the regrets in the world couldn't change what had happened, couldn't bring Russell back to life.

And no matter how hard she tried, she would never be able to trust Joe. Never again. She had trusted him completely once, and not only had he betrayed her trust in him, but he had run away instead of staying and facing the consequences of his actions.

"Maybe it's best if you and I don't see each other again after today," Joe said. "Any information I have, I can pass along to you through a third party. Kate or—"

"Wrong." Andi glowered at him, her heartbeat drumming inside her head. "If you think, for one minute, that I'm going to let you go after Russ and Eddie alone, then you'd better think again. Wherever you go and whatever you do from now until the moment we find those boys, I'm going to be your shadow."

"No, you won't. I don't need you or want you..." Joe hesitated, shifted mental gears, then cleared his throat. "You'll just get in the way."

"I don't care what you want. I'm coming with you and that's that."

"No. J.T. and I can handle things. We are both trained for this type of situation. You are not. So just get any ideas you have of tagging along with us out of your head. You are not going."

Andi punched him in the center of his chest with her index finger. "You just try to stop me."

Chapter 3

I have no intention of giving Joe a choice in the matter! He's not leaving me out of the search for Russ and Eddie. Andi was determined to be involved in every aspect of the hunt. She couldn't trust Joe, not when it came to her brother's life. The initial meeting at Kate and Ed Whitehorn's earlier today had been less than productive. She'd found Joe to be as stubborn and unbending as he'd been five years ago, when his go-by-the-rules-at-any-cost attitude had destroyed her father.

Remembering Russell Lapahie still evoked a mixture of emotions within Andi, but foremost a great sense of loss. The man had been a father she'd barely known, and to this day she felt cheated by his death. Only six months before that fateful day when Russell had taken his own life, she had been living in South Carolina, the daughter of wealthy, socially prominent parents, with her life as a socialite all mapped out for her. She'd been practically engaged to a childhood friend, Tyler Markey IV, an up-

and-coming young state senator. But everything had changed when her parents decided to divorce, the result of her father's adulterous affair with a girl half his age. Distraught and filled with rage, Rosemary Stephens had blurted out to Andi that Randall Stephens wasn't even her real father. At that moment, Andi realized why she'd always felt different, as if she didn't quite fit into her parents' neat little world. And it had suddenly made sense why she had never felt loved by the man she'd thought was her father.

"It happened while I was in New Mexico with friends, shortly before I married your...before I married Randall," Rosemary had explained. "He was a handsome young Navajo man, and we were instantly attracted to each other. The affair lasted for one glorious week. He was so smitten that he asked me to marry him. But, of course, that was out of the question. He was poor. I was rich. He was an Indian and I was—"

"You were a bigot," Andi had all but screamed at her mother. "He was good enough to have sex with, but not good enough to marry."

"I didn't love Russell," Rosemary had admitted. "It was hot sex and nothing more. I'm sorry, Andrea, but that's the truth."

"Russell? His name is Russell...what?"

"Lapahie. Russell Lapahie. He lived on the reservation. His dream was to be a Tribal police officer."

"Is he still alive?" Andi had asked.

"I have no idea." Rosemary had gasped when she realized her daughter's intentions. "You aren't thinking of trying to find him, are you? Darling, he has no idea you even exist."

Two weeks after that revealing conversation with her mother, Andi had headed west. In search of a father who didn't know his brief affair with a vacationing Southern belle had resulted in a child. In search of a heritage that had been denied her, a birthright she had every intention of claiming. That had been five-and-a-half years ago.

As Andi drove her white Ford Expedition up to the open gates at the end of the long stretch of road leading from the main highway, the Blackwood's house came into view. A sprawling, Spanish stucco built only seven years ago, the home of her dear friend Joanna seemed as welcoming as ever. But just how welcome would she be, now that Joe was back and J.T. was joining forces with him to find their young kinsman, Joe's nephew and J.T.'s cousin?

The moment she pulled up beside the vehicle she recognized as Joe's rental car, Andi's stomach knotted painfully. He'd said his goodbyes to her at his sister's house and had assured her that he'd contact her when he had any news of Russ and Eddie. Despite her protests, Joe Ornelas had dismissed her and left for the Blackwood ranch shortly after lunch. If he'd thought she wouldn't follow him, then he didn't know her very well. *Of course, he doesn't know you!* an inner voice taunted. *He never did.*

Before Andi's foot even hit the ground, Joanna Blackwood, round and rosy in her eighth month of pregnancy, came waddling out of the house. Her long red hair hung down her back in a cascading ponytail. Turquoise-and-silver earrings dangled in her ears, and a flowing white-and-aqua striped tent dress hit her mid-calf. Andi had always thought that Joanna was a lovely woman, and the bloom of pregnancy only added to her beauty.

"You were expecting me, weren't you?" Andi smiled as she approached her friend, who waited on the wide, expansive veranda.

Grinning, Joanna nodded. "Joe arrived about an hour ago, so I assumed you wouldn't be far behind."

"Where is he?" Andi hugged Joanna, then pulled back, looked at her swollen tummy and gave it a gentle pat. "You're bigger than you were last week."

"If the ultrasound hadn't shown us differently, I'd swear I was having twins again." Joanna placed both hands atop her stomach. "Joe's in the den with J.T. They're talking strategy. Want to join them?"

Andi laughed as she laced her arm through Joanna's. "You know that Joe all but forbid me to interfere. He told me that he'd keep in touch through you or Kate, and inform me when he had any news about the boys."

"Typical macho man." Joanna led Andi inside, into the large, terra-cotta tiled foyer. "But my guess is that neither Joe nor J.T. will be surprised to see you. Especially not my J.T. He's gotten to know you pretty well these past five years and he's acquainted with your mile-wide stubborn streak."

"I'm not going to let Joe bully me. I have every right to be involved in the search. I may not have his qualifications, but—"

"Save your arguments for Joe. I'm on your side, remember? We women have to stick together against our ultra-masculine Navajo males."

"Joe isn't *my* Navajo male," Andi reminded her friend.

Joanna eyed the silver-and-turquoise bracelet that adorned Andi's wrist. "Then why are you wearing his brand?"

Why, indeed! Andi fingered the magnificent piece of jewelry, handcrafted by Joe and J.T.'s great-grandfather, Benjamin Greymountain. The sentimentally priceless bracelet had been a gift from Joe on her twenty-fifth birthday, shortly before her father's death.

"It's the most beautiful piece of jewelry I own, but I wore it today for a reason. I'm going to give it back to Joe. I would have given it to him five years ago, if he hadn't left in such a hurry. He didn't stick around long enough even to say goodbye."

"And you still resent his speedy departure," Joanna commented. "Admit it to yourself, even if you won't admit it to me—you still care about Joe. Otherwise, you'd already have found someone else."

"I think we've had this conversation before, haven't we? But I'll tell you again—I don't care about Joe. He means nothing to me. And as you well know, I've had several interesting men in my life during the past few years, so that should prove I haven't been pining away for some lost love."

"Just how many of those interesting men lasted longer than a couple of months?" Joanna asked. "Not one of those relationships got beyond the kissing—"

Much to Andi's relief, Joanna's assessment of her love life, or lack thereof, was cut short by the interruption of two redheaded twin toddlers. Annabelle grabbed her mother's right leg as her brother Benjamin manacled the left. They gazed up at Andi with their father's dark eyes. Then a tall, lanky boy of six entered the foyer, halting abruptly when he saw his young siblings attached to Joanna.

"Hi, Andi," the black-haired, green-eyed boy said. "Sorry, Mama, but they got away from me before I knew what was happening." John Thomas Blackwood acted if he were a grown-up, though he was nothing more than a child himself. J.T. and Joanna's eldest had been born an old soul, a protector and a caretaker. Every time Andi was around the boy she sensed his ancient spirit.

"It's all right, honey. No one can keep up with these

two.'' Joanna pried the twins away from her legs and grasped each one by a hand, keeping them separated by her body. Then she turned to Andi. ''It's almost supper-time, so I need to get my brood cleaned up and ready to eat. You know where J.T.'s den is. Feel free to interrupt, and tell Joe and him that Rita will be serving dinner in about thirty minutes.''

''I intend to tell them more than *that*.'' Andi's voice was edged with tension.

''What's wrong, Andi?'' John Thomas asked. ''Are you angry with my daddy?''

''Good heavens, no,'' Andi said. ''I'm angry with—''

Joanna cleared her throat.

''I'm a little annoyed with your cousin Joe,'' Andi amended.

''I like Joe,'' John Thomas told her. ''He brought me an Atlanta Braves cap and a baseball signed by Chipper Jones.''

Andi forced a smile. Joanna chuckled under her breath, then shooed her brood down the hall, leaving Andi alone in the foyer. *Okay, get this over with,* she told herself. *Walk right into J.T.'s den and tell those infuriating, old-fashioned, domineering men that in order to represent the Lapahie family, you insist on having a personal involve-ment in the search for Russ and Eddie.*

J.T. handed Joe a bottle of beer, then sat across from him in a huge wing chair upholstered in a striking Navajo blanket-style fabric, a mate to Joe's chair. Joe liked the masculine look of the room, which he thought reflected his cousin's mixed heritage and his own unique person-ality quite well. It was obvious that the woman who had decorated this room not only knew J.T. well, but cared deeply for him. His cousin was a lucky man to have found someone like Joanna.

Crossing one leg over the other, J.T. shook his head. "There's no evidence that the boys were involved in the crime."

"Circumstantial evidence at best," Joe agreed. "They were seen running from Bobby Yazzi's home shortly after gunshots were fired, which places them with Bobby at the time of his death. And they haven't turned themselves in to the police, which makes them look guilty of something, even if they're not."

"Do you think they're guilty of something other than being scared kids?" J.T. asked, then took a swig from his beer.

Joe circled his thumb around the mouth of his bottle. "Eddie's never been in any kind of trouble. I know he couldn't have killed Bobby or even been a party to his murder. I'm sure he was just in the wrong place at the wrong time."

"What about Russ?"

"I don't know about that boy. The last thing I want is to believe that Russell's son has committed a crime. If I have to bring in Russ, it'll be like arresting Russell all over again. Is anybody going to believe that I want to help that boy, and not condemn him?"

"'Anybody' being Andi Stephens?" J.T.'s lips curved up in a hint of a smile.

"I saw her today," Joe said. "She was at Kate and Ed's when I arrived. She still hates me. Still blames me for what happened to Russell."

"Russell Lapahie was a good man who made a bad mistake." J.T. rubbed his beer bottle back and forth between the palms of his hands. "You did the legally responsible thing. You were a police officer with a sworn duty. Russell committed a crime. He was wrong. You were right.''

"Yeah, sure.'' Joe set his beer on the round wooden side table that separated the matching chairs, then stood and walked over to the big window facing the U-shaped veranda that circled the back of the house. "If I was right, then why did everyone I knew—except you and Joanna and Kate and Ed—turn against me? Why did even my fellow officers look at as if I'd been the one who committed the crime?''

"Everyone liked Russell. He was a respected man in the Navajo community. At the time Russell killed himself, people reacted emotionally. Today, I don't think anyone blames you for what happened. In retrospect, they realize that Russell took the easy way out and that what you did took courage and strong convictions.''

"Andi still blames me. And I'm sure Doli and Russ do, too. I doubt I can ever redeem myself in their eyes.''

"And is that what you want to do—redeem yourself with Russell's family?''

"Maybe. I don't know.''

J.T. stood, walked over and laid his hand on Joe's back. "When we find Eddie and Russ and prove they weren't involved with Bobby's murder, that should go a long way in helping you get back into Andi's good graces.''

"What Andi thinks of me doesn't matter. Not anymore. But what happens if when we find the boys, it turns out that Russ did kill Bobby Yazzi? What do I do then? I'm not a police officer now. To whom do I owe my allegiance?''

When Andi approached J.T.'s den, she found the door standing wide open, revealing the backs of the two men silhouetted by the late-afternoon sunshine pouring in through the window that faced west. J.T. was tall and lean, an inheritance from his *bilgaana* father. Joe, a full-blood Navajo, was an inch shy of six feet and more stockily built. His skin was a shade darker, his hair a rich blue-black. There had been a time when her heart skipped a beat whenever she saw him. Even now, she could not control the unwanted attraction she felt.

Should I knock? she wondered. Or should I simply barge in? They seemed deep in conversation. The polite thing to do was knock, announce her presence and state her business. But before she could follow through with her intention to use the good manners her mother had drilled into her since childhood, J.T. spoke to Joe.

"Your allegiance is to yourself," J.T. said. "If Russ is guilty, then you have to do what you believe is right, not what will gain you popularity points. You know that as well as I do."

"I made a huge mistake telling Kate and Ed that they should let Eddie remain friends with Russ. If only I'd advised them to keep Eddie away from Russ, then my nephew wouldn't be in the situation he's in now. On the run. Wanted by the police."

Andi had heard all she could endure. It was just as she had suspected—Joe and J.T. both thought Russ had killed Bobby Yazzi. Their objective was to find and save Eddie, even if that meant tossing Russ to the wolves. They didn't care what happened to her brother.

"Russ did not kill Bobby Yazzi!" Andi stormed into the room, anger boiling inside her.

Both men snapped around to face an enraged woman. Noting the startled expressions on their faces, she glared at them, hoping they felt as guilty as they looked.

"Andi, we didn't know…that is, you should have let us…" J.T. stammered. "I'm sorry you overheard that part

of our conversation and misunderstood. Neither of us believes that Russ is guilty. It's just that we know he's been
in trouble quite a bit the past couple of years.''

''And Eddie is a saint, who wouldn't be in this mess
if it weren't for my brother.'' Andi paused several feet
away from the two men, planting herself firmly in front
of them.

''You're putting words into our mouths,'' J.T. told her.

''Andi's very good at doing that.'' Joe mumbled, but
Andi understood what he'd said.

''I'm here to tell both of you that whatever type of
search y'all instigate to find the boys, I'm going to be a
part of it.''

''We don't need you interfering and creating problems,'' Joe said, his dark gaze narrowing on her.

''We'll keep you informed about—'' J.T. tried to explain.

''No!'' Andi walked right up to the two men, who
stood side by side, stiff and unyielding. With only inches
separating her from them, she pointed her finger right in
Joe's face. ''Just being informed isn't good enough.''

''J.T. and I will be splitting up the job of looking for
Eddie and Russ,'' Joe said. ''I'll be following up most of
the leads that require any traveling, while J.T. spearheads
a local investigation for the family. Since Joanna is so
close to giving birth, he doesn't want to get very far away
from her.''

''It seems y'all have everything all figured out.'' Andi
frowned. ''Eddie's family is well represented by the two
of you, and I intend to make sure Russ's interests aren't
forgotten. Wherever Joe goes, I go. He can look out for
Eddie, and I'll look out for Russ.''

''Andi…'' J.T. held out his hand in a gesture of friendship. "Come on. Sit down and we'll talk this thing through until we reach a satisfactory decision."

"I don't need to sit down or talk anything through. The only decision that will satisfy me is to be included in the search."

"You're being unreasonable," Joe said, his voice deadly soft. Then he added in a growling whisper, "But then, you always were."

"Is it unreasonable to want to protect my brother?" Andi asked. "Is it unreasonable of me not to trust you to do what is best for Russ as you will for Eddie? And it is unreasonable for me to believe that you will not protect our family from further disgrace?"

"You honestly believe that when the time comes, I won't do the right thing, the honorable thing?" Joe broke eye contact with Andi and gazed down at the floor, avoiding her intense scrutiny. "Before we've even begun the search, you've condemned me. How do you think you and I can work together? It would be impossible."

"Impossible or not, we must work together." Andi looked to J.T. for confirmation, but before he could speak, Joe did what he was so very good at doing. He ran away. Again.

"Give my regrets to Joanna," Joe said. "I'll have dinner with your family another time. I need to get settled into my old place. You can follow through and get that ad placed in the *Navajo Times*. Maybe the boys will see it and contact us. We'll start out first thing in the morning questioning anyone who has a connection to either Eddie or Russ."

"It won't do you any good to run," Andi said. "You're just postponing the inevitable. I know how to find you, and from now until the boys are safe, you won't get away from me."

Joe nodded to J.T., gave Andi a hard, menacing glare and strode out of the den, leaving behind a fuming Andi and a somber J.T.

Joanna Blackwood stood in the doorway, glancing back and forth from her husband to Andi. "Isn't Joe staying for dinner?"

"No," Andi said. "I think I ran him off."

"What happened?" Joanna asked.

"A difference of opinion," J.T. replied.

"I'm sorry," Andi said. "Under normal circumstances I would never have... I'm only doing what I must. If I don't protect Russ, no one else will. Please understand."

Huffing disgustedly, J.T. shook his head. "Andi, you act as if everyone is against Russ, as if our family—Eddie's family—would be willing to sacrifice Russ in order to save Eddie."

"Not the entire family. Just Joe."

"Why is it that you can't seem to realize that Joe wasn't the one who committed a crime five years ago?" J.T. looked Andi square in the eye. "I liked Russell as much as anybody did, but Joe wasn't responsible for his death. Joe didn't make Russell kill himself. Your father chose—"

Joanna rushed to her husband's side and grabbed his arm.

"J.T., I think you've said enough."

"No, it's all right," Andi assured her friend. "J.T. has every right to defend Joe. Just as I have every right to defend my father and my brother."

"There isn't any reason why we can't all work together, is there?" Joanna gazed pleadingly up at J.T. "Andi needs to be with Joe throughout his search. If Russ were my sixteen-year-old brother, I'd insist on going along."

"Thank you, Joanna, for seeing my side of this situation," Andi said. "I appreciate the predicament y'all find yourselves in and I don't want to cause any friction between the two of you. I think it's best if I leave, too."

Lacing her arm through J.T.'s, Joanna smiled at him and said, "Don't you agree that Andi should go with Joe when he sets out searching for the boys?"

J.T. looked as if he'd been cornered by a grizzly bear. He shrugged, huffed loudly, and then nodded. "You have to do what you think is right, just the same as Joe does."

"Now, Andi, why don't you stay for dinner?" Joanna said.

"I'm afraid I can't. I have somewhere I need to go."

"Right now?" Joanna asked.

"Right now," Andi replied.

J.T. groaned, but then his lips curved into a smile. "You could give him until morning to cool off before you go after him."

"If he gets any information on the boys' whereabouts tonight, he could be long gone by morning," Andi said. "I'm not going to give him the opportunity to go anywhere without me."

Chapter 4

Joe knew the minute he walked into his four-room stucco house that Kate had been there earlier. She had cleaned the place and aired it out. A fire had been built in the fireplace, and both living room windows remained cracked open a couple of inches. He dumped his suitcase just inside the front door and quickly closed the windows, blocking out the cool evening air. He would check out the kitchen, bedroom, bath and back porch later. Right now, all he wanted was a few minutes of peace and quiet. No one asking, demanding, questioning. Back home less than ten hours, and he was already caught up in the same emotional storm from which he had run five years ago.

He slumped down in a comfortable tan leather chair to the right of the fireplace, lifted his feet and rested them on the matching ottoman. These two pieces of furniture had been his first buy, right after building this small house for himself. He had loved his home, his job and his way of life. He'd been a Native son whom the Navajo youths had admired and emulated. Joe Ornelas had been the Native American equivalent of the hometown hero. Handsome. Intelligent. A star athlete. A Tribal police officer. A man dedicated to the *Dine* and traditional ways. He had greatly appreciated and enjoyed having the respect of his people and the high esteem of his family.

He had always been proud of his Native American heritage, his clan and his family. As part of a matriarchal society, a Navajo is born into his or her mother's clan. Joe had been born into the *K'aahanaanii* clan. The Living Arrow People.

To the Navajo, the land is everything, and they believe that all living things are equal and sacred. He had lived his life by that code, respecting not only other humans, but animals and birds, trees and mountains. With each passing year, it became more and more difficult for the *Dine* to hold on to the old ways, to remain true to an ancient heritage. The boarding school experience, the *Livestock Reduction Act* and the land dispute issue with the Hopi, had divided the people over the years, making it almost impossible to blend traditional ways with a modern lifestyle. Joe had tried to do just that, but he had failed.

Friends and family alike had been divided in their opinion of what Joe should or should not have done when he discovered that Russell Lapahie had not only been covering up his sister-in-law Lucille's husband's criminal acts, but had actually taken money for his silence. In a matter of days, Joseph Ornelas had gone from being a hero to being a traitor. Even one of his own cousins, Ray Judee, a friend since childhood, had turned against him. When swarms of area and national news media had shown up on the reservation after Russell's death, Ray had told Joe that by revealing what Russell had done, Joe had allowed the white world to see the worst side of the Navajo.

Every unkind, unsympathetic word hurled at him had hurt, but none so much as Andi's bitter accusation that he'd been responsible for her father's death. She had turned against him completely. He had thought that they could share their grief and console each other. But Andi hadn't given him a chance to explain why he'd arrested her father, why he believed he had done the right thing. Less than a week after Russell's death, Joe had known he couldn't stay in New Mexico, couldn't remain on the Tribal police force. Raw with pain, anger and resentment, Joe hadn't known where to go or what to do. It had been his cousin J.T. who had gotten him the job with the Dundee agency in Atlanta, where J.T. himself had once worked. Without looking back, Joe had packed and taken the first available plane to Georgia. He'd left behind everything he'd once held so dear—his heritage, his lifestyle, his family, and the woman he had loved.

Seeing Andi again had been even more difficult than he'd imagined it would be. He had expected her unforgiving attitude, but he hadn't expected still to feel something for her.

It's just lust, he told himself. *From the moment you first met her, you reacted to her like a rutting bull. You wanted her in a way you'd never wanted another woman. And you still do. Admit it to yourself and deal with it. Whatever you might have had with Andi died the day Russell killed himself.*

Andi had made it abundantly clear that she didn't trust him. Hell, she even believed that he didn't care what happened to Russ. But he did care. A part of him felt as if he owed it to Russell to help his son. *Even if the boy is guilty?* an inner voice asked. Now there was the rub. What would he do if evidence showed up indicating Russ had pulled the trigger? He'd be confronted with a similar di-

lemma to the one he'd faced when he decided to do the
lawful thing and arrest Russell. Damn! The only way he
could come out of this without hurting Andi and her family even more than they'd already been hurt was if he
could prove Russ was innocent.

Eddie Whitehorn wished that he was home in his own
bed. Warm. Well fed. Safe. With his parents keeping
watch over him. With Summer and Joey pestering him.
With a school day ahead and hard work on the sheep
ranch to keep him busy and out of trouble. He wanted his
boring, uneventful life back. He realized he had never
appreciated how good things had been for him. Until now.

If only he could go back twenty-four hours and change
what had happened. Why hadn't he vetoed Jewel's idea
of stopping by Bobby Yazzi's to pick up some beer? He'd
known Bobby's reputation as a drug dealer. But Russ had
assured him that he'd gotten beer from Bobby before, that
lots of the kids did. Even the ones who didn't buy some
weed or any of the hard stuff.

Idiot, Eddie chided himself. What was he going to do
now? He couldn't leave Russ, couldn't turn himself in and
let Russ hide out on his own. They'd been best buddies
since they were babies. Even when his uncle Joe had arrested Russ's dad, they had somehow managed to remain
friends. Eddie understood Russ better than anybody else
did. Russ wasn't a bad person. He was just a little mixed
up. And he was a bit of a show-off. He liked being the
center of attention, liked defying his elders, and loved
having the girls think he was a real bad-boy. Guess he
and Russ were as different as night and day. The last thing
Eddie ever wanted to be was the center of attention. But
right now, he'd bet he and Russ were the talk of Castle
Springs, probably of the whole reservation.

Eddie glanced across the interior of the stolen pickup truck at a sleeping Russ. They'd pooled what little money they had and filled the tank with gas, all the while hoping nobody at the trading post on the outskirts of Sawmill would recognize them. They'd kept to the back roads as much as possible and had prayed they could make it to their destination without running into the law. Every Tribal police officer on the reservation was probably looking for them. Did the police have orders to bring them in dead or alive? Eddie wondered. Stupid assumption. He knew better. The police wouldn't kill them—unless there was no other choice. Not unless Russ lost his cool and shot at the police.

Eddie cringed at the thought. Russ had found a rifle in the truck. And a box of ammunition. Somehow Eddie would feel safer if Russ didn't have a weapon.

Russ woke with a start. When he opened his eyes he saw nothing unusual. Only the moonlit interior of the truck's cab. So what had awakened him? Eddie sat with his head resting against the window, his mouth open as he breathed evenly in sleep. The only sounds were nighttime noises particular to the desert regions of the reservation. They were as safe as they could possibly be, considering the police were looking for them. He'd chosen this spot, off the road, hidden from the view of passersby, so that they could get a few hours of rest before going on to his uncle Jefferson's home, in a remote area in Arizona.

If anyone could help them, his mother's uncle would. Russ was counting on the old man to hide them out for as long as necessary. If he could get in touch with Jewel without tipping off the real killer, and she agreed to admit being with him and seeing who really killed Bobby, then he'd surrender to the police. But without Jewel to back up his story, there was no way he'd trust the law. In the meantime, he intended to do everything he could to protect himself and Eddie from the man who had killed Bobby and was sure to either come after them himself or send someone to hunt them down.

Russ imagined his mother was awfully upset. She hadn't been well since his father's death, and finding out that her son was wanted for questioning in a murder case was sure to be rough on her. If he could change what had happened, he would. But he and Eddie were in this mess up to their eyeballs. They had gotten themselves into a no-win situation. Correction—*he* had gotten them into a no-win situation.

He supposed he should have called Andi. Eddie had wanted to phone his parents. But what good would it have done? Andi and Mr. and Mrs. Whitehorn would have insisted they come home and turn themselves in to the police. He knew Andi loved him and wanted what was best for him, but sometimes she acted more like a parent than a big sister. He supposed that was because he didn't have much parental guidance—not that he listened to his mother, anyway.

I'm not a bad kid, he told himself. *I don't mean to keep screwing up. It just seems that I'm always making the wrong decisions. But this time, I've done the smart thing. I've made sure that Eddie and I are safe. For the time being.*

He promised himself that he wouldn't let anything happen to his best friend. Eddie had stood by him time and again, when everyone else had turned against him. He owed Eddie a lot.

Russ glanced out the window, up at the half moon in the dark night sky. He wished he were home. He wouldn't even mind listening to Andi come down hard on him for messing up so bad.

Joe didn't realize that he'd fallen asleep in the chair until he heard the loud banging on his front door. Who the hell—? But before he even rose to his feet, he'd figured out who his uninvited guest was. Who else would it be?

Damn! What was he going to do with her? She was as tenacious as a bulldog with a bone. Getting rid of her would be just about impossible. All he needed to further complicate this already complicated situation was to be trapped with a woman who made his blood boil and thrust his libido into overdrive.

Joe swung open the door. There she stood. Tall, slender and gorgeous, a phony smile plastered on her pretty face.

"May I come in?" she asked, as pleasant and civil as if he'd sent her a handwritten invitation to visit.

"Do I have a choice?" Despite his annoyance, he just barely kept himself from grinning. As aggravating as she was, he couldn't help admiring her spirit, her determination and her plain old stubbornness. Joe stepped aside to allow her entrance into his humble home.

Andi barged past him into the house, then waited just past the threshold while he closed and locked the door. "We need to get things settled tonight. As you can plainly see, I'm not going away. Where you go, I go. And there's nothing you can do to stop me, short of killing me. Do I make myself clear?"

"Crystal clear."

"Then let's set down some ground rules."

"By all means." He waved his hand in a gesture of welcome. "Have a seat."

"Thank you." She plopped herself down on the brown

corduroy sofa directly in front of the fireplace. "I hope
you realize that I don't relish spending time with you any
more than you look forward to enduring my presence. But
we have a common goal, don't we? We both want to find
Russ and Eddie. You have Eddie's best interests at heart
just as I do Russ's."

Joe nodded, but he kept some distance between them
as he looked at her. How was it possible that she'd grown
more beautiful? More tempting? He hadn't exactly been
celibate the past five years, but he'd never met a woman
he'd wanted more than he did Andi. Maybe if they had
consummated their relationship, he wouldn't be feeling
this hunger right now. Could it be that the great unknown
made her all the more alluring?

And what the hell was she doing wearing the bracelet
that he'd given her? He had inherited several pieces of
silver-and-turquoise jewelry from his mother, the grand-
daughter of Benjamin Greymountain, who had been a re-
markable silversmith long before the Navajos were known
for that specific craft. Joe had chosen the bracelet from
his collection with great care, wanting something that
would appeal to Andi and yet at the same time brand her
as his own. Primitive emotions? Old-fashioned male pos-
sessiveness? Yes, he was guilty of both.

Her twenty-fifth birthday had been special. A night out
with her father and Doli, then a private celebration, here
at his home. They had come so close to making love that
night. But Andi had called a halt, asking him to be patient,
to give her more time. She wanted him, she'd said, but
she also needed to be sure that their relationship had a
future. Despite her Navajo blood, he and she had come
from two different worlds, and she wasn't sure they could
ever reconcile the two. He had loved her all the more for

eing a woman to whom lovemaking meant a commit-
ent.

"You aren't saying anything." Andi snapped her head
round and glared at Joe. "Are we in agreement or not?"

"Sorry," he said. "I'm not quite sure what we're sup-
osed to be in agreement on."

Andi huffed indignantly. "Weren't you listening? I was
roposing that you look after Eddie's best interests and I
o the same for Russ."

Here we go, Joe thought. She was accusing him of lay-
ıg all the blame on Russ again. Why was it that she
ouldn't believe he cared about what happened to her
rother? It was as if five years hadn't been long enough
ır her to come to terms with her father's death and Joe's
art in the tragedy. Would she never realize that Russell
ad had other options? He chose to commit suicide, to
ısgrace his family and leave them bereft.

"Sure. That's easy enough," Joe said in order to pacify
ir, then added, "but it would be a lot easier if we agreed
at we both care about the boys and want what's best for
em. After all, it's going to be hard enough spending time
gether, without the two of us being constantly at odds.
we trusted each other—"

"Ah, but we don't, do we?"

Andi's gaze connected with Joe's, and for one split sec-
ıd he felt as if someone had hit him in the stomach with
two-by-four. He knew he was fighting a losing battle.
e'd have to let Andi come along, join him in the search
ır the boys. If he went out alone and something happened
 Russ, she'd blame him; she would convince herself that
 was at fault. By letting her tag along, he ran the risk
 either making love to her or strangling her. But some-
ıw, he had to find the strength to avoid both.

"J.T. is putting an ad in the *Navajo Times*. Maybe the

boys will see it and contact us." Joe made his way close
to Andi and sat beside her, he on one end of the sofa an
she on the other. "He's also been questioning all o
Eddie's and Russ's friends. If they've contacted anyone
then no one's admitting it."

"What about the girls they had a date with that night?
Andi said. "Do you have any idea who they were? I'v
asked Doli, and she doesn't know."

"Kate and Ed said that Russ arranged the date, but a
Eddie told them was that they were a couple of nice gir
who lived in Castle Springs."

The moment he heard Andi grunt, Joe realized that
verbal attack was imminent. She was too damn touch
about Russ, taking everything he said about the boy th
wrong way.

"Before you jump down my throat," Joe said, "I wan
you to know that I wasn't accusing Russ of anything, ju
because he was the one to arrange the double date."

Andi slapped her hands down on her thighs, huffe
loudly and took a deep breath. "Okay, this time I'll tak
you at your word. And I'll even admit that I might b
overreacting about your blaming Russ. But you have
realize that I have good reason to not trust you."

"I'll agree that we both believe we have good reason
to not trust each other."

"What's our next move? Where do we start?"

"We start by questioning family and friends again, se
ing if anyone has any idea where or to whom the bo
might run. They're a couple of sixteen-year-old kids, wi
maybe twenty-five dollars between them. How far ca
they get without help?"

"You're right." Andi curved around so that she face
Joe as she relaxed her back against the arm of the sof

"Is there anyone Eddie would go to for help, other than his parents?"

"I can't think of anyone, other than some cousins, and J.T. has checked with all our relatives. What about Russ?"

"My little brother is a loner. He isn't really close to anyone except Doli and me. And Eddie, of course."

"We'll double-check with Doli, as well as with Kate and Ed, in the morning." Joe stood. "It's late. I'm tired, and no doubt you are, too. I don't mean to rush you, but why don't you go home and get some rest. You can meet me back here—"

"I'm not going anywhere."

"What?"

"I said—"

"I heard you." Joe scowled at Andi. "You aren't suggesting that you spend the night here, are you?"

"I'm not 'suggesting' anything. I'm telling you. But obviously you haven't been listening." Andi patted the sofa cushion at her side. "You're not going to get more than a few feet away from me until we find Russ and Eddie. Starting tonight, I'm—"

"I have only one bedroom, but if you'd like to share, I have no objections." He knew before he spoke that his words were inflammatory, that she'd go off on him the moment she heard his suggestion. If she could torment him by harassing the hell out of him, then he could damn well give her back a little of her own.

When she glowered at him, her topaz eyes wide and glimmering with anger, Joe grinned. She hopped up off the sofa and gave him an eat-dirt-and-die glare.

"I wouldn't share a bed with you if you were the last— I'll be quite comfortable right here on the couch, thank you."

"Going to sleep in your clothes? I think I have an old T-shirt you can borrow."

"I have an overnight bag in my SUV," she told him. "I drove back to my house in Gallup and packed, then called my assistant to take care of the shop for me while I'm gone. That's why it took me so long to get here."

"I see." Joe held out his hand. "Give me the keys, and I'll go get your bag for you."

"No, thank you. I can get my own bag." She headed toward the door.

"Fine." He slashed his hand across the air as if to say, *I give up.* "You get your bag, and I'll get myself a blanket and a pillow for the sofa."

Andi halted halfway across the room. "I'm sleeping on the sofa, not you."

"You'd be more comfortable in my bed."

"I'll be just fine on the sofa."

"Okay by me." He shrugged. "I was just trying to do the gentlemanly thing."

"I don't want you to put yourself out for me. After all, I am an uninvited and unwelcome guest."

Before he could reply, she flung open the door and disappeared outside. Joe grumbled to himself as he went into his bedroom and rummaged around in the closet, searching for a blanket and an extra pillow. How was he going to endure days—maybe weeks—with Andi, when the tension between them sizzled? Anger mixed with desire was a deadly combination.

Andi took her own sweet time retrieving her bag from the back of the Expedition. She needed a few extra minutes outside in the cool night air to clear her head, calm her nerves and let the smoldering emotions raging inside her die down a bit. Being around Joe aroused too many memories, too many old feelings that she'd thought long dead. A part of her despised him, and yet another part of her ached for him, wishing that he could erase the past and make things right again.

If Russ's future—perhaps his very life—didn't depend on her acting as his protector, then she wouldn't put herself through the torment of spending endless days with Joe Ornelas.

She wanted to be able to look at Joe, have a conversation with him, spend time with him—and not be consumed with emotions she could barely control. She wavered between wanting to pummel him with her fists and longing for him to take her into his arms. If only she could vent her frustration and demand an explanation for his actions five years ago. *Why did you leave me? Why didn't you stay and fight for our relationship? Why didn't you try harder to make me understand why you betrayed my father's friendship?*

Don't do this to yourself! an inner voice advised. She was not here to reconcile with Joe, to forgive him or to ask his forgiveness. She was here to help her brother. She must never forget that she couldn't trust Joe. Not when it came to her family.

Andi lifted the vinyl bag out of her SUV, closed the hatch and locked it. Squaring her shoulders, she marched to Joe's front door, turned the knob and reentered his house. The overhead light had been turned off and only the glow from the fireplace illuminated the room. She skidded to a stop when she saw him bent over in front of the fireplace, replenishing the logs. She had always loved Joe's back—wide shoulders, thickly muscled and tapering into a narrow waist. His hair hung long and straight to just below the neck of his sweater. Cut blunt and straight, it glistened a shiny blue-black in the firelight.

Without saying a word, she tossed her bag over and onto the sofa. It landed with a resounding *thump*. Joe glanced back at her, then rose to his feet and replaced the iron poker in the rack alongside the other rustic fireplace utensils.

"Found you a pillow and a couple of blankets," he said. "You should be cosy enough by the fire. You remember where the bathroom is, don't you?"

"Yes." Why did he have to look so good? Every feature of his face was chiseled perfection, from high cheekbones to a strong, square chin. And he had the most incredible eyes. Deep, dark brown ovals, slightly slanted and extremely expressive. There had been a time when she'd known what Joe was thinking by just looking into his eyes.

"If you happen to wake before I do in the morning, how about putting on a pot of coffee?"

"Sure thing," she said.

"If you need—"

"I won't. I'll be fine."

"Good night, then."

"Good night."

She waited until he disappeared into his bedroom before she rifled through her bag, searching for her pajamas. She quickly found the set—yellow cotton shorts and an oversize matching top. With the pajamas thrown over her arm, she took her small cosmetics case with her to the bathroom. It was then, just when she started to remove her blouse, that she realized she was still wearing the bracelet. She'd had every intention of returning it to him.

You can do that in the morning, she told herself. *No! Do it now. Don't put it off any longer,* her conscience insisted. Joe must have seen the bracelet on her wrist. He had to be wondering what it meant. She didn't want to give him the wrong impression.

Leaving her pajamas and her cosmetics case on the back of the commode in the tiny bathroom, she scurried into the living room and over to the closed door of Joe's bedroom. She lifted her hand and knocked.

"Yeah, come on in," Joe said.

She opened the door. Moonlight shining through the window blended with the muted light from the lamp on the bedside table and outlined Joe's big, hard body. He turned around and looked at her. Bare-chested, wearing nothing but a pair of unsnapped jeans, he stood before her, gloriously, magnificently male.

Andi swallowed hard.

"Something wrong?" he asked.

"No. Nothing's wrong." She took a couple of hesitant steps in his direction. Her other hand hovering over the bracelet, she said, "I meant to give you this at Kate and Ed's today."

He glanced down at her hand covering her wrist. She eased the antique piece of handcrafted jewelry from her arm and held it out to him. He stared at the gleaming silver object lying in the palm of her hand.

"It's the bracelet you gave me for my—"

"I know what it is," he said. "Why give it back to me, now?"

"I had intended to give it back to you years ago, but you left town before I had a chance."

"You could have given it to Kate at any time."

"Yes, I suppose I could have," she admitted. "But I felt I should return it personally."

"Okay."

She hurried over to him, grabbed his hand, turned it over and deposited the bracelet in the middle of his palm.

"You could keep it," he said, but didn't make eye contact with her.

"No, I can't." She didn't move away from him for several seconds, but stood there waiting. Waiting for what? she wondered. "You'll want to give this bracelet to someone else one day."

"Yeah. Sure."

He looked at her then, and she thought her heart would break. What had she expected? Had she honestly believed that he would say or do something that would miraculously make everything all right between them? He was no more a magician than she was. Neither of them were capable of turning back the clock to a time when they'd had a chance at spending a lifetime together.

Joe lifted his big, dark hand and caressed her cheek. Softly. A featherlight touch. She gasped quietly as every nerve ending in her body cried out with pleasure.

As quickly as he had lifted his hand, he let it drop to his side.

Andi stared at him, praying that the longing she felt didn't show. Then, while she still had the strength to move, she turned around and walked away from temptation.

Chapter 5

Andi thought she heard a telephone ringing. She roused herself from sleep slowly, groggily, stretching her arms over her head when she sat up on the sofa. She groaned as she rubbed the back of her neck. Realizing she was at Joe's house, she wondered if Kate could have gotten his phone line reconnected so quickly. As she shoved back the blankets to the end of the couch, she heard murmuring coming from another room. Joe was definitely talking to someone. Padding across the wooden floor in her bare feet, Andi made her way to the kitchen.

Seated at a small, square table, Joe clutched a cup of coffee in one hand and used the other to hold his cellular phone to his ear.

"Yeah, she's here," Joe said. "Yes, she stayed the night. Slept on my sofa."

Andi wondered who had called Joe at the crack of dawn. It was definitely too early for casual chitchat.

"Sure thing. I'll pass on the message," Joe said. "And I will let you know what we decide to do."

Joe closed his phone and laid it on the table, then put the mug to his lips and drank. Andi cleared her throat.

Joe glanced over his shoulder. "Morning."

"Who was that on the phone?" she asked.

"J.T."

"Why did he want to know if I was here? And what message are you supposed to pass along?"

Joe surveyed her from head to toe, taking in every inch of her long, lean body. Within Andrea Stevens ran the blood of two races that had combined to create perfection. Her hair was a shade lighter than his—not a true black, more a deep, smoky brown. And her soft, smooth skin was shades fairer than his and yet still a rich olive. But it was in her eyes that Andi was unique. He'd never seen eyes quite the color of hers. Golden eyes. Like mixing the brown of the earth with the yellow of the sun.

Andi frowned. "Didn't you hear what I asked?"

"Yeah, sure. J.T. called. Doli is looking for you. She phoned your house and when you didn't answer, she contacted Joanna."

"Is something wrong? Is Doli all right?"

"She's all right, as far as I know. She told Joanna it was urgent that she talk to you."

"May I use your phone?"

He picked up the cell phone and held it out to her. "Maybe she's heard from Russ."

"Dear God, I hope so."

Andi grasped the phone and quickly dialed Doli's number. Joe got up, refilled his cup with hot coffee and poured a second cup. He remembered that she liked her coffee black, just as he did. He set the cup down in front of Andi. She nodded and mouthed the words *Thank you.*

Andi took a sip of the strong brew as she listened to the phone ringing. Ah, Joe made great coffee and he'd served it to her without cream or sugar. He'd remembered. She cast a quick glance in his direction and saw that he was watching her. Their gazes met and held, then Lucille Chalon, Doli's sister, answered the phone.

"Hello."

"Lucille, this is Andi Stephens."

"Yes, Doli needs to speak with you."

"Is something wrong? Has she heard from Russ?"

"No, she has heard nothing from her son," Lucille said. "But she has thought of a place where Russ might go."

"Where?"

"She must speak with you herself. Wait. I will get her."

Holding the phone against her cheekbone, Andi tapped the back of the small black telephone with her fingertips as she waited.

"What's going on?" Joe asked.

She put her finger to her lips. "Shh. Doli might not tell me anything if she thinks I'm with you."

"What is it—"

Andi glowered at him and repeated, "Shh."

"Andi, is that you?" Doli asked, her voice pitifully weak.

"Yes, Doli. Your sister told me that you've thought of a place where Russ might have gone."

Joe's eyes widened as he stared directly at Andi. She shook her head, warning him to keep quiet.

"Yes, I believe Russ might have gone to my uncle Jefferson Nastas, who lives in a secluded area of the reservation. Over in Arizona. Russ has been there many times and he has great respect for my uncle."

"Doli, why don't you call your uncle and find out if Russ is there?"

"You do not understand," Doli said. "My uncle has no telephone, no television, no electricity. Neither he nor the families of his three daughters who live close by have telephones."

"Give me directions to his home, and I'll find out if Russ has gone to your uncle for help."

Joe scrambled around in a kitchen drawer until he found a pad and pencil. He plopped them down on the table and shoved them over to Andi. She nodded to him, grabbed the pad and pencil, and wrote hurriedly as Doli gave her the directions.

"You must not trust Joe Ornelas," Doli said. "If you do, you will regret it."

"Believe me, I know that better than anyone." Andi glanced over at Joe, who stood propped against the wall, his unbuttoned shirt hanging open to reveal the sleek, dark flesh of his muscular chest. "I'll get in touch after I've seen your uncle. Thank you. And Doli, please take care."

The minute Andi ended her conversation and laid the phone down on the table, she took another sip of her coffee and faced Joe.

"Want to make a trip to Arizona?"

"Sure thing. I'd say Doli's hunch that Russ might have gone to a relative is our best lead yet. Actually, our only lead. Let me tell J.T. where we're going, and then we can head out within the hour."

Andi grabbed Joe's arm and gazed into his eyes. "If the boys are there at Doli's uncle's home, Russ is going to balk when he sees you. He still blames you for what happened to our father."

"Just as you do."

"It's different for Russ. He's only a boy and he doesn't deal with his emotions rationally sometimes."

"Are you saying Russ might shoot me on sight?"

"No, damn it, that's not what I'm saying." Andi gritted her teeth. "I'm asking that when we get to Jefferson Nastas's home, you stay in the SUV and let me go in and check things out. Okay?"

"Sure. You know your brother better than I do. The last thing I want is to scare him off."

"Why don't you pack us a couple of sandwiches, and we'll pick up some bottled water at a store somewhere. I need to get dressed so we can leave as soon as possible."

"Go." Joe waved his hand, shooing her from the kitchen. "I'll fix the sandwiches and a thermos of coffee, after I call J.T."

Charlie Kirk had tailed people before, so he knew what he was doing. His main objective was to not let the boys catch on that they were being followed. He'd been damn lucky that a friend of a friend had spotted the stolen truck early this morning and had called Mr. Lanza instead of getting in touch with the police. But then, Mr. Lanza paid better for information than the police did.

His orders were to kill the boys. And to do it inconspicuously. Hit them when they were alone, if possible, or when they were around the fewest number of people. Eliminate all witnesses. And make sure nothing pointed a finger at Mr. Lanza.

If he'd found Russ Lapahie and Eddie Whitehorn last night, he could have done the job quickly and easily. But now they were on the move, going northwest and still within the reservation boundaries. Where the hell were they headed? Charlie wondered. He'd just have to wait and see, and then, when the time was right, he would strike.

Jefferson Nastas lived in the foothills of the sparse Navajo land and was the proud owner of a small cattle herd. His sons-in-law and grandsons now worked the cattle for him. A widower for three years, he was all but retired and had moved into a small house that had been built for him by his family. His days were filled with peace and contentment. Occasionally he would ride his horse the three miles that separated him from his grandchildren and visit them for an afternoon. From time to time, a relative or a friend would come by to pass the time with him, and he would always make them welcome. But for the most part, he preferred his solitude.

Today, he sat outside in an old rocking chair, the midday sun warm on his face, as he finished his daily meditation. Although his eyesight was not what it used to be, his hearing had not diminished. He heard the vehicle long before it reached his home. A truck, he surmised, going at top speed around the winding dirt road. Within minutes he noted a cloud of dust rising into the air, coming toward him like a whirlwind. He didn't move from his chair as he awaited his visitors' arrival.

He did not recognize the truck or the two Navajo youths who emerged from it. But they were several yards away, and he did not wear his glasses when he meditated.

"Uncle Jefferson," the taller boy called to him.

He recognized that voice, and when the boys drew nearer he saw that one of them possessed a familiar face.

"Russell Lapahie, Jr.," Jefferson said. "The son of my sister's daughter. You are welcome here."

"Thank you," the boy replied.

A look of fear showed plainly in the eyes of both young braves. The fear of those being chased by evil.

"You will introduce me to your friend?" Jefferson's gaze traveled over the skinny, silent boy.

"Oh, yeah, sorry. Uncle Jefferson, this is my friend, Eddie Whitehorn."

Jefferson nodded. "You are thirsty? Or hungry?"

"Yes, but food and water can wait," Russ said. "Eddie and I need your help. We have gotten ourselves into some trouble, and I didn't know where else to go."

Jefferson rose slowly, lifting the cane propped against the side of his rocker. Using the cane to aid his unsteady steps, he showed the boys into his humble home.

"We will eat and drink first, and then you will tell me what trouble has sent you to me."

Reluctantly the two boys joined him in his noonday meal, the three of them gathered about the small wooden table. Jefferson saw that the boys were hungry, but too nervous to eat much.

"Does your mother know that you have come to see me?" Jefferson looked directly at Russ.

"No, sir."

"You have run away from home?"

"No, sir. Not exactly. You see Eddie and I...well, we were someplace we shouldn't have been and I saw something...I saw a man kill another man. And now the police think Eddie and I were involved."

"Why did you not go to the police and tell them what happened?"

"Look, maybe I'd better start at the beginning and tell you everything. That way, you'll know why we can't go back. It's not just the police who are after us, but the man who shot this other man—he's after us, too."

"Yes, it is good that you begin at the beginning and tell me everything."

Andi wasn't sure she would ever get used to the odd combination of desolation and colorful beauty that comprised a great section of the Navajo land. As they approached the turnoff to the cattle ranch owed by Jefferson Nastas and his family, several windmills sprang up alongside the road. Towering metal sentinels. Wind-driven pumps used to gather drinking water in tanks for the herds.

"Look," Andi said. "There's a truck parked there beside the house. And it has New Mexico license plates. Do you think it might be Russ and Eddie?"

"I can't believe we'll be lucky enough to find the boys still here," Joe replied. "Seems too easy. Besides, where would they get a truck?"

"They could have borrowed the truck."

"Or stole it."

Andi gave Joe a hard look, then pulled her Expedition up alongside the truck. "You stay here. If Russ is inside, he's not going to want to see you."

"I'll wait. But you be very careful." He grabbed her arm. "I think you should take my gun with you."

"What?"

"I have a rifle, too," he reminded her. "But just in case—"

"I don't need protection from my own brother!" She jerked free from Joe's hold.

"I wasn't thinking about Russ being a threat. You need to remember that if the boys didn't kill Bobby Yazzi, someone else did. And that someone will want the boys to keep quiet."

"There's no way the real killer could know where the

boys are.'' Andi opened the door, jumped down and headed toward the house. Before she reached her destination, an old man appeared from inside and, shading his eyes from the sun, greeted her.

''*Ya'at'eeh,*'' Jefferson Nastas said.

''Mr. Nastas?'' Andi asked.

He nodded. ''*Hash yinilye?*''

Andi didn't speak Saad, but she knew enough of the language to understand that the old man had asked her name. Using her limited knowledge of the language, she replied, ''*Yinish'ye* Andrea Stevens. Russ Lapahie is my brother. I was born in my mother's world of the white people. And I was born for the Red Running Into the Water clan.''

''Yes, Doli has spoken of you. She tells me you are a good woman.'' The old man inspected Andi thoroughly, then said, ''You are looking for young Russell.''

''Is he here?''

''He and his friend, Eddie Whitehorn, were here a few hours ago. That is their truck—the truck they borrowed.'' Jefferson nodded toward the old vehicle.

''Where are they now?''

''Who is that you have with you?'' Jefferson, who wore a pair of silver-rimmed glasses, studied the occupant of the SUV.

Now what? Andi wondered. Did she tell Doli's uncle the truth? If Doli had spoken to him about the man she held responsible for her husband's death, how would Mr. Nastas react to meeting Joe?

''He is a friend who has come with me to search for Russ and Eddie. He is Eddie's uncle and is as concerned about the boys as I am.''

''Tell him to get out of the car, and I will tell you both where I have sent the young braves.''

"You know where they are?"

"Yes, I know."

Andi motioned to Joe, her hand gestures inviting him to join her. While Joe introduced himself, Andi held her breath, wondering if Jefferson Nastas would refuse to help them once he knew Joe's identity. To her surprise, the old man's facial expression didn't alter in the least, but she did note a change in his cloudy brown eyes.

"You are working together to save these young braves from the *Ladrones.* Yes?"

Joe nodded. "Yes, *Hosteen,* we need to find Russ and Eddie before these bad men harm them."

Andi noticed Jefferson Nastas's expression soften slightly when Joe referred to him with the word meaning "old man," a term of great respect.

"I have sent Russell, Jr. and his friend up into the mountains to see Edmund Kieyoomia. He is a wise *ya-taalii* and will know the right way to guide two such as they."

"You sent them to see a shaman?" Andi had spent five years trying to understand her father's people, but at times like this she wondered if she ever would. Of course, sending the boys to a shaman was the Native equivalent of sending them to a minister or rabbi or priest for spiritual advice. And yet, seeking out a revered shaman entailed much more, which was understood completely only by a people who believed in the magic and the power these men possessed.

"How far away does this shaman live?" Joe asked. "And did the boys go on foot?"

"Edmund's hogan is in the mountains. On horseback you can reach it in perhaps two hours," Jefferson said. "I let the young ones take my horses."

"And if we drive the Expedition, how long will it—"

"You cannot drive your vehicle. There are no roads. Only pathways."

Great! Andi thought. Russ's great-uncle had given his horses to the boys to ride, so just how were she and Joe supposed to follow them? "Now what?" she asked Joe.

"*Hosteen* Nastas, is there somewhere we can get horses, so that we can follow Russ and Eddie to Edmund Kieyoomia's?"

"I will ride with you in your vehicle to my eldest daughters', and there you may get two horses."

Charlie Kirk wasn't a horseman, but it didn't take an expert to handle the mare he'd stolen. However, he wasn't accustomed to tracking his prey up into the desolate hills or trying to stay a discreet distance behind when it was possible to lose his quarry at any given moment. This godforsaken land might be the home of his grandmother and her ancestors, but he'd been born and raised in the white man's world and only a quarter of his blood tied him to the Navajo. Some folks didn't even know he had a drop of Indian blood flowing in his veins.

When the boys dismounted and began leading their mounts, Charlie did the same. Where the hell were they going—and why? Had the old man they'd gone to see sent them to some sort of hideout up here in the mountains?

He had intended to go in and kill the boys and the old man, but before he'd gotten a chance to make a move, another truck had shown up, the bed filled with half a dozen kids. They hadn't stayed long, but long enough for young Lapahie and Eddie Whitehorn to saddle up and head out. The old man had to be a relative. Only a relative would be helping the boys run from the police. And seeing as neither Russ nor Eddie panicked and ran when the others showed up out of nowhere meant they had to be family, too.

Charlie tied the reins around a tree to secure his horse, then climbed up the rocky pathway. When he reached the top he saw an old stone hogan, a smokestack protruding through the mud roof. Wonder who lives here? Charlie mused. Another relative?

He waited while the boys tied their reins to a wooden hitching post outside the hogan, then went to the door and knocked. A couple of minutes later, the door opened and the boys went inside.

He figured that as small as the hogan was, there couldn't be more than two or three other people inside, but more than likely it was just some old hermit living way up here in the middle of nowhere. Charlie would simply bide his time and see if anyone else came or went. Then, when his instincts told him it was time to act, he'd move in—for the kill.

Joe dismounted and then assisted Andi. They led the horses, borrowed from Jefferson Nastas's son-in-law, the rest of the way up the uneven slope. The first thing Joe noticed when they reached the top and saw the stone hogan was that the shaman's home had been constructed according to tradition, the builder following the Navajo Way. One doorway, facing the east. East was the direction of all beginnings.

"Look—" Andi pointed. "The door is open."

"I don't see any horses around, do you?"

"No. And I don't like it. Something's wrong here. I can just feel it."

"We couldn't be more than a few hours behind those boys," Joe said. "Damn it! I was sure they'd still be here."

"They're taking us on a wild-goose chase, aren't they. If only we could catch them and talk to them. We have to make them understand the danger they're in from the real killer."

"They're a couple of frightened boys who obviously aren't thinking straight and don't realize that they would be safer in police custody than running around on their own." Joe grasped Andi's arm. "You stay out here while I go in and talk to Edmund Kieyoomia. It's possible that he advised the boys to give themselves up to the Tribal Police, and they're headed back to civilization right now."

"We can only hope that they're safe and that the shaman did advise them to do the right thing." Andi clutched Joe's hand and forcefully removed it from her arm. "Why should I stay out here?"

"I want you to wait until I check things inside. You're right about something being wrong. Things don't seem quite right to me, either. I've got an odd feeling."

"What sort of odd feeling? Mine's a sick churning in my stomach, as if we're walking into big trouble."

"Mine's a gut reaction, too." Joe visually surveyed the area around the hogan. "It'll be dark in a couple of hours, so why didn't Eddie and Russ just stay the night and then head out at daybreak? They couldn't know that we were following them. This is unfamiliar territory to them, and they could easily get lost once the sun sets."

"You think something—"

"I'm not thinking anything," he told her. "Not until I've spoken with the shaman."

"All right. I'll stay here. You go on in and then come right back out and let me know that everything is all right."

Joe nodded, then removed the rifle from the leather

sheath attached to the saddle. Andi gasped. He gave her a warning glare to stay where she was and to be quiet.

The door stood wide open. Carefully, ever mindful that anything or anyone could be waiting inside for him, Joe entered the hogan. It took his eyes a couple of minutes to adjust to the semidarkness inside the round structure. The sparsely furnished interior had been ransacked. Tables and chairs overturned. A kerosene lamp broken. Unease ate away at Joe's gut like a strong acid.

Then he saw the figure of an ancient Navajo sprawled half on the bed, half on the floor, his long white hair matted with red blood, barely dried. On closer inspection, Joe realized that this weathered man of indiscernible age must be Edmund Kieyoomia. The revered shaman had been shot—once in the head. But his body showed signs of having been severely beaten. Joe would bet his life that this was not the handiwork of two scared boys on the run. Whoever had killed the old *yataalii* had fought with him first, and from the looks of the room it appeared that Edmund Kieyoomia had put up quite a struggle.

Joe knew that once the shaman's body was removed, through a corpse hole made in the north side of the hogan, the house would be boarded up, but the corpse hole would be left open as a warning. A body could be taken away from the house, but the evil *chindi* would remain forever.

"Joe!" Andi called from the doorway. "What's keeping you so long?"

Damn! Why couldn't she have stayed outside where he'd left her? "Don't come in—"

She rushed into the hogan, took one look at the scene before her and let out a bloodcurdling scream.

Chapter 6

Joe rushed to Andi, grabbed her and dragged her outside, then pulled her into his arms and held her while she shivered uncontrollably. "Calm down." He rubbed her back, comforting her as best he could. "The old shaman is dead. There's nothing we can do to help him."

Andi sucked in several deep breaths, then lifted her head and stared into Joe's dark eyes. "I'm okay. Honestly. It's just...well, seeing..." She disengaged herself from Joe's hold. "What do you think happened? You don't believe that Russ—"

"Neither Russ nor Eddie killed the shaman," Joe reassured her. "My guess is that Bobby Yazzi's real murderer, or someone he has hired to hunt down the boys, did this."

"Oh, God!" She grabbed the front of Joe's jacket. "Does that mean he—he...? If he caught Russ and Eddie here, he would have killed them, too."

"We can't be a hundred percent sure that the boys were

even here," Joe told her. "But my guess is that whoever's tracking them followed them here. From the looks of the shaman, I'd say he fought his attacker. Since there would have been no reason for the boys to leave before morning, I figure that Edmund Kieyoomia detained the tracker so that Eddie and Russ could get away."

"You think he saved their lives?"

"I do."

"Now what? Where could the boys have gone from here? Where do *we* go from here?"

"We return to Jefferson Nastas's home," Joe said. "My guess is that Russ and Eddie will go back there to pick up the truck. They don't know these hills and I think they're smart enough to realize their best bet is to get away from this part of the country as fast as possible."

"So what are the odds the boys will still be at Mr. Nastas's when we get back there?"

"I'd say not good," Joe admitted. "I think we probably crossed paths with the boys on our way up here. They could have seen or heard us and kept out of sight until we passed and then they went straight down to get the truck."

"Maybe they'll tell Mr. Nastas where they're going," Andi said hopefully.

Joe shook his head. "They'll know that not only are we looking for them, but that the person who killed the old shaman is still after them, too. If they're gone when we get back, our best bet is to go straight to the nearest Tribal Police station and report the murder scene we found here and let the authorities know the boys have a truck. Possibly a stolen truck. And that someone—probably the person who killed Mr. Kieyoomia—is following Eddie and Russ."

"I can't believe you're willing to trust the police."

"I want to find the boys and I'd like to do it before the police do," Joe said. "But the police aren't our enemy and they aren't the boys' enemy either. They're in a position to help us locate the boys. It's better for Eddie and Russ if the police find them first and not the killer. If you have a better suggestion on where to go from here, then tell me."

Andi balled her hands into tight fists. "I don't know." Andi fumed. "But I do know that if we go to the police and tell them we found the shaman's body, then they're going to ask us what we were doing and—"

"And we will tell them the truth."

"What if the police think the boys killed Mr. Kieyoomia? Aren't they in enough trouble already?"

"Withholding the truth will not help Eddie and Russ."

"Oh, yes, by all means, let's make sure the truth comes out. It doesn't matter who gets hurt by the truth. You haven't changed at all. You still have to do everything *by the book!*" Andi stormed away from Joe, stomping around the side of hogan in an effort to vent her frustration.

Hell! He couldn't say or do anything right as far as Andi was concerned. Her problem was that she always thought with her heart and not with her head. But she was a woman. What else could he expect? She said that he hadn't changed—hell, she hadn't changed any, either. She was still only too willing to prejudge him, to assume the worst about him. Why couldn't she understand that helping Eddie and Russ was as important to him as it was to her? Yes, he did hold Russ responsible for dragging Eddie into a bad situation, but that didn't mean he blamed the boy for anything else. Certainly not murder.

Joe looked around and didn't see Andi, so he circled the hogan and found her on the far side, bent over, picking something up off the ground. He halted and waited until she had the object in her hand before he approached her.

"What did you find?"

She jumped and gasped. "Damn it, you scared me half to death."

"Sorry." He glanced down at the square brown wallet she held.

"What have you got there?" When she hesitated and clutched the object all the tighter, Joe suspected she recognized the item. "Does it belong to Russ?"

"Yes," she replied, her gaze meeting Joe's, her expression issuing him a warning. "It's Russ's. I gave it to him this past Christmas. It's handmade and one of a kind."

"Look through it and see if you find anything that might help us."

"I'm surprised you trust me. I'd think you'd want to do it yourself."

"I trust you a lot more than you trust me." He nodded to the wallet. "Take a look."

She opened the wallet and inspected it thoroughly. "Four dollars. His driver's license. A picture of Doli and me. One of our father. A library card. That's it."

"Nothing to help us. Nothing to give us a clue as to where they might be going from here."

"Joe?"

"Yes?"

"Will you tell the police about this wallet?"

"It's evidence," he replied, then turned and walked away.

He had to contact the police as soon as possible and tell them about finding the shaman's body. Of course, the authorities would want to know why he and Andi had made a trek up into the mountains to see the old man. He wouldn't lie about that. Besides, it wouldn't do any good to lie. Too many people knew about his and Andi's search for their kinsman.

But did he have to mention that Andi had found Russ's wallet? If he were totally honest, he would. But in what way would telling the police about the wallet help them track down Edmund Kieyoomia's murderer? If he said anything about the wallet, Andi would see it as yet another betrayal.

What the hell was he going to do?

"They left my horses and took the truck," Jefferson Nastas said. "I could see that they were frightened, but when I asked, they would not say why."

"How long ago were they here?" Joe asked.

"Just as the sun set, they came. I asked them to stay the night, but they would not. They said they must go, that if they stayed I would be in danger, too."

"Did they tell you where they were going?" Andi asked.

"No. They only said to tell you both that they will not come home. Russ said this to me. The other one, he said nothing."

Andi eyed Joe, waiting for his response, knowing that Mr. Nastas's comment only gave credence to Joe's assumption that everything was Russ's fault, that her brother had dragged Eddie into this intolerable situation, into inescapable danger.

"Mr. Nastas, Andi and I are going from here to the police station in Echo City," Joe explained. "We will report the murder of Edmund Kieyoomia. I'm sure the police will want to question you."

"The young braves did not do this bad thing," Jefferson said. "I will tell the police I believe this."

''Thank you,'' Andi said. ''We, too, know that Russ and Eddie aren't murderers.''

At least, *she* knew it, Andi thought. And surely Joe did, too. He kept saying that he didn't think Russ was capable of murder, but was he only telling her what he thought she wanted to hear? If he gave the police Russ's wallet, she'd know how he truly felt. If Joe believed Russ was innocent, there would be no need to implicate him, to give the police evidence that would prove her brother had been at the scene of a second murder. Was Joe capable of bending his principles just a fraction in order to protect someone she loved?

They said their goodbyes to Jefferson Nastas and headed out for Echo City, the nearest town. Joe asked to drive, and she gladly handed over the keys. She didn't know how to get to Echo City without a map and she hated trying to find an unknown place when she was driving in the dark.

Where were Russ and Eddie? she wondered. And just how long would it take before the police caught them in the stolen truck? All it would take was for one policeman to spot the truck. And if her brother resisted arrest, what then? The thought of Russ being shot, perhaps fatally wounded, flashed through her mind. She hadn't realized that she'd gasped aloud until Joe questioned her.

''Are you all right?'' he asked.

''What?''

''Is something wrong?'' He kept his gaze fixed on the dark, lonely highway.

''Joe, we've got to find them. Sooner or later, either the police or the real killer is going to catch up with them. We have to get to them first.''

''Keep one thing in mind,'' he said. ''There are a lot of places those boys could hide out and keep safe for quite a while. Just hold on to the thought that even if they're acting irrationally by running away, they're both pretty smart. They're well aware that they are only two steps ahead of both the law and a killer.''

"I know we have to report the shaman's death, but I can't help feeling as if we're wasting precious time.''

"Andi, we have no idea where to look next. We don't know if the boys even stayed on the reservation. They could be anywhere. We're going to have to regroup and hope we get another break, something that will lead us to them again. And we can pray that if we don't find them first, the police will.''

"And what happens if they resist arrest?''

"Eddie would never—''

"But Russ might,'' she said. "That's what you were going to say, isn't it?''

"If you're honest with yourself, you'll admit that it was what you were thinking.''

Andi crossed her arms over her chest and scooted up against the door. Yes, that was exactly what she'd been thinking, but she would never admit it to Joe. Never! She closed her eyes and uttered a silent plea. *Please, God, please, keep Russ and Eddie safe.*

"We've got to ditch this truck,'' Russ said. "The police can recognize it too easy. We're just lucky we've gotten this far in it.''

"Why don't we go home? Or at least, let's call our mothers,'' Eddie said. "Believe me, my uncle Joe won't stop looking for us until he finds us.''

"I don't trust your uncle Joe, and you know why. I'd no more turn myself over him to than I would to the police.''

"You trust your sister, don't you? Mr. Nastas said that

she's with Uncle Joe. She wants us to turn ourselves in.
She knows we can't keep running forever. She and Uncle
Joe just want to help us. We should have waited for them
at Mr. Nastas's house.''

"Will you quit being such a crybaby!'' Russ screamed
as he gripped the steering wheel with white-knuckled fe-
rociousness. After taking a deep breath, he said, "I'm
sorry, Eddie. It's just that Andi is crazy if she thinks Joe
Ornelas gives a damn about me. Yeah, sure, he cares what
happens to you, but he's probably already got me pegged
as guilty. He's not going to give me a break.''

"Uncle Joe's not like that.''

"Yeah, well, tell that to my father. Joe sure didn't give
him a break, did he.''

Eddie grabbed Russ's arm. "That guy who's after us
killed the *yataalii* and he would have killed us, too, if
Hosteen Kieyoomia hadn't held him off until we could
get away. For all we know, that guy is right behind us,
following us, just waiting to kill us.''

Russ tugged on his arm, but Eddie held fast. "Let me
go, will you? Nobody is following us. Don't you think
I'd know if somebody was right behind us?''

"I want to go home,'' Eddie said. "If you want to keep
on running—''

"No! You aren't going home and neither am I. Not yet.
I have to call Jewel again. Maybe this time she won't
hang up on me. Until she can back up our story, we have
no way to prove that I didn't kill Bobby. And I can hardly
go to her house. Her family knows the police are looking
for us. Besides, I don't want to lead the killer to her and
put her life in danger.''

"The police don't have any proof that you shot
Bobby.'' Eddie tugged on Russ's arm again. "I thought

we'd be safe at your great-uncle's house, but we weren't. We aren't safe anywhere.''

"Damn it, Eddie, will you quit bellyaching.''

When Russ jerked his arm free of Eddie's hold, he momentarily lost control of the truck. The vehicle went careening across the highway and straight through the guardrail. Both boys bounced forward. Russ's chest slammed into the steering wheel and Eddie's head thumped against the windshield as the truck came to a halt in a deep, rocky ditch.

Joe wished he could read Andi's mind. After they left the Echo City police station, she didn't say two words to him and hadn't been particularly talkative since. But what had he expected? Had he thought she would thank him for not mentioning the fact that they had found Russ's wallet at the scene of the crime? Even now, he wasn't one hundred percent sure why he'd withheld the information. Was it because, just this once, he wanted to look like a hero in Andi's eyes again? Or was it because he thought he owed it to Russell to protect Russ? Hell, maybe it was just because he knew that telling the police he had evidence Russ was at the scene of the crime wouldn't help them solve Edmund Kieyoomia's murder. The police already suspected that the boys had been at the shaman's hogan, so why cloud the issue by throwing unjust suspicion on Russ? Whatever his true motivation had been, Joe felt guilty for not being totally honest.

He and Andi had been on the road all night, after leaving the police station at well past one in the morning. He was taking them straight to his house where they could shower and change clothes, then they'd head out to J.T.'s ranch for a strategy meeting. He figured they would probably reach his place within the next fifteen minutes. Dawn sunlight streaked across the eastern horizon in front of them, painting the sky with vivid color. He glanced quickly over at Andi and noted that she was still asleep. She was huddled in a ball, her knees drawn up and her arms crisscrossed over her stomach. She was lovely. Tired, probably hungry, with her hair slightly disheveled and her face void of makeup, Andrea Stephens was still a beautiful woman.

Just catching shadowy glimpses of her in his peripheral vision as he'd been driving had whetted his appetite to see more of her. Despite her obstinance and hostility, he couldn't convince his body that she was the wrong woman for him. He wanted her. As much now as he had five years ago. Back then, he had been patient, willing to wait for her to decide when the time was right for them to become lovers. But that was when he had hoped they might one day marry. Now, there was no hope for the future, no possibility that they would ever become husband and wife. Too many obstacles stood between them— far more now than in the past.

On some instinctive level Joe knew that if he never made love to Andi, a part of him would remain incomplete. He would always wonder. And he would always long for what had never been. But did Andi feel the same?

When Joe pulled the Expedition up in front of his humble home, Andi didn't move. He reached out to nudge her, then stopped himself. He got out, rounded the SUV and opened Andi's door, then shoved her car keys into his pocket and retrieved his house key. She didn't move, didn't open her eyes. He slid one arm beneath her and lifted her up and into his arms. She moaned softly and snuggled against him, wrapping her arm around his neck. His body reacted in a typical male fashion, and he admitted to himself that he would like nothing better than

to take her inside to his bed and make passionate love to
her.

Maneuvering awkwardly, still holding Andi securely,
Joe fiddled with the door lock, inserting the key and trying
to balance the sleeping woman in his arms. The lock
clicked. He turned the knob and the door swung open.
Andi mumbled. Her eyelids flickered. "Joe?"

"Yeah?"

"Oh, Joe." She nuzzled his neck with her nose and
buried her face against his shoulder.

As much as he wished she were consciously reacting
with pleasure to being in his arms, he realized that she
wasn't fully awake, that she wasn't aware of what she
was saying or doing.

Joe carried her through the living room and into his
bedroom. When he deposited her on his unmade bed, she
clung to him, her arms tugging him down to her. His
muscles strained. His body yearned. *Kiss her,* an inner
voice advised. *Even if she wakes and slaps your face afterward, won't it be worth it?* Joe came down over her,
bracing himself with his hands as he sat on the edge of
the bed and lowered his lips to hers. For a split second
he almost stopped himself, but the urge to take her mouth,
to taste her sweet lips, overpowered his conscience.

Her mouth was soft and warm and inviting. She partic-
ipated in the kiss, from first tender touch to the hot, moist
tongue-mating. Joe's sex hardened. He wanted more. He
wanted everything she had to give. He couldn't resist
touching her. Bracing himself with one hand, he lifted the
other and slid it just inside her collar, his fingertips caressing her neck as his thumb stroked her throat.

As if his touch had brought her to full consciousness,
alerting her to reality, Andi's eyelids flew open and she
stared up at Joe. Just for a moment she smiled at him, and

he saw the desire in her eyes. But in a heartbeat, the smile faded, replaced with a frown. The hunger in her eyes vanished.

"What do you think you're doing?" she demanded.

"Nothing you didn't want me to do."

Andi shoved against his chest. "Get off me!"

Joe lifted himself up and off the bed, then stood and glared down at her. "You were asleep when we got here, so I decided not to wake you. But when you wrapped yourself around me and kept calling my name, I took it as an invitation to—"

"To take advantage of me?" Andi shot straight up in bed, glanced around the room and then groaned. "I'm in your bedroom."

"So? It's the only bedroom in the house."

"If you thought I was going to…that we were going to…I'll have you know that you're the last man on earth I'd have sex with." She jumped out of bed and confronted him. "What's happened to you? You used to be a gentleman. When we were dating you never would have…well, you didn't ever try to push me into doing something I wasn't ready to do."

"Maybe I should have."

"What?" She glared at him, an incredulous look on her face.

He wanted to grab her by the shoulders and force her to admit the truth—that despite all the obstacles that kept them apart, the old chemistry between them still existed. Stronger and more compelling than ever before. But he didn't touch her. Instead he captured her with his intense gaze.

"I always treated you with respect and I let you set the rules that governed our relationship. I gave you your way in every situation, about everything that concerned us."

Joe had never voiced his resentment. And certainly never to Andi. "I was so afraid I'd lose you before you were truly mine. I didn't want to do anything that would scare you off. I thought that if I were patient and understanding, you'd come to see my life on the reservation as a life you wanted to share with me.

"But what good did catering to your wishes do me? The first time I did something you disapproved of, you turned against me. I did what I thought was the right thing—the honorable thing—and you wouldn't even let me explain my side of the situation."

"My father killed himself because you arrested him, because your actions shamed him before his family and his people. I was in shock and mourning my father's death. How did you think I should have reacted? You didn't give me time to deal with anything before you tucked tail and ran."

"Your father's own actions shamed him," Joe said, barely able to control the rage seething inside him. "He disappointed everyone who knew and respected him. But by doing my duty, by being a good lawman, you and many others treated me as if I were the one who had committed a crime. Don't you think that every day of my life, I mourn Russell Lapahie? He was like a father to me. He didn't have to kill himself. He could have faced up to his actions and made amends."

"And you could have stayed here on the reservation and given people a chance to forgive you, but instead you deserted us. You ran away and never looked back."

"Maybe I didn't think I'd done something that required forgiveness," Joe said. "And if you believe that I never looked back, then you're wrong. Not a day passed that some part of me didn't remember my old life, didn't long to return."

Andi looked at him for a moment longer, then broke eye contact. Squaring her shoulders, she stiffened her spine and walked around Joe and across the bedroom. Pausing in the doorway, she said, ''I'm going to take a shower and change clothes.''

''Go ahead. I'll fix us some breakfast, then call J.T. and let him know we'll be there in a couple of hours. After we eat, you can clean up the dishes while I shower and change.''

''Fine.''

When Andi disappeared from view, Joe smashed one fist into the palm of his other hand and cursed under his breath. Their frank discussion had accomplished nothing. They were exactly where they had been—at an impasse.

He headed toward the kitchen, thankful that Kate had filled his refrigerator and cupboards with supplies. But before he had broken the first egg into a bowl, his cellular phone rang. He removed the telephone from the holder attached to his belt, flipped the phone open and answered.

''Ornelas here.''

''Joe, I've got some bad news.''

A shudder racked Joe's body. ''Has something happened to the boys?''

''I haven't had any word on Eddie and Russ,'' J.T. said. ''But it seems the police have found the murder weapon.''

''How is that bad news?''

''They found the gun in a water trough in one of the corrals next to Doli Lapahie's barn.''

''Damn!''

Chapter 7

Rita Gonzales, the Blackwood family's housekeeper, served coffee in the den, where Joe and Andi sat on opposite sides of the room, each occasionally glancing the other's way. Joanna had tried her best to include them in conversation, but her efforts had been futile. Andi assumed that after their confrontation at his house earlier this morning, Joe's emotions were as raw as hers.

She still couldn't believe that she had thought she was dreaming about Joe kissing her, only to waken fully and discover that it had been no dream. Even now, a couple of hours later, she still felt embarrassed by the incident. Had she said anything that Joe could have taken the wrong way? She had definitely done something that had prompted his actions—she hadn't resisted when he'd put his lips on hers. She had given herself over to that kiss and enjoyed it with total abandon.

"Elena and Alex are returning this afternoon, from Alex's one-man show in Albuquerque," Joanna said.

"Why don't you two stay for dinner? Joe, you haven't seen them in years and—"

"Honey, I'm sure Joe will see my sister while he's back in New Mexico," J.T. said. "But right now, we have more urgent matters to take care of."

J.T. smiled at his wife, his one-eyed gaze resting lovingly on her. Joe's cousin had lost his left eye years ago when he'd been in the Secret Service. Andi had always thought that the black eyepatch he wore gave him a roguish quality. She greatly envied the Blackwoods—their marriage, their children, their good fortune to have found each other and fallen in love. Joanna was one of the first friends Andi had made when she arrived in New Mexico five-and-a-half years ago. Perhaps it was because Joanna, as another *bilagaana,* had originally been seen as an outsider, too—just as Andi had been, despite the fact that she was half Navajo. Or maybe it was because both she and J.T.'s wife had been raised in wealthy Southern families, she in South Carolina and Joanna in Virginia.

When Andi had opened her arts and crafts gallery in Gallup, she had commissioned several paintings from Joanna, a talented and renowned artist, and a couple of sculptures from Alex, another *bilagaana,* who was married to J.T.'s younger sister, Elena. Over time, as they'd become close friends, Joanna had shared the story of how she and J.T. had met and that when they had married, he had built her a new home and deeded the original ranch house to Elena.

"I'll make a point of stopping by to see Elena and Alex," Joe said. "After all, I've never met their little girl, and she's how old now—almost two?"

"She'll be three in July," Joanna corrected.

"Honey, I know that you're in nest-building mode right

now," J.T. said, "but Joe and I really need to get down to business here and discuss—"

"Yes, I know." Joanna lifted her rotund body from the sofa before J.T., who'd been standing by the windows, hurried across the room to assist her. She caressed his hands affectionately when he touched her. "Andi, I'm sure you'll want to stay here and get all the news firsthand. But I'm afraid my husband has given me strict orders that since I'm an emotional wreck these days—" she patted her protruding belly "—I have to avoid any stress."

"J.T. is a wise and caring husband," Joe said. "A man who loves his wife wants only to take care of her, especially when she carries his child."

A sudden hush fell over the room. A tender quiet. Joe looked directly at Andi, whose gaze instantly met his. The two of them shared a singular thought: a picture of Andi pregnant with Joe's baby flashed through his mind and hers.

How could she even consider such a possibility? she wondered. She and Joe didn't belong together. Not now. Even if her body still yearned for his. Even if he wanted her. Even if she couldn't imagine spending her life with anyone else.

"I'll see y'all at lunch." Joanna walked out of the room, taking her time and being very careful with each step.

The moment his wife was out of earshot, J.T. turned to Joe. "Did you tell Andi about the gun?"

"No," Joe said.

"What gun?" Andi asked.

J.T. huffed. "The murder weapon, the gun that was used to kill Bobby Yazzi, has turned up."

"Where?" Andi steeled herself for the answer, instinct telling her that she wasn't going to like what she heard.

"In a water trough at the corrals beside Doli Lapahie's barn," J.T. replied.

"No!" Andi spun around and faced Joe. He lifted his gaze and met her questioning stare head-on. "You think this means that Russ killed Bobby, don't you." When Joe didn't reply immediately, she yelled at him. "Answer me, damn it! You think that finding the gun on Lapahie property proves Russ is guilty."

"Andi, neither Joe nor I—" J.T. tried to explain.

Without breaking eye contact with Joe, Andi said, "Joe can speak for himself, can't he?"

"The police are going to see this discovery as evidence against Russ," Joe admitted. "But it's possible that the real killer had the gun planted near Russ's home for that very reason."

"There were no fingerprints on the gun," J.T. said. "So whoever disposed of it had wiped it clean."

"If Russ had used the gun, why would he wipe off his fingerprints and then toss the gun into a water trough on his family's property?" Andi glanced over her shoulder at J.T. "That doesn't make any sense, does it?"

"Not to me," J.T. said. "And not to Joe."

Andi looked back at Joe.

"At this point we can't be certain of anything," Joe said, "but I tend to agree with J.T. And with you. Someone probably planted the weapon. The same someone who caught up with the boys at *Hosteen* Keiyoomia's."

"I'd say this guy is a hired gun," J.T. surmised. "He knows his business. That means he could still be following Russ and Eddie, and perhaps..." J.T. paused, obviously not wanting to verbalize his thought.

"He could have caught up with them," Andi finished. "That is what you're thinking, isn't it?"

"It's possible," J.T. replied.

"So where does that leave us?" Andi asked.

"It leaves us trying to figure out where the boys would have gone next." J.T. rubbed his chin. "Andi, is there anywhere else Russ might go for help? Anyone other than Doli's uncle, whom Russ might think would hide Eddie and him?"

"No one comes to mind." Andi sighed. "I can call Doli and see if she has any other ideas. But I'm not sure she'll be much help. After that gun was found on her property, she probably went into a tailspin."

"I've given it a great deal of thought," J.T. said. "And if we don't get some sort of lead soon, I think Joe and I will have to call in some favors and bring in a few Dundee agents to help in the search. The more men on the job, the better our chances."

Eddie Whitehorn had torn a piece of material from the hem of his shirt and tied it around his forehead, covering the gash and the swollen bruise that resulted from his head hitting the windshield. He'd bled quite a bit, but after he'd applied the makeshift bandage, the blood finally clotted and dried. The impact with the steering wheel had momentarily knocked the breath out of Russ, but he didn't seem to be badly hurt. They'd had no choice but to leave the truck there in the ditch, since Russ couldn't get it to start up again.

Luckily they hadn't been far from another sheep ranch that adjoined Eddie's family's property, that of his mother's cousin. Even in the dark, Eddie had been able to find the way there. They had hidden in the small lean-to that the family used as a tool shed. Exhausted from their mad run from Arizona back to New Mexico, they'd slept for several hours, until Eddie's cousin, Clara Gilbert, who was only twelve, discovered them.

"I promise I won't tell anyone that I've seen you," Clara said. "But you'd better stay here out of sight for now. I'll bring you some food and water, and then you'll have to go before Mama finds out you're here. She'll be sure to call Kate."

Russ grabbed Clara's thin, brown arm. "Would you do me a favor?"

"What sort of favor?"

"Call somebody for me, would you?"

"Who do you want me to call? I thought you and Eddie didn't want anyone to know where you are."

"I want you to call Jewel Begay. She's sort of my girlfriend. Tell her that you're Eddie's cousin and that I need for her to go to the police and tell them what really happened the night Bobby Yazzi was killed."

"Your girlfriend was there?" Clara's large brown eyes widened with interest. "I thought you and Eddie went there alone."

"Yeah, well, we didn't," Eddie said. "The truth is that we had a couple of girls with us, and they drove off and left us there."

"I'll have to wait until Mama comes out to feed the chickens, to make the call and get you some food." Clara pointed to the rag tied around Eddie's head. "What's that for? Are you trying to look like an Indian?" She grinned, showing a set of perfect white teeth.

"Ah, I got a scratch when we wrecked our truck," Eddie said. "It wouldn't stop bleeding."

"Are you okay?" she asked.

"I'm okay."

But he wasn't. Eddie didn't think he'd ever be okay

again. Whenever he allowed himself to think about what was happening, he felt hopeless. He and Russ could stay on the run for only so long before someone caught up with them. The police. The killer. Or Uncle Joe. He prayed it would be his uncle. If he did what he really wanted to do, what he knew he should do, he'd go home. Then his parents could drive him to the police station to turn himself in. But Russ was determined to keep running, and there was no way Eddie would desert his best friend. They were in this together. To the end, whatever that end might be.

"Stay out of sight," Clara repeated. "I'll be back as soon as I can. By the way, what is Jewel's phone number?"

"Don't you need to write it down?" Russ asked.

"No, just tell it to me and I'll remember."

The very second Russ finished reciting the number, Clara rushed out of the lean-to and ran toward the back door of her house.

Russ released a long, loud sigh of relief. "Man, that was close. Lucky for us your cousin isn't going to turn us in. She's a pretty good kid."

"You have to know it's only a matter of time before somebody finds that truck we stole," Eddie said. "The police will search my parents' place and here, too, since it's so close to where we left the truck. Unless we intend to turn ourselves in, we'd better get going soon."

"Yeah, you're right. It's just, I haven't figured out yet where to go from here."

"I know a place where we can hide out for a while," Eddie said. "It's someplace nobody ever goes anymore. But we'll have to borrow a couple of horses, and I hate the thought of stealing from Clara's family. I wish we had some money."

"I had four bucks in my wallet, before I lost it." Russ patted his hip pocket. "But that wouldn't have bought us a ride on a horse, let alone the horse itself."

"I'll tell Clara to tell her parents that we— No, I can't do that. If she tells them that we only borrowed the horses, then they'll know we were here."

"Look, when this is all over, you can explain. They're family, right? They'll understand that we only did what we had to do."

Fifteen minutes later, Clara sneaked out the back door of the house and scurried toward the lean-to. Eddie held his breath as he watched her heading in their direction. When her foot tripped over a large rock, she almost dropped the sack she held in her arms.

The minute she entered the shack, she thrust the paper bag at Eddie. "Here's some candy bars and canned colas and fruit. That's the best I could do."

"Did you call Jewel?" Russ asked.

"Yes, I called her, but the minute I told her I was Eddie Whitehorn's cousin, she told me never to call her again— and then she hung up."

"Damn!" Russ kicked the dirt floor, stirring up dust.

"I called her right back," Clara said.

Hope glimmered in Russ's eyes—momentary hope dashed by Clara's next words.

"She hung up on me again."

"Well, I'm screwed. She's the only other eyewitness to what happened at Bobby Yazzi's." Russ nodded toward the rickety wooden door. "We'd better get going."

Eddie laid his hand on his cousin's shoulder. "Clara, Russ and I need to borrow a couple of horses."

"My father takes me to school on his way to work. We usually leave about the same time Mama and Uncle Will herd the sheep out to graze," she explained. "Wait here until you hear the truck start up, then it should be safe to take two of the horses from the corral.''

''Thank you for helping us.'' Eddie squeezed Clara's arm.

''You are family,'' she said, as if no other explanation was necessary.

Becoming more and more frustrated by the minute, Joe paced the floor. Andi and J.T. had been making phone calls for the past two hours, contacting every friend, acquaintance and relative on the reservation and asking them to pass along the word that any clue to the boys' whereabouts was desperately needed. In the meantime, Joe had phoned Ellen Denby and lined up a contingency force—four Dundee agents would be on ''ready'' for the next twenty-four hours and could fly to New Mexico the moment Joe gave the word.

Andi slumped down in one of the wingback chairs, dropped J.T.'s cell phone in her lap and let out a long, low sigh. ''Where are they? Where the hell *are* they?''

Leaning his hip against the edge of his desk, his booted feet crossed at the ankles, J.T. replaced the receiver on the telephone.

Before he had a chance to comment on Andi's rhetorical question, the phone rang.

''Blackwood Ranch,'' J.T. said. ''Yeah? When? Are you combing the area?''

Andi shot up out of the chair. Joe ceased his pacing. They approached J.T. just as he said, ''Thank you,'' and hung up.

''Who was that?'' Andi asked.

''Was it word on the boys?'' Instinctively Joe reached out to touch Andi, a gesture of comfort and support, but stopped himself short of placing his hand on her back.

"That was Bill Cummings," J.T. said. "They found Mr. Lovato's stolen truck in a ditch. Looked like it had gone through a guardrail and wrecked. No sign of the boys, but there was blood on the windshield, probably from where one of the boys hit his head."

"Oh, God, what if one or both of them are hurt?" Andi grabbed J.T.'s arm.

"If they'd been seriously hurt, they wouldn't have gone far," J.T. told her.

"Where did the police find the truck?" Joe asked.

"About fifteen miles from Ed and Kate's place." J.T. patted Andi's hand. "About five miles west of Arthur and Frances Gilbert's ranch."

"Have the police contacted the Gilberts?" Andi released her hold on J.T.'s arm.

"They didn't find anyone home, but since Frances and Will take care of the sheep, Bill said his men were out looking for them."

"The Gilberts are relatives. There's a good chance that Eddie might have felt safe going there." Joe had attended the Navajo Community College with Frances's husband, Arthur Gilbert, and the two had once been friends. He and his sister had grown up with their cousins, Frances and Will, and Kate and Frances remained close friends to this day.

"Wouldn't the Gilberts have notified Kate if the boys showed up at their house?" Andi glanced at Joe.

"I'm sure she would have." Joe wished he could erase the worry he saw in Andi's eyes, wished that he could find a way to make things right for her. "But at this point, we don't have another lead. I think we should head out to the Gilberts' ranch and see if the police have found Frances."

"I agree," Andi said. "I'll go crazy if we have to sit around here waiting."

"You two go ahead." J.T. hitched his thumb toward the door. "I'll hold down the fort here, and if I get any word on the boys I'll call you immediately."

"Thanks, J.T." Joe nodded curtly and exchanged a knowing glance with his cousin, each understanding that J.T. didn't want to leave Joanna alone for very long, just in case she went into labor.

Frances Gilbert was a petite woman with huge dark eyes and a round, full face. She offered her guests refreshments and when they declined, she sat with them in her small living room cluttered with mismatched furniture. Navajo blankets adorned the back of the worn sofa and hung on two walls.

"I told the police that we have not seen Eddie and his friend, Russ," Frances said.

"Although we have not seen them, we think they were here." Will looked directly at Joe. "We believe that Clara may have helped them."

"Clara?" Andi repeated.

"My daughter," Frances replied. "She and Eddie have known each other all their lives, and if he came here, she would have done what she could to help him and she would have kept his presence a secret."

"What makes you think Clara helped Eddie?" Joe asked.

"There are canned colas, candy bars and some fruit missing from the kitchen," Frances told them. "And two of our five horses are gone. Clara probably 'loaned' them the horses so they could get away."

"Or maybe they just took the horses," Joe mumbled

under his breath. "You didn't tell the police about the missing horses?"

"No," Will said. "We waited to tell you so that you could decide if this is something the police should know."

"Thank you." Joe stood. "Now all we have to do is figure out where the boys went from here."

"In my estimation, they were heading southwest when they left here," Will said. "Once the police were gone, I looked for signs and followed some tracks for several miles. I believe the tracks were made by our horses."

"That means they're going toward Painted Canyon," Joe said. "Eddie knows that region like the back of his hand." He grabbed Andi's arm, jerked her up out of the chair and held her wrist. "Come on. I've got a good idea where they've gone."

"Thank y'all so very much." Andi glanced back and smiled graciously at Frances, before Joe led her out into the yard. As they neared her SUV, she snatched her wrist from his grasp. "You could have just asked me to come with you. You didn't have to manhandle me."

"Stop complaining about everything!" Joe opened the SUV's passenger door. "Get in."

"What's turned you into the grouch of the century?"

"If I'm the grouch of the century, then you are the shrew of the century."

"Touché." Andi shrugged. "Okay, so now that we agree that you're a grouch and I'm a shrew, how about telling me where we're going?"

"I'm fairly certain I know where Eddie and Russ have gone. And if I'm right, they could be in big trouble if the guy hunting them finds them before we do."

Andi jumped into the Expedition and slammed the door, while Joe circled behind the vehicle, got in and slid behind the wheel. Before he started the engine, Joe removed his cell phone and tossed it to Andi.

"Call J.T. and tell him to meet us at the old abandoned uranium mine." Joe revved the motor, shifted into reverse and backed out onto the road.

"An old mine? What makes you think the boys went there?"

"Because seven years ago, a madman held Joanna Blackwood captive in the abandoned mine, which is southwest of here. Eddie will remember the incident and recall that the old mine is a good hiding place."

"If it's a good hiding place, then why won't the boys be safe there?"

"Because there is only one way in and one way out," Joe told her. "There was a cave-in at the back entrance a few months after J.T. rescued Joanna. So, if the man following Eddie and Russ finds them in the mine, they will have no escape route, except straight into him."

They traveled over the rough terrain, jostling up and down as the Expedition whipped up a cloud of dust behind them. Andi gasped when Joe took the turnoff onto a dirt trail, which she assumed lead to the old mine.

"How much farther?" Andi gripped the edge of the seat on either side of her thighs.

"Not far. A couple of miles." His gaze focused on the hills spreading out in front of them.

The last time Andi had prayed this fervently had been when her father died. She knew Joe well enough to realize that he was worried—very worried. And his concern only added to her own.

As they neared the mine, Andi recognized J.T.'s truck parked alongside an older model black Jeep Cherokee. Had he brought someone with him? she wondered.

Joe flew in beside J.T.'s truck, stopped, released his seat belt immediately and hopped out of the Expedition. J.T. met him in front of the SUV. Andi struggled with her safety belt, her hands trembling and her heart racing madly. She could hear the men talking in hushed tones. What were they saying? Damn it! Finally the catch gave on the seat belt and she hurriedly flung open the door and rushed to join Joe and J.T.

"No sign of the horses," J.T. said. "Either the boys aren't here or the horses ran off by themselves."

"Whose Jeep?" Andi nodded to the nearby vehicle.

"Good question," J.T. replied. "Don't suppose the boys stole it, do you?"

"Let's hope so," Joe said, his mouth curving into a mockery of a smile. "But my gut instincts are telling me something else."

"You think the man who killed the old shaman tracked the boys here and has them trapped inside the mine, don't you." Andi shuddered at the thought that Russ and Eddie might both be dead.

"There's only one way to find out," Joe told her.

"I brought an extra rifle," J.T. said.

"Get it," Joe told him. "I'll leave mine with Andi, just in case she needs a weapon with a long range."

"What do you mean you'll leave your rifle with me?" she demanded. "Are you planning on leaving me here, going in the mine without me?"

"Yeah, that's exactly what I'm planning to do."

Assessing the situation quickly, Andi accepted defeat without putting up too much of a fight. The odds were two-to-one against her. If she'd thought she could reason with J.T., she'd have given it a try, but she understood only too well that these two Navajo men were in agreement; neither was willingly going to allow a woman to put her life at risk.

"Do you have any idea how to use a rifle?" Joe asked her.

"Believe it or not, that's something I've learned how to do in the past five years. My little brother taught me."

"Good." Joe grabbed her arm and dragged her back to the SUV's open passenger door. "Get in, lock the doors and keep my rifle handy. And if someone comes out of the mine—someone other than J.T. or me—do not try to capture him yourself. Do I make myself clear?"

"Clear as a bell!"

Joe boosted her up and into the SUV, then slammed the door. She did as he had commanded. She locked the doors. After watching Joe and J.T. for several minutes as they headed up the hill toward the entrance to the mine, she reached down and ran her hand over the rifle that lay on the floor, then lifted it onto her lap. She returned her attention to the two men climbing up the hillside.

An odd feeling of foreboding washed over her, almost drowning her with fear. She wanted to get out of the SUV, run toward Joe and J.T. and shout a warning. But she forced herself to stay put.

The sensation of danger inside her intensified until she felt as if she were unraveling from within. Of its own volition her hand reached for the door handle. She couldn't stay here another minute. Disregarding Joe's instructions, Andi opened the SUV door, clasped the rifle to her chest and jumped down onto the ground.

A shot rang out loud and clear in the distance, the sound carrying for miles in the desert. Who had fired the shot? Andi's nerves zinged like live wires. Joe? J.T.? Or a murderer out for another victim?

Chapter 8

Acting purely on instinct, Andi ran toward the mine, rifle in hand. As she drew nearer, she saw Joe and J.T., each backed up flat against either side of the mine entrance. Both appeared unharmed. She breathed a sigh of relief. What was going on? Had they cornered someone inside the mine? Oh, God, what if it was Russ and Eddie? Did Russ have a weapon? Had he fired the shot?

Joe must have heard her approaching because he turned abruptly, his rifle pointing in her direction, and moved his lips in what she suspected was a silent curse. Before she knew what was happening, he rushed toward her, grabbed her arm and dragged her behind the nearest protective barrier, a rusted-out piece of equipment that had been left to the elements when the mine was abandoned. A couple of rifle shots whizzed over their heads, striking the decaying metal, bursting off razor-sharp chips. He tightened his grip on her arm. She winced.

''What the hell are you doing here?'' He glared at her,

both anger and concern evident in his expression. "Didn't I tell you to stay in the Expedition?"

"I heard a rifle shot. I thought maybe—"

"It's not the boys," he said. "We got a glimpse of the guy when we first approached the mine entrance. It looked like he was getting ready to leave, and we surprised him."

"Do you think it's the man who's been hunting Russ and Eddie?"

"Maybe."

"Does that mean you think—"

"No, it doesn't mean he's killed the boys," Joe reassured her. "It's possible Eddie and Russ didn't even come here."

"Then why—"

"We don't have time to hash all of this out right now. I want you to stay here, keep down and do not move. Do you think, just this once, you can do as you're told?"

"Yes." She looked into his eyes, and for a split second an inexplicable understanding passed between them. "Where are you going?"

"We can't wait around until that guy runs out of ammunition," Joe said. "That could take days. If there's any possibility that he has Eddie and Russ in there with him, then we have to make a move soon."

"I thought you said the boys might not even be here."

"They may not be, but if they are…"

"I know. I'll stay right here and I won't move until you tell me to," she promised.

Joe nodded, then eased out from behind the barrier. When he glanced back at Andi, she whispered, "Be careful."

From her hiding place, she could see very little, unless she raised her head. But she had vowed that she wouldn't move from the spot. With a tenacious hold, she gripped

her rifle and prayed. Moments passed slowly. She could
almost hear the ticking of every second inside her head.
Or maybe it was just her erratic heartbeat. A myriad of
concerns flickered through her mind, each mini-scenario
worse than the previous one. What if J.T. was killed and
Joanna was left a widow with four children? What if Russ
and Eddie were already dead? What if Joe lost his life in
an attempt to save the boys?

A sudden barrage of gunfire alerted her to a battle going
on several yards away. While she sat there in comparative
safety, J.T. and Joe were putting their lives on the line.
When more gunshots rang out in the stillness of the hot
New Mexico desert, Andi's mind waged its own war.
Should she stay put as Joe had instructed, or should she
join their fight?

She stayed where she was, all her instincts telling her
she should be helping, not sitting back waiting for the
outcome. *What is happening? Maybe they need me.* The
blood rushed through her body, pounding her heart. The
thunderous beat of her pulse deafened her to every sound
except the continuing gunfire.

Enough! She couldn't stay put a minute longer. But she
wouldn't just rush out and chance getting herself shot. She
must be careful and think before she acted.

The minute Andi exposed herself, placing herself in
danger, a rush of adrenaline flooded her system. She
rolled, then crawled across the parched desert floor until
she found cover behind the edge of the mountain wall.
Lifting her rifle, preparing to use it, she surveyed the area
around the mouth of the old mine. Where were Joe and
J.T.? Had they gone inside the mine to hunt down the
shooter? Andi's nerves screamed. Her heartbeat accelerated alarmingly.

Suddenly, there was silence. No more gunfire. Creeping

along the edge of the mountainside, she made her way carefully toward the dark opening that led into the mine. Should she call out to Joe? If she cried out, would she warn the shooter of her presence? But if she went inside without making Joe and J.T. aware that she was coming in, they might shoot her by mistake.

She eased closer and closer to the entrance, then stepped inside, into the gloomy, dank cavern. She could see nothing ahead of her. Pitch black. But within minutes, when she edged her way farther inside and her vision refocused in the semidarkness, she saw the backs of two men, both on their knees, huddled over something. Or someone. Her heart caught in her throat. Then she realized that the two men were Joe and J.T.

"Joe?" she called softly.

Joe and J.T. looked over their shoulders. Joe groaned.

"Why don't you wait outside for us," J.T. said.

"Did you capture him?" she asked. "Do you have the man who was shooting at you?"

"Yes," Joe replied. "Now get the hell out of here."

Andi halted, angered and hurt by Joe's brutal command. Ignoring his orders, she headed straight toward them. The wounded man lay stretched out on the ground. The sight of his bloody shirt, which had been ripped open to expose his gaping wound, turned her stomach. She glanced away quickly, trying her best to keep the nausea from overwhelming her.

"Where are Russ and Eddie?" Joe asked the wounded man.

Andi forced herself to look down, over J.T.'s shoulder, at the shadowy figure of the shooter. She could tell he was young, no more than thirty. Lean. And even in the dimness of the mine, his eyes appeared a sky blue against the darkness of his skin.

"Why would I tell you anything?" the man asked, wheezing slightly. Suddenly he coughed up blood and spit it out of his mouth onto the ground beside him. When he lifted his hand, he didn't seem to have the strength to wipe his bloodstained lips and cheek. His hand fell limply to his side.

"You'll talk to us, tell us what we want to know, because your life is in our hands," Joe said.

The man gazed up at Joe and smiled. A weak smile, yet somehow sinister all the same. "If I tell you what happened to the two boys, then you'll get me to a doctor. Is that the way it works?"

"Yeah. You cooperate, and we'll do what we can to help you," Joe hovered closer to the man, less than a foot separating their faces. "But if you choose to keep your mouth shut, we could just leave you here to die a slow death."

Andi almost gasped, but caught herself. Joe was using a threat to get information. He didn't really mean what he'd said. He wouldn't leave this man here to die, would he?

"They got away. Both of them," the man said. "Got clean away. Again." He coughed up more blood. "Almost had them."

"How did they get away?" Andi said. "You had a gun."

The man's gaze settled on Andi, and she realized he might be able to see the fear in her eyes. She glanced away from his face and down to his bloody stomach.

"Answer her!" Joe demanded.

"Damn rotten timbers in there—" he rolled his eyes back "—gave way and crashed in on me." *Cough. Cough.* "They hit me across the shoulders and knocked me to the ground. By the time I dug my way out—" *Cough.*

Spit. Cough. "—the boys were gone. I was heading out after them when you showed up."

"I guess you know that you aren't going anywhere," J.T. said. "Except maybe to jail."

"I'm not going to jail," the man said. *Cough.* Blood trickled out of the corner of his mouth. "But you're right. I'm not going anywhere. I'm dying, aren't I."

"Probably," J.T. said.

The man looked straight up into the darkness. "Hell of a place to die."

Andi tried to look away, tried to shut out the sight, but some sick fascination kept her fixated on the badly wounded man.

"Who sent you after Eddie and Russ?" J.T. asked.

"Somebody you don't want to mess with." *Cough. Wheeze. Cough.*

"How about giving us a name?" Joe clamped his hand down on the man's shoulder.

"Now, why would I do that?"

"Ease your conscience, maybe," J.T. suggested.

The man laughed, then quickly broke out in a cold sweat and began coughing again. When the coughing subsided, he took one deep, final breath and went limp. His bright blue eyes were wide open.

Joe checked his pulse. "He's dead."

"Damn!" J.T. shot to his feet. "He could have given us a name."

"At least, we know that Russ and Eddie got away," Andi said.

"That's the only bit of good news we got." J.T. ran his hand through his short, black hair. "But we'd better look around, just to be sure. I wouldn't take that bastard's word for anything."

Andi gasped. "Do you think he lied and that he might have killed—"

"He could have tied them up in here but not had a chance to kill them before we showed up."

Joe rose slowly. "Then let's bring out the flashlights and have a look around."

Andi heard a hint of something in Joe's voice. Concern? Anger? Or was it pain? Something wasn't right with him. She couldn't pinpoint the exact emotion.

Within a few minutes, they had found the still warm ashes from a fire, as well as empty cola cans, candy wrappers and a couple of apple cores. But no sign of the boys.

"They've been here, all right. Or, at least, someone has." J.T. kicked the embers and sent the ashes flying into the air.

"Colas and candy and apples," Joe said. "Those are the items that were missing from the Gilberts' kitchen— the exact food that Clara probably gave Eddie and Russ this morning."

"Well, I guess it's safe to assume Eddie and Russ were here and that they did get away," J.T. said.

"We need to get in touch with Bill Cummings and let him know what's happened here." Joe leaned against the rock wall beside him. He held his left arm across his stomach while he clutched the rifle in his right hand. "The police should be able to ID the guy we shot. And once we know his identity, it will be easier to figure out who he was working for."

"What about Russ and Eddie?" Andi wondered how in the world they were going to figure out where the boys had gone. Would Joe and J.T. be able to track them, since they were undoubtedly traveling on horseback? Or would whatever clues they might have left be blown away in the wind by now?

"We might as well head out." J.T. motioned to his cousin. "He—" J.T. inclined his head toward the corpse "—isn't going anywhere. I'll call Bill and let him know what's happened, and if he doesn't need you and Andi to hang around, you two can see if you can pick up the boys' trail."

"Depending on where the boys are headed, we might need horses," Joe said. "If we do, we'll make a stop by Ed and Kate's."

When the three of them emerged from the dungeon-like mine, Andi noticed that Joe moved slowly and kept his arm hugged to his left side, resting it from elbow to fingertips across his stomach. And he held back, keeping some distance between himself and her.

J.T. climbed down the ladder leading from the mine to the desert floor, then motioned for Andi to follow.

"Toss me your rifle," he said. "It'll be easier for you to climb down."

She tossed the rifle, which he caught and then laid at his feet, along with his own weapon. When she reached level ground, she looked up to where Joe was backing down the ladder. That's when she noticed a bright red stain seeping through his shirt between his armpit and his waist. She stifled a gasp, covering her mouth with her hand. Joe was injured. Why hadn't he mentioned it to them?

When Joe stepped off the last rung of the ladder, Andi ran over to him, then reached out and grabbed his left arm. He winced. Their gazes met and held for just a moment, then he looked away, but not before she saw the pain in his eyes.

"You're hurt," she said.

"It's nothing." He kept his voice low, speaking barely above a strained whisper.

"What happened?"

"Nothing." He glanced over at J.T., who was picking up Andi's rifle. "I'll be okay. Don't say anything to J.T."

Andi persisted, determined that Joe not dismiss his injury as insignificant. "Were you shot?"

"Damn it, Andi, I said I'm okay." He deliberately kept his gaze riveted on the far horizon as he turned and walked away from her.

"Joe!" She hurried after him.

He acted as if he didn't hear her and just kept walking toward their parked vehicles. The faster she walked, the more he increased his speed to keep a distance between them. She paused and waved to J.T., who was following several yards behind her. Just as she opened her mouth to tell J.T. that Joe had been wounded, a sudden, powerful sensation hit her and she knew Joe was in trouble.

She cried out for J.T. just as Joe slumped to the ground, clutching his left side. She broke into a run, rushing to Joe. J.T. caught up with her, as she sank down on her knees and laid her hand on Joe's shoulder. Huddled there on the ground, his body clenched tightly as if he were struggling to remain conscious, Joe looked at Andi. He ground his teeth. Andi tried to lift his arm, but stopped immediately when he groaned deep in his throat. When she clasped his hand in hers, she felt a warm wet stickiness. She gently flipped his hand over and saw that it was covered with blood.

"Why didn't you just tell us that you were wounded?" Andi slid her hand beneath his arm. "Where were you hit?"

"Who the hell do you think you are, a superhero?" J.T. bent on one knee, lifted Joe's right arm, eased it around his neck and then placed his arm around Joe's waist. "You're going to have to help me get you on your feet."

Joe nodded, then cooperated with his cousin, groaning quietly as he came to his feet.

"What can I do?" Andi asked.

"Open the door of your Expedition," J.T. said. "We need to get him to the clinic in Castle Springs as quick as we can, and, if necessary, they can arrange for a medflight from Albuquerque."

"You're making too big a deal out of this," Joe told them. "It's not that bad. I'm sure the bullet didn't hit anything vital—just one of my lower ribs."

Andi scowled at him as she opened the Expedition's front passenger door. "Not serious? You're bleeding like a stuck hog and you are in so much pain you nearly passed out. Stop being such a jackass and let us take care of you."

"I do love your Southernisms." Joe's momentary smile turned into a grimace when J.T. hoisted him up into the passenger seat.

"Oh, shut up!" Andi hopped in on the other side of the car and slid behind the steering wheel. "You're going to do exactly what I tell you to do. Do I make myself clear?"

"As always, you've made yourself crystal clear."

J.T. stuck his head into the SUV on Joe's side. "Follow me out of here and into Castle Springs. Once we get Joe to the clinic, I'll contact Bill Cummings."

Andi nodded. Joe opened his mouth to speak. She glared at him, her expression warning him not to say a word. He leaned back, relaxed against the headrest and closed his eyes. Andi started the engine, shifted gears, put the SUV in motion and followed J.T. She stole a quick glance at Joe. Sweat beads covered his forehead.

"Don't you dare die on me, Joe Ornelas!"

* * *

"I want to leave. Now!" With a pained expression on his face, Joe sat up in his hospital bed. "The bullet's out. I'm conscious. And we're wasting precious time."

Andi laid her hand in the middle of his chest and pressed gently. "Lie back down and stop being such a...a..." She struggled for the right word, then smiled when she recalled the Navajo word for jackass. "Stop being such a *tkele-cho-g*. You're not going anywhere until Dr. Harvey says you can."

"Where's J.T.? He'll get me out of here."

"He's at home with his wife, where he should be."

Joe hated being incapacitated, hated having someone else in control of his life. When he'd awoken about fifteen minutes ago, the first thing he'd seen was a half-asleep Andi sitting at his bedside. What was she doing here? he'd wondered. Then, when he discovered that an entire twenty-four hours had passed since he'd gone into surgery, he had started demanding answers to some important questions, but Andi had put him off, cautioning him to take it easy.

After a nurse that Andi had summoned came in and checked his vital signs, he had decided that what he needed was to get the hell out of this place. He hated clinics and hospitals, and avoided them at all costs. Only bad memories resided inside the Castle Springs Clinic. Here was where, when he was six, his mother had died in childbirth, along with his infant brother. And five years later, the family had brought his father here to die, after the cancer that had reduced him to mere skin and bone finally conquered him.

"What's happened since I've been out of it for the past twenty-four hours?"

"Cooperate with me, and I'll tell you everything I know."

"I'll lay back if you'll find the button that raises the head of this damn hospital bed."

Andi hit the button, raised the head of the bed and then hovered over Joe, who grunted and then lay back in a half lying, half sitting position. Andi grabbed his pillow, which had fallen to the side, fluffed it and lifted his head so she could replace the pillow.

"How's that?" she asked.

"Fine. Now tell me what's going on. Any word on Eddie and Russ?"

"J.T. sent a couple of his ranch hands, both good at tracking, out after the boys, but all they found were the horses."

"They set the horses free and headed in a different direction on foot," Joe surmised. "They couldn't get far on foot, so that means they had to be looking for alternative transportation. They probably stole another truck or car."

"That's what J.T. thinks."

"What about the guy we killed in the old mine?" Joe asked. "Did the police ID him yet?"

Andi nodded. "His name was Charlie Kirk. He's a quarter Navajo, but he's never lived on the reservation. He's been in and out of trouble with the law since he was a teenager."

Joe could tell by the expression on Andi's face that there was more. "What aren't you telling me? Do you know who hired him?"

She shook her head. "No, not yet. But…well, J.T.'s been doing some checking and it seems Charlie Kirk had quite a reputation throughout the area, in this state, Arizona and Colorado as a…a hired gun."

"You mean he's a professional killer."

"Yes."

"You know what that means, don't you?"

"J.T. explained," she said. "Whoever hired this guy will simply replace him with someone else."

"I need to get out of here and find those boys."

When he started to sit up again, Andi quickly lowered the rail on his bed and sat down beside him. She grabbed his shoulders and looked him square in the eye.

"J.T. has put out feelers throughout the reservation. If anyone catches a glimpse of Russ and Eddie, they'll notify us immediately." Andi loosened her grip on Joe, but didn't release him. "You'll be of more help to your nephew and my brother by getting well as quickly as possible. And that means following orders."

"Whose orders?"

"Mine!"

Russ lifted a bottle of water to Eddie's lips and held it there until his friend had drunk his fill, then he wiped Eddie's mouth with his shirttail. This was all his fault. He'd gotten them in this mess in the first place. Why hadn't he listened to Eddie? If he'd just listened, then Eddie would be home right now, instead of hiding away in this damn cave, running a fever and bleeding from a gunshot wound. Of course, if they had gone to the police, Russ didn't doubt for a minute that he'd be behind bars now, accused of Bobby Yazzi's murder.

He had to get some help for Eddie and he had to somehow get Jewel to talk to him. If she would just corroborate his story and tell the police the truth about what happened that night, he might have a chance. But without Jewel to back him up, he'd wind up spending the rest of his life in prison. He couldn't run the risk.

"Look, Eddie, I'm going to leave you here, and when I get to a phone, I'll call and tell the police where to find you."

Eddie grabbed Russ's arm. "No, don't leave me. Don't run off by yourself. If we can just get this bullet out of me, I'll be okay."

"And how are we going to do that, without a doctor?"

"You could get it out." Eddie laid his hand over his wounded shoulder. "I don't think it's too deep. You could take your knife and—"

"I can't!" Russ sprang to his feet. "I could kill you if I try."

"I could die before help gets here." Eddie ripped open his shirt sleeve. "Just take a look, will you, and see what you think."

Russ poured some water from a glass jar Clara Gilbert had given them over Eddie's shoulder, erasing some of the blood. Fresh blood oozed from the wound. Nausea swelled inside Russ's stomach. *Damn it, don't puke right here in front of Eddie!* Already Eddie's arm had turned blue and was swollen. Did that mean infection? Russ wondered. Or was that normal for a bullet wound? The only other time he'd seen someone shot was when he had found his father's body. But it hadn't been quite the same. His father had put a gun in his mouth and pulled the trigger. Russ shuddered as he recalled the horrific sight.

"You have to help me," Eddie said. "There's no one else."

How could he do it? How could he gouge around in Eddie's wound and try to remove a bullet embedded in his shoulder? "All I've got is my pocketknife, and we don't have any way to sterilize it."

"Build a fire and do it that way," Eddie suggested.

"We don't have anything for you to take for the pain—not even some aspirin."

"Yeah, I know." Eddie tried to grin. "I hear that if the pain gets bad enough, you just pass out."

Russ rubbed his hand over his mouth, removing the perspiration from his upper lip. "I'm sorry I got you into this. You didn't want to run. Now look what's happened to you."

"You have to do it," Eddie said. "If you don't get the bullet out, I'm going to die."

"Yeah, I know. I know."

Chapter 9

Crash! The decorative metal tray hit the floor, spilling the contents across the glossy wood. Black coffee splashed into the air and spread out over the handwoven rug beside the bed. The cup splintered into fragments. The dinner plate cracked in two. A grilled chicken breast slid under the dresser. The baked potato, butter oozing out all around it, landed with a dull *splat.* And green beans scattered everywhere, like leaves in the wind.

"Woman, leave me alone!"

Andi jumped away from the bed, then planted her hands on her hips and glowered at Joe Ornelas. Confined to bed since he'd left the clinic yesterday, he was driving her crazy by refusing to take care of himself. She had never dealt with a more cantankerous man in her life. He had to be the worst patient in the world. Recovering from a gunshot wound might have given any other man a reason to take it easy, but the opposite seemed true of Joe. It was as if getting shot had only fueled his determination to find

Russ and Eddie. J.T. had told Joe that not only were the police diligently searching for the boys, but that family and friends were staying on top of things by sharing information. They were all waiting for word, hoping someone would spot the boys and new evidence of Russ and Eddie's whereabouts would surface to give them a fresh lead to follow. J.T. not only had his entire ranch staff on "ready," but he had also put in a call to the Dundee agency and arranged for a squad of agents to be sent to New Mexico at a moment's notice.

Andi had pointed out to Joe that if she had any idea where to search, she would be hot on the boys' trail herself. In the meantime, the only thing that reassured her was the certain knowledge that everything possible that could be done was being done to find Russ and Eddie.

J.T. and Joanna rushed into the guest bedroom. Each surveyed the scene. J.T. covered his mouth and coughed in an obvious effort not to laugh. Joanna smiled as she glanced back and forth from Andi to Joe.

"I'll get Rita to clean up the mess," Joanna said.

"No, I'll clean it up." Andi focused her gaze on Joe, glowering at him. "However, I'm tempted to just leave it and let Joe clean it up himself when he gets well."

"The damn tray wouldn't be on the floor if you had just left me alone and stopped trying to feed me," Joe snapped.

"All I did was offer to cut the chicken breast into pieces for you. Is that such a crime?"

"I can feed myself." Joe refused to look her way. He kept his gaze fixed on the foot of the bed. "And if everyone would stop treating me like an invalid, I could get up and come to the table."

"The doctor said—"

"Don't you think I'm a better judge of how I feel than the doctor is?"

"I think you're an infuriating grouch and an A-number-one pain in the ass. You were nearly killed less than forty-eight hours ago and you're trying to act all macho, as if that wound in your side isn't anything more than a mosquito bite."

"And you're—issuing orders, telling me what I can and can't do, fussing and fuming and treating me as if I were addle-brained just because I got shot."

Andi marched over to the bed, grabbed Joe's chin between her thumb and forefinger and forced him to look at her. "If you dislike my taking care of you, then why didn't you go home with Kate and let her be your nursemaid? She wanted you to go straight from the clinic to her house."

"You know as well as I do that Kate has enough to deal with right now." Joe jerked free of Andi's hold, but didn't break eye contact. "I thought that staying here was a good idea. I wanted to be on hand when new information came in, and I mistakenly believed that J.T. would protect me from any female *hovering*."

"Sorry to have disappointed you." J.T. shrugged. "But in this case, I'm on Andi's side. You need to stay in bed and let us take care of you until—"

"The bullet is out. No major damage was done. There's no infection. I should be fine in a couple of days," Joe said. "And in the meantime, I'd feel better if I could keep busy in some way instead of lying in bed doing nothing."

J.T. eyed the stack of magazines on the nightstand. "Not into reading, I see."

"I'd prefer a telephone," Joe said. "That way I could keep involved in the search for Eddie and Russ."

"Don't you dare plug in a telephone by his bed," Andi warned.

"Stay out of my business." Joe lifted his right hand, manacled Andi's wrist and tugged her down until she was leaning over him, nose-to-nose. Then he whispered so quietly that only she could hear, "If you don't leave me the hell alone, I might start thinking you still love me."

Andi trembled from the shock of his accusation. "Go ahead and kill yourself. See if I care." She pulled loose from his grip, then glanced hastily at J.T. and at Joanna before rushing out of the room and down the hall. Tears filled her eyes. She swatted them away with her fingertips.

J.T. shook his head. Joanna took a deep breath and then approached Joe, who waited for the tongue-lashing he knew he deserved.

"I don't know what you said to her, but I'm sure you owe her an apology," Joanna told him. "Andi has been 'hovering' around you since she and J.T. brought you here from the clinic yesterday. She's done everything possible to make things easier for you. Do you realize that she actually slept in that chair last night—" Joanna pointed to the overstuffed striped chair in the corner of the room "—just in case you needed something? Who do you think woke you to give you your medicine at two this morning—the tooth fairy?"

Joe aimed his gaze at J.T. "Is that true? Did Andi sleep in here last night?"

"Of course, it's true. She's been reluctant to leave your side, even to eat or take a bath," J.T. explained. "I've had to insist that I sit with you whenever we thought she needed a five- or ten-minute break."

"But why? Why would she—"

"Men!" Joanna threw up her hands in frustration. "I'll send Rita to clean up the mess and then I'll check on

Andi and find out if she's all right.'' Joanna gave Joe a disapproving glare before she left the bedroom.

"Looks like I've got two women angry with me," Joe said.

"What's really bothering you?" J.T. asked. "And don't give me any crap about not liking the way Andi is waiting on you hand and foot."

"I don't need to be wasting time recuperating. I need to be out there finding those boys."

"And where would you look?" J.T. asked. "They seem to have disappeared quite effectively. Once they set those horses free, they could have headed in any direction."

Joe picked up on something in J.T.'s voice. Just a hint that something wasn't quite right. "What aren't you telling me?"

"I've told you everything you need to know. Now settle down and get some rest."

"I'll rest better if I know."

"I haven't told Andi yet, so—"

"What is it?"

"When we tracked the horses, we found drops of blood along the trail. But once the boys were on foot, the blood stopped and they started covering their tracks. I figure, they spotted the blood dropping on the ground once they were on foot and made sure they didn't leave any more signs for us." J.T. paused, as if he couldn't bare to think about the obvious conclusion. "We took a sample of the blood and sent it off to Albuquerque, but the police haven't gotten the results back yet."

"Either Eddie or Russ is wounded. That's what you think, isn't it."

"Yeah. I figure Kirk shot one of them."

"Damn. Whoever's hurt needs to see a doctor. Without proper treatment, he could die."

"We'll have to tell Andi, eventually," J.T. said. "But she's been so worried about you that I didn't have the heart to tell her that one of the boys was probably injured, too."

Andi found a sanctuary in the sunroom that faced north. This section of the house was on the opposite side from the wing containing the bedrooms and far enough away from the children's playroom that it possessed a quiet serenity absent throughout the rest of the busy household. She might have shed a few tears, but she was determined not to cry her heart out. Not over Joe Ornelas's brusque, inconsiderate treatment. She had allowed his past actions to hurt her more than enough. Hadn't she learned her lesson five years ago? All she had wanted was to help him, to take care of him and make sure he recovered fully. But was he grateful? No. Did he appreciate anything she'd done for him? No.

"Andi, are you all right?" Joanna Blackwood asked as she entered the secluded room.

"I'm fine. Sorry about that little show Joe and I put on for y'all. Has he calmed down any?"

"I left J.T. with him." Joanna smiled warmly. "If I'd stayed another minute, I might have given Mr. Joe Ornelas a piece of my mind."

Andi grinned. "Why does he have to be so stubborn and aggravating?"

"You rub him the wrong way," Joanna said. "Don't you know that?"

"Well, the feeling is mutual. He certainly rubs me the wrong way."

"And why do you suppose that is?"

"If you're implying that Joe and I are still...that there's something between us, then you're wrong. Whatever we had together has been over a long time. The only reason we can even tolerate each other's presence is because we have a common goal—to rescue Russ and Eddie.''

"I'll bet that Joe is telling J.T. exactly what you just told me. And I imagine J.T. doesn't believe him any more than I believe you.''

"I love you dearly, Joanna,'' Andi said. "You're my best friend. But if you think you're going to finagle some sort of confession out of me, then you're wrong.''

"I'm not asking you to confess anything to me, but I am asking you to be honest with yourself. What went through your mind when you realized Joe had been shot? How did you feel when you thought he might die?''

No fair! Andi wanted to shout. *What I thought and how I felt at those moments have nothing to do with reality. I do not love Joe. He does not love me. And we have no future together.*

"All right,'' Andi said. "I do still care about Joe. But it doesn't mean anything. It can't.''

"Why can't it? If the two of you could forgive each other for past mistakes and—''

"That's not possible.'' Andi slumped down on the antique green wicker settee that faced the rock garden. "It's too late for us. And even if it wasn't...I realized something after Joe left the reservation. Even back then, it would have been impossible for us to have come together as one. Even before my father...before he died, Joe and I were at odds over the differences in our lifestyles. Don't you see, with the two of us, there would always be something keeping us apart.''

"Only if you and Joe let it be that way.'' Joanna sat beside Andi. "If the two of you truly love each other, y'all will find a way to make it work.''

"But we don't love—''

"Tell that to someone who'll believe you." Joanna patted Andi's shoulder. "Remember, I've been watching the two of you together. If ever two people desperately needed to be together—as one—you and Joe do."

"Are you saying what I think you're saying?"

A wide, all-knowing smile spread across Joanna's pregnancy-plump face. "I'm saying that what you and Joe need to work off some of that sexual tension is to have a lot of hot, sweaty sex."

"Joanna Blackwood!" Andi couldn't stop herself from giggling. "You're awful."

"If after you and Joe make love, you can still honestly tell yourself that you don't love him and don't want to spend the rest of your life with him, then fine. At least, you won't go to your grave wondering what it would have been like."

"What makes you think...okay, so there's this sexual chemistry between us. That doesn't mean we could have anything more than a physical relationship."

"You'll never know unless you try."

LeCroy Lanza traced the sweat lines down the frosted glass of beer sitting in front of him. He did not like it when his employees let him down. Charlie Kirk had proved to be a great disappointment. LeCroy had been so sure that the man was a competent killer, able to do the job for which he'd been hired. The idiot might have been able to outsmart the law, but this time he'd had to deal with more than the local Tribal Police. Joe Ornelas and J. T. Blackwood weren't ordinary Navajos. They'd both had experience as professional security agents. And to make matters worse, they were both related to Eddie Whitehorn, so they had a personal interest in finding and protecting the boys. Kirk had no doubt underestimated these men. But LeCroy wouldn't make the same mistake.

He supposed he could hire another hit man, but what good would that do when no one knew where the boys were right now? No, he'd just bide his time and let Ornelas and Blackwood find the boys. What he needed was a tracker, someone to keep tabs on the people searching for the boys. Once their whereabouts was discovered, he could move in for the kill. And even if he couldn't get to the boys before they told the police what they knew, he still had plenty of time to eliminate them before they actually testified against him. Hell, he'd bring in a damn army of assassins, if that was what it took to protect himself.

One thing LeCroy knew for sure—he wasn't going to let a couple of punk Navajo kids take him down. And if that meant destroying Ornelas and Blackwood and even Lapahie's gorgeous half-sister, then so be it.

The following day, only two days after Joe had been released from the Castle Springs Clinic, he was out of bed, dressed and ready for action, albeit with his left side still heavily bandaged. And although *he* would never admit it, Andi knew he was still in pain. Her greatest worry was that he would reopen his wound by physically overexerting himself. But who could tell that mule-headed man anything? He certainly wouldn't listen to her. She'd given up on him yesterday when he had all but tossed his dinner tray at her.

She had focused her attention on working tirelessly with J.T. to garner all the information they could on Charlie Kirk. And by keeping busy, she'd been able to avoid thinking about her feelings for Joe. About why she was so concerned with his well-being. And she *was* concerned.

Deeply concerned. More than she would be for anyone else. Did that mean she still loved him? No, of course not. Despite what Joanna thought, she *did not* love Joe. But Andi had to admit that she was still emotionally involved with him and he was with her, even though neither of them wanted or needed that kind of extra baggage weighing them down.

But what if Joanna had been at least partially right? Andi asked herself. What if the hostility between Joe and her would diminish if they released some of the sexual tension that kept them both on edge? Was she willing to have a brief affair with Joe in order to maintain peace between them while they worked together to save Russ and Eddie?

Andi carried two tall glasses of iced tea out to the pool area, where Joe sat alone in a lounge chair, shaded by a huge umbrella. The late-afternoon sun had begun its descent over the western horizon. She had steered clear of Joe for the past twenty-four hours. But now, she had no choice but to return to the role of nursemaid, at least until J.T. and Joanna returned tonight.

"We've got the place all to ourselves," she told him as she handed him a glass.

"Where is everyone?" He lifted the chilled tea to his lips and drank, then sighed contentedly.

"Didn't J.T. tell you? He took Joanna into Trinidad to her OBGYN for her weekly checkup. They're staying in town for dinner and won't be back until late."

"Where's Rita?"

"This is her day off."

"Where are the children?"

"With Alex and Elena," Andi said.

"Whose idea was that?"

"Not mine, if that's what you're implying."

"I wasn't implying anything. I was just asking a simple question."

"Humph!" Andi sat in the cushioned wooden rocker situated across from Joe's reclining lounger. "Nothing is simple with you. There's always a hidden meaning in your questions."

"So you say."

"So I know."

"All of this arguing isn't good for my recovery," Joe told her, just a hint of a sardonic smile lifting the corners of his mouth.

"Bull. You seem to be thriving on our little confrontations," Andi countered. "I'll bet you've missed me, haven't you?"

"Maybe," he admitted. "After all, I need something for entertainment while I'm recuperating. But if you think you're going to put me back in bed and keep me there, then you'd better think again."

Andi felt the blush as it crept up her neck. Before it reached her cheeks, she looked down at the tiled patio floor, deliberately avoiding Joe's eyes. What he'd said could easily be interpreted in more than one way. She had immediately thought of keeping Joe in bed for a couple of days, and the two of them making love.

When she heard him chuckle, she jerked her head up and glared at him. "What's so funny?"

Damn it, why had she asked him something so stupid? He was bound to respond with a caustic remark. But instead, he surprised her.

"*We* are what's funny. You and I," Joe said. "There's so much tension between the two of us that everyone around us can't help but notice. We've been fighting ever since the first day I returned, when I came to Kate's house and found you there. Why can't we stop arguing?" He sipped on the iced tea, then set the tall, perspiring glass down on the wooden Mexican-style table to his right.

"We argue because we disagree. I'd think that's obvious."

"Okay, I'll give you that. But we seem to be disagreeing over everything. If I say up, you say down. If you say black, I say white."

"So what are you suggesting? Do you want to lay the reason out on the table and examine it?" she asked. "Are you sure that's what you really want to do?"

"It might help us if we did just that. It might clear the air."

"Or it could get us in trouble."

"We're already in trouble and we both know it. That's part of the problem. We're trying so hard to avoid the truth that it's become the size of an elephant, just sitting there between us. How do we continue avoiding something that big?"

Andi stood, looked directly at Joe and said, "I'm not ready to—"

Joe grabbed her wrist and jerked her down onto his lap. When he winced and groaned, she tried to pull away, but he reached out and wrapped his arm around her waist.

"Please, let me go." The steely determination she saw in his eyes momentarily rattled her. "I—I hurt you when I fell into your lap. You must be more careful."

"Stay where you are." He spoke with authority, his words a command instead of a request. "In the past, I let you postpone things one time too many. You were never ready to take the next step in our relationship. Well, Andrea, this time you're not going to put off facing the inevitable. You're as ready right now as you'll ever be."

Andrea? Dear God, he had called her Andrea. In the past, the only time he had used her given name instead of her nickname was when he had been aroused and intent on making love to her.

"This can wait until you're better," she told him.

"No, it can't wait. So, I will go first. I will speak the truth," he said. "I have wanted you, as a man wants a woman, since the first time I saw you. That one thing has not changed."

Andi sucked in a deep breath as his words settled over her and a tingling awareness spiraled outward from the feminine core of her body. "All right. I can be totally honest, too. I knew you felt that way. I felt it, too, from the very beginning. But I was afraid of that feeling. I had never experienced anything so powerful."

"Is that why you kept putting me off?" he asked. "Because you were afraid?"

"Yes," Andi admitted. "I thought that if I gave in to what I was feeling and we became lovers, I would love you too much to leave you. And that frightened me. We weren't sure if we had a future together. I didn't want either of us trapped in a relationship that might eventually bring us both a great deal of unhappiness. And I was right, wasn't I?"

Joe frowned, but nodded agreement. "It seems you were. But things are different now. We aren't falling in love and hoping for a future together. We're just two people trying to resist a physical attraction."

"For once, you and I are in total agreement." Andi glanced away, uncertain what secret truths might be revealed in her eyes.

Joe loosened his hold around her waist and let his arm drift lower to drape her hip. "I never wanted to hurt you. I still don't."

Andi trapped the lump of emotion in her throat, stemming the tide of tears threatening to erupt. "I don't want to talk about the past. Not right now. Discussing what happened five years ago will only confuse me more than I'm already confused.''

Joe eased Andi over to his side, so that she rested half on the lounge chair and partly against his right side. Her heartbeat accelerated when he reached under the fall of her long hair and clamped his big hand around the back of her neck. As she drew in a startled gasp, their gazes linked and they shared an utterly spellbinding moment of recognition. Man to woman.

She melted against his uninjured side when he brought her face down to his. Their breaths mingled, warm and sensual. Waves of anticipation washed over her as Joe touched his lips to hers. Tender and tentative. She sighed. His fingers spread through her hair and gripped the back of her head, then pressed her closer as he claimed her mouth in a ravaging kiss.

Passion too long denied controlled their actions. The kiss deepened quickly, becoming a heated mating dance. Andi lifted her hand to his chest and laid it flat atop his shirt, over his erratically beating heart. She longed to touch his bare flesh, to run her fingertips over the solid muscles of his shoulders and broad chest. Seemingly of their own volition, her fingers opened the top four buttons on Joe's shirt and inched their way beneath the parted folds. The moment she encountered one tight male nipple, Joe groaned.

''Am I hurting you?'' she asked.

''Only if you stop touching me,'' he replied, his lips brushing hers.

''We can't... If we try to... Your wound could reopen and—''

Joe silenced her with another kiss, longer and more powerful than the first one. Within seconds her body took control, eliminating all rational thought. She wanted nothing more than to stay here in this glorious moment forever. On the verge of unparalleled satisfaction. The promise of fulfillment almost as great as the fulfillment itself. Her body and her mind awaited the inevitable, yearning with an uncontrollable hunger.

She wanted Joe. She had always wanted him. Her soul recognized him as its mate. Denying this truth was useless. She had lied to herself long enough. She could lie to Joanna and even to Joe, but her heart knew the truth. She loved Joe Ornelas. She had loved him since the first moment she saw him, and she probably would love him until the day she died. And beyond.

''Joseph,'' she murmured as she lifted her fingertips to caress the lips she had only moments ago kissed. ''Oh, Joseph.''

He grabbed her hand, squeezing her fingers tightly. ''Don't,'' he cautioned her. ''Don't say anything.''

She realized that he knew she had been about to confess her love and had stopped her before she spoke the words aloud. He didn't want her love, only her body. He was wise enough to understand that there was no place in their relationship for love. Too many unresolved issues stood between them.

Andi withdrew from him, first on an emotional level and then physically. He tried to hold on to her, to bring her back to him, but she resisted. And when she pulled away and stood, he made no move to stop her. He only looked at her, a sad compliance in his dark eyes.

''When we find Russ and Eddie...'' Andi studied Joe's face, needing to read his expression as much as to hear his reply. ''When they are safe and this is all over, you'll go back to Atlanta, won't you.''

''I suppose I will,'' Joe said. ''Unless...''

"Unless?"

"Unless something changes and I have a good reason to stay."

"You should stay," she said. "For Kate and J.T. and their families. For Eddie, in particular. But mostly, you should stay for yourself. This is where your heart is, isn't it? In New Mexico, on the reservation? If only you hadn't run away—"

"I would never have left, if you hadn't…"

"You blame me. I blame you. We always come back to that, don't we."

Joe stood. Andi backed away from him.

"Just stay the hell away from me for the next few hours, will you?" Joe stalked past her, leaving her alone on the patio.

She felt as if he'd slapped her. She wanted Joe. She could even admit that she loved him. But unless they could come to terms with the pain and disillusionment of the past, they would continue going around and around in the same vicious circle that bound them together and yet kept them apart.

Chapter 10

"Tell him that he can't go," Andi said. "He hasn't recovered enough to be gallivanting all over creation."

J.T. shrugged. Joanna's eyes widened as she shook her head in a noncommittal gesture.

"Woman, I am going. And if you want to go with me, then stop giving me such a hard time." Joe narrowed his gaze until his eyes were mere slits. "I can and will leave you here."

"You're certainly not going alone. You aren't going at all." Andi huffed, completely aggravated with Joe. "J.T. can send someone else with me. One of the Dundee agents who flew in from Atlanta this morning."

"I am one of their agents," Joe informed her. "We'll call Wolfe and Hunter in if we find anything in Black Rock."

J.T. interjected himself into the conversation as he laid his hand on Andi's shoulder. "Look, Andi, I don't think it's going to hurt Joe to ride over to Black Rock and take a look around. You can drive and he can rest.''

Andi could have gone to Black Rock alone or with one of J.T.'s ranch hands or one of the Dundee agents, but Joe was being a stubborn jackass, as usual, and insisted on going. The phone call had come in thirty minutes ago, from a distant relative of Joe's father, a man named Aaron Tuvi, who lived in a small Arizona village on the reservation, just over the New Mexico border. Black Rock had a population of about three hundred and whenever strangers showed up, residents were bound to take notice. Aaron had overheard some men talking at the trading post about squatters having moved into an abandoned house on the outskirts of town. Someone had caught a glimpse of a teenage boy entering the old shack. Aaron had immediately thought about Russ and Eddie, because word had traveled throughout the reservation about the missing boys. Since Aaron was ''family,'' he had gotten in touch with J.T. instead of the Tribal Police.

''I'm glad Aaron didn't try to confront the boys,'' Joe said. ''If he had, they might have bolted and run. Or he could have frightened them and somebody might have gotten hurt.''

''Since the rifle we found at the mine belonged to Mr. Lovato, same as the stolen truck, then we can assume the boys aren't armed, except possibly with knives.''

Joe nodded.

''Let's just hope that someone else in Black Rock doesn't put two and two together and call the police,'' Andi said.

''All the more reason why we shouldn't waste time arguing,'' Joe told her. ''If we head out now, we can be in Black Rock within an hour.''

''Oh, all right.'' Andi knew when she'd lost a battle,

and she had most definitely lost this one. Although he was still healing from a gunshot wound, Joe had no intention of letting anyone else spearhead the search for the boys.

J.T. and Joanna walked with them out to the Expedition, and waved goodbye as Andi headed the SUV westward. With every mile that took them closer to Black Rock, she prayed that the squatters Aaron Tuvi had heard about really were Russ and Eddie. And that she and Joe could reach them before they either fled or ended up in a standoff with the police. *Or were tracked down by Bobby Yazzi's killer.*

Joe seemed as reluctant as she to indulge in idle conversation. They hadn't gotten more than five miles from Blackwood Ranch before he'd reclined his seat, pulled the Stetson he'd borrowed from J.T. down over his eyes and gone to sleep. The drone of the tires on the asphalt hummed a monotonous rhythm, mile after mile. Taking the back roads cut their traveling time by nearly fifteen minutes, and Joe had told her that they were less likely to be followed that way, since they could more easily detect a tail. J.T. had pointed out that it was only a matter of time before the police started keeping an eye on Joe and her, if they weren't already. Since the deaths of Edmund Kieyoomia and Charlie Kirk, half the law enforcement agencies in the two states had become involved, including the New Mexico State Police, the Arizona Highway Patrol and the Law and Order Division of the Bureau of Indian Affairs.

Andi checked the clock on the dashboard. Noon precisely. She was making good time and had passed only three vehicles since leaving the main highway. She slowed the Expedition when she saw a narrow wooden bridge ahead. The old bridge spanned Chiz Creek, which meandered downstream between terraced limestone cliffs.

A coppice of willows and alders edged the long, sleepy waterway.

"Something wrong?" Joe lifted the Stetson and glanced at Andi, but didn't raise his head.

"No, nothing's wrong. Just making sure there isn't anything coming from the other direction. That's definitely a one-way bridge." She nodded at the old wooden structure.

Joe raised his head just enough to take a look. "Want me to drive?"

"No, I do not want you to drive."

"Hmm."

Andi took the Expedition across the bridge. Slowly. Carefully. Then she breathed a sigh of relief when they reached the other side. Joe covered his eyes once again with the Stetson. Andi inhaled deeply and then exhaled, thankful that they had avoided another argument.

"You shouldn't have a problem finding the trading post," Joe said. "This road will take you straight into Black Rock. There's only one street in town, and the trading post is the largest of the four buildings."

"Mr. Tuvi is meeting us there, isn't he?"

"Yes. He will show us the way to the abandoned house."

"You think the squatters are Russ and Eddie, don't you."

"I think there's a good chance that it's them."

"Maybe, when we get to the house, you should let me go in first and see—"

"It's too dangerous for you to go in alone," Joe said. "If these squatters aren't the boys, anything could happen."

"And if the squatters are Russ and Eddie, Russ isn't going to react in a positive way—"

"I know, I know. Then we'll go in together." He lifted

the Stetson, pushing it back on top of his head as he sat up and glanced at Andi. "When we get to the house, you will stay behind me." When she opened her mouth to protest, Joe narrowed his gaze and said, "You stay behind me or you stay in the Expedition."

"Oh, all right. I'll stay behind you."

Within twenty minutes they arrived in Black Rock, which was by most standards nothing more than a wide place in the road. She pulled the SUV up in front of the trading post and killed the engine. When she started to open her door, Joe grabbed her arm.

"You stay here."

"Why?"

"People will ask fewer questions if I go in alone," he told her. "Aaron is the son of my grandfather's brother. He has no doubt mentioned that a cousin of his is coming by to pick him up today."

"Okay," Andi agreed. "It makes sense to me. Navajo sense, anyway." She understood that to the Navajos, family was everything.

While Joe got out of the SUV and went into the trading post, Andi bided her time. She thumped her fingertips on the steering wheel, then curved her head just enough to take a good look at Black Rock, which comprised Johnson's Trading Post and three other weather-worn buildings. And one of those structures appeared to be empty. There wasn't a sign of human life on the street—only a stray mongrel that looked as if he needed a good meal and probably a flea bath.

As the minutes ticked by, Andi became restless. What was taking Joe so long? All he had to do was bring Aaron Tuvi outside.

Suddenly, the door to the trading post opened. Andi sat up straight and peered through the windshield. A man and woman, each carrying a sack, came outside and headed toward the lone truck parked alongside the Expedition. The couple stared at her, but neither spoke nor acknowledged her in any way. She smiled at them. They did not return the friendly gesture.

A few minutes later, after the Navajo couple had driven out of town, Joe emerged from the trading post. At his side was a small, dark man with long gray hair hanging almost to his waist. When they approached the SUV, Joe motioned to Andi, and for just a second she didn't catch his meaning. But when she did, she huffed disgustedly. He was instructing her to get into the back seat. A typical macho maneuver.

Don't lose your cool, she cautioned herself. *Just get in the back and keep your mouth shut. You can always voice your opinion later, when you and Joe are alone.*

She opened the driver's door, hopped out, and then opened the back door. Before she had a chance to get in, Joe laid his hand on her shoulder. She tensed, then turned to greet Mr. Tuvi. Joe made the introductions hurriedly before the three of them got in the SUV. Then Joe drove out of town, following their guide's directions.

"This old house is out by itself," Aaron said. "There was another house close by, but it burned down ten years ago. No one has lived in this house for more than three years."

"We appreciate your contacting J.T.," Joe said. "We haven't gotten many leads."

"Then I hope those who are staying in the house are your nephew and Miss Lapahie's brother." Aaron glanced over his shoulder at Andi.

She didn't even consider correcting his error in calling her 'Miss Lapahie.' She might not bear her father's name, but she was as much a Lapahie as Russ was. She offered

Mr. Tuvi a fragile smile. He nodded his head, acknowledging Andi in a friendly manner.

"Turn here," Aaron said. "You can see the house. There, to your right."

House? Andi thought. *Shack* was a more apt description. A small structure probably containing no more than four rooms. The outer clapboard walls had once been painted a brick red, but had faded and peeled until the color was a reddish mud-brown. The roof had caved in on one side and the two front wooden steps had rotted.

Joe parked the SUV in front of the crumpling building. When he got out, Andi quickly followed him. He didn't wait for her to catch up before he leapt to avoid the dilapidated steps, bounding directly onto the porch. She reached his side just as he tried the doorknob. The rusty hinges creaked when the door swung open. With utmost caution, Joe entered the hot, shadowy interior. Andi's heartbeat drummed inside her head.

"Call out to Russ," Joe whispered.

"Russ? Are you in here? It's Andi. I'm here to help you."

Utter silence.

With Andi directly behind him, Joe strode from one room to the next and found the first three empty. Then, when he entered the fourth and last room, he stopped dead still. Instinctively Andi knew something was wrong.

"What is it?" she asked.

He didn't reply.

Andi sidestepped and went around him, then skidded to a stop when she saw the bloody rags lying in the middle of the floor. She moved forward and bent down, intending to pick them up, but Joe clasped her arm and pulled her away.

"That's blood on those rags, isn't it?" She could tell

from the odd expression on his face that he was hiding something from her. But what? What did he know that she didn't?

"Yes, I suspect that it's blood."

"If the boys were here, then one of them is hurt."

"Yes."

"Damn it, Joe, you'd better tell me what you know, and you'd better tell me right now!"

He grasped her shoulders and met her furious gaze with his calm, concerned expression. "We believe that Charlie Kirk shot one of the boys, back at the uranium mine."

Andi sucked in a deep breath as she tried to control her emotions. She wanted to strike out at something or someone, and if she didn't stop herself that someone would be Joe Ornelas.

"How do you know?" she asked through clenched teeth.

"J.T. found drops of blood along the path the horses took when the boys left the mine," Joe explained. "The police sent a sample to Albuquerque, but they haven't gotten the results back yet."

"You knew all this time and didn't tell me."

"You would only have worried."

"You had no right to keep this information from me."

Joe nodded. "Probably not. But now isn't the time for another argument. We have to see if we can find any signs of where the boys might have gone from here."

"If they stole another car—"

"There hasn't been a car parked near this house anytime recently. If the boys were here—and I believe they were—then they're probably on foot."

"What can I do to help?" she asked.

"Go back to the Expedition and wait."

She started to protest but thought better of it, and hes-

itantly followed his orders. She waited in the SUV with
Aaron Tuvi, a man of few words. When the afternoon sun
beat down unmercifully, Andi moved into the driver's
seat, cranked the motor and started the air-conditioning.

Joe came around from the back of the shack and walked
over to her side of the vehicle. She opened the door and
started to get out, but he stopped her.

"No sign of horses," he said.

"Does that mean they're on foot?"

"That's my guess. And if they are, they can't get very
far, especially with one of them injured."

"So what now?" she asked.

"First, I call J.T. to give him an update. After that, we
will start looking for the boys."

Andi blew out an exasperated breath. "What do we do,
just drive up and down every road near here? Or do we
head out on foot, too?"

Joe glanced around Andi and looked straight at Aaron
Tuvi. Without saying a word, the old man nodded, then
opened the passenger door and got out of the SUV.

"What's going on?" Andi asked.

"Aaron will help me try to pick up the boys' trail,"
Joe said. "In his day, Aaron was a well-known tracker."

"And if y'all pick up any signs of which way they
went, what then? Do the three of us head out together?"

"Just wait here. And stop asking so many questions.
One thing at a time," Joe mumbled as he withdrew his
cellular phone from its belt sheath.

Joe felt certain that unless Russ and Eddie had found
someone to help them, they couldn't have gone far. The
blood on the rags inside the old shack appeared to be
fresh. He punched J.T.'s number and waited.

"Blackwood, here."

"J.T., we are pretty sure the boys were here in Black

Rock. We found some bloody rags in one of the rooms, but no sign of either Eddie or Russ. Aaron is going to help me try to pick up their trail. We think they're on foot."

"I was just going to call you," J.T. said, then paused briefly. "One of our sources, admittedly a less than reputable source, came through with some interesting information."

"Information on what?" Joe glanced at Andi. With the SUV door open, she sat sideways in the driver's seat and watched him like a hawk zeroing in on its prey.

"The guy gave us a name," J.T. said. "LeCroy Lanza. He's a known drug dealer and has a reputation for eliminating his competition and seeking revenge against anyone who crosses him. Word has it that Bobby Yazzi had dealings with Lanza."

"So you think Lanza killed Bobby and then hired Charlie Kirk to track down and kill Eddie and Russ?"

"Bingo."

"Then I hope we can get to the boys soon."

"If Lanza's our man, then a call to the DEA might be in order. Sam Dundee has connections within that agency."

"Why don't you give Sam a call and see what he can find out."

"Will do," J.T. said. "I'll be in touch if I find out anything else, and you keep me posted on your search."

Joe closed his phone, slipped it into the belt clip-on and turned to Andi, who waited impatiently. He relayed J.T.'s message to her. When she simply sat there, very still and quiet, he realized she was struggling with her emotions. His hand hovered over hers, but he waited, unsure whether to touch her. But his need to comfort her overcame his sense of uncertainty, and he clasped her hand in his.

"We're going to find them," Joe assured her. "They're on foot. They can't have gone far."

"I don't understand why they keep on running, especially now that one of them is hurt."

"They're more scared and confused than ever." Joe squeezed her hand tenderly. "Just sit here until Aaron and I check things out. We shouldn't be gone long. You've got a cell phone and a rifle." Reluctantly, he released her hand.

"Joe, please…I want to go with you."

"If we find their trail, I'll come back for you." Joe glanced at the stoic Aaron. "He can't make a long trek. I just need him to help me pick up any signs."

"I cannot stay here and wait."

"Damn," Joe muttered under his breath. "I shouldn't have wasted time trying to make you stay here. Come on. Let's go."

Twenty minutes later, the trail that Aaron Tuvi had easily picked up at the back of the old shack came to an end at a roadway intersection.

"Here is where the signs end," Aaron said.

"How is that possible?" Andi asked. "They couldn't have just disappeared."

"Someone picked them up." Joe glanced in each direction, but saw no sign of a vehicle on the lonely roads. "It's the only explanation."

Andi grabbed his arm, tugging on his shirt sleeve. "You don't think—"

He shook his head. "Don't think the worst. They could have just hitched a ride with someone." Joe turned to Aaron. "Where do these roads lead?"

"This road—" he pointed west "—will take you to a

highway that goes to the Hopi Reservation. The north road circles around and takes you back to Black Rock. And to the south, the road will end at Interstate 40.''

"Well, what do we do, flip a coin?" Andi's shoulders slumped.

Momentarily, Joe shared her feeling of hopelessness. "No, we call in some help."

"Not the police."

"No, not the police, although my guess is that they'll catch up with us sooner or later." Joe nodded west, the direction from which they'd come. "We'll take Aaron back to Black Rock, then I'll call J.T. and have him send us some help. Wolfe and Hunter, along with some of the ranch hands. You and I will make the circle from Black Rock back to this point, and then we'll head toward the Hopi Reservation. J.T.'s searchers and the Dundee agents can take the road to I-40 and then the interstate itself."

"Sounds like the only reasonable plan."

"Then, for once we're in agreement."

At two the following morning, Joe and Andi found themselves on a long, virtually deserted stretch of road. Endless searching had brought them to one dead end after another. Wherever they'd gone, they had questioned people and come up with nothing. Andi couldn't understand how two teenage boys, one of them injured and bleeding, could simply vanish. At last report, J.T.'s men had fared no better.

Joe pulled the Expedition from the road onto a dirt lane, killed the motor and turned off the headlights.

"What are you doing?" Andi asked.

"I'm stopping so we can get a few hours of rest," he said.

"But the boys will get away if we—"

Joe put his hand on her shoulder. "Let's face it, Andi, the boys have already gotten away again."

"I know you're right. I just didn't want to admit the truth to myself. We've searched everywhere and come up with nothing."

"Maybe J.T.'s men will unearth something. And don't forget that Wolfe and Hunter are still out there searching." He squeezed her shoulder, then released his hold. "Don't give up hope. With so many people looking for the boys, somebody's bound to find them."

She shook her head. "No, I won't give up hope."

The full moon partially illuminated the interior of the SUV, at least enough so that she could see Joe's silhouette. She watched while he undid his safety belt and reclined the seat. He removed his Stetson and tossed it in the back, then crossed his arms behind his head and relaxed. Andi followed his lead, quickly releasing her belt and reclining the seat. But lying beside Joe, with only the console between them, Andi felt as if they were sharing some enormous canopied bed.

She was bone weary and longed for a warm bath, her own bed and something to eat that hadn't come out of a vending machine. Each time Joe had stopped for gas, he'd picked up snacks. She couldn't remember the last time she'd eaten three candy bars in one day. Her mind immediately skipped from her concern over her own well-being to wondering how the boys were faring. Were they hungry? Cold? Sick? Whichever boy had been shot—if, indeed, Charlie Kirk had shot one of them—how was he able to keep running? Odd, she thought, that it didn't really matter to her whether the injured boy was Russ or Eddie. She could no more bear the thought of Eddie Whitehorn dying than she could of losing her own brother.

Did Joe feel the same way?

She glanced at Joe's still form. That hard, masculine body within arm's reach. She had accused Joe of not caring about Russ, but in her heart she knew that wasn't true. There had been a time when Joe had been to Russ the Navajo equivalent of a godfather.

And there'd been a time when Joe had loved Russell Lapahie like a father, she reminded herself. Unfortunately, that love hadn't stopped Joe from doing his duty.

But her father had been the one to choose death over facing the dishonor his actions had brought on his family, his clan and his people. The pain of that admission clutched Andi's heart. She had allowed that thought to enter her mind on numerous occasions, but she had always pushed it aside, unwilling to fault her father for his own actions. It had been so much easier to lay all the blame on Joe's wide shoulders. After all, Joe had chosen to desert her, as her father had done. When she had just begun to love them, they had exited her life without any explanation—without proper goodbyes.

She had hated them both. Joe. And her father.

A lone tear trickled down her cheek. She pulled in a deep breath, then released it on a whimpering sigh.

Joe stirred, inclining his body toward hers. "Are you all right?"

"No, not really," she admitted.

"Worried about Eddie and Russ?"

"Yes, but…" *Just say it,* she told herself. *Admit the truth to Joe. After all you've put him through—five years ago and during the past few days—you owe him complete honesty.* But what exactly would complete honesty entail? she wondered.

"Is there something else?" Joe asked.

She turned toward him, but in the semidarkness couldn't make out his features. It didn't matter. Her heart had, long ago, memorized the bold, arrogant structure of his handsome face.

"You care about what happens to Russ, don't you. You came back to the reservation as much for Russ as for Eddie."

She sensed Joe suddenly tense. Even in the darkness, their bodies not touching, she and Joe were connected. They always had been. Both of them had recognized that bond the first moment they met. And neither time nor distance had altered that mystical link.

"Yes."

"I'm sorry that I doubted your motives," she said. "You and I want what is best for both Russ and Eddie."

"Yes."

"I've hated you for a long time. You broke my heart, you know."

"Yes, I know."

"And I broke yours, didn't I, when I turned against you and blamed you for my father's death?"

"Yes."

"Damn it, Joe, can't you say anything except 'yes'?"

"What do you want me to say?"

"Tell me how you feel."

"I'd rather show you."

He reached across the console, grabbed her into his arms, lifted her up, then over and into his lap. A startled gasp whooshed out of her as she landed against him, her bottom solidly pressed against his blatant arousal.

Chapter 11

With his face so close to hers, Andi could see the sparkle in his black eyes. "Joe?"

"Yes?"

She understood what he was saying, what he was asking. *It's too soon,* her mind told her, but she didn't listen to her mind. Instead she heard her heart's plea—*you love this man*—and obeyed her body's command not to wait, to take what she wanted, now.

She said, "Yes."

He pulled her closer, until they were soft breasts to hard chest. She lifted her arms and wrapped them around his neck. Breathlessly she waited for him to make the next move. For endless moments, Joe gazed into her eyes. Waiting. Giving her time to reconsider her decision.

She brushed her lips against his, inviting him to further action. As if the touch of her mouth on his ignited some barely controlled fire inside him, Joe claimed her lips with possessive greed. His breathing grew harsh and ragged with desire as he plunged and pillaged. She clung to him, whimpering and squirming, her femininity clenching and unclenching in preparation. Hot moisture. Puckering nipples. Throbbing need. Intense longing to be taken hard and fast quickly overwhelmed common sense.

Joe tore his mouth from hers and moved his lips downward, nipping, licking and kissing her throat. Then he stopped his exploration at the top of her bra. With his breath warm between her breasts, he hurriedly unbuttoned her shirt and jerked it free from her jeans. She drew in an expectant breath, yearning for the feel of his hands and mouth on her body. And wanting just as badly to touch him with equal intimacy.

Following his lead, she undid his shirt and slid her hands inside to clutch his broad shoulders. He was big and muscular and devastatingly male. As she caressed him, leisurely, seductively, her hands moved over his chest. When her fingers encountered his bandaged side, she gasped, suddenly remembering that he was injured. Badly injured. And still recuperating.

"Your wound," she said. "I forgot all about—"

"It's okay. We'll be careful. You won't hurt me." He lifted her hands back to his shoulders. "Hold on."

When he eased his hands between their bodies and covered her breasts, pure pleasure spiraled through her. Her short nails bit into his shoulders, the action urging him to take her mouth once more. She needed little prompting. When he kissed her again, she gave as good as she got, devouring him with the same urgency.

Joe released the front closure of her bra and spread the garment apart to reveal her high, round breasts. Her nipples tightened almost painfully. He took one begging nipple into his mouth. She keened with pleasure-pain as he sucked hard. When she pushed against his chest in a con-

fused effort to end the glorious torment, he held her
tighter, forcing her to accept him. He worked with the
snap on her jeans, freeing it quickly, and then jerked down
the zipper. When he delved with his hand inside her panties, she threw back her head and rested her shoulders
against the steering wheel. While the fingers of his right
hand worked their way through the nest of dark curls between her thighs, his left hand grabbed her wrist and laid
her open palm over his crotch. His sex strained and pulsed
against her hand. The combination of his mouth on her
breast and their hands placed so intimately on each other's
bodies heightened Andi's senses.

Joe's fingers danced over her feminine folds, urged
them apart, and sought the center of her sexuality. The
moment he stroked that hard nub, she unraveled. His ar-
dent attention soon had her writhing, her body wanting
and needing only a little more to achieve fulfillment.

Mindless with passion, she undid and unzipped Joe's
jeans, then reached inside his briefs to cup his sex. He
was big and hard and ready. She shivered with anticipation.

Her last rational thought was that she had never expected their first time to take place inside her Expedition.
But where really didn't matter. Nothing mattered except
that at long last she would belong to Joseph Ornelas as
she was meant to belong to him.

His talented fingers worked their magic, and he soon
had Andi on the verge of release. She fought the moment,
wanting these pre-climactic feelings to last, but with one
final stroke, Joe sent her over the edge to a shattering
conclusion.

Crying out with pleasure, she shuddered and then fell
limp. Before she had time to fully recover, Joe urged her
jeans and panties down over her hips, ripping off her

clothing, shoes and socks. Hurriedly, he freed his sex, lifted her up and around until she straddled him. Then he thrust into her damp, swollen sheath, so receptive to him. The moment he entered her, renewed sensations began to build inside her.

"I want you," he murmured. "Only you."

She savored his admission of need as well as the hot, sultry words that followed. Erotic. Crude. Words a man spoke while in the throes of passion.

"Love me," she told him.

He withdrew from her, only to plunge deeper. When she whimpered, wanting more and yet uncertain of her ability to accommodate him entirely, he filled her. Big and hard and demanding.

"It's all right, Andrea. I promise I won't hurt you."

With every powerful thrust, Andi felt his shaft embedding itself more and more completely within her, until she knew they were truly one. Two bodies joined together in the oldest and most profound way a man and woman can physically unite.

Everything dissolved, faded away to nothingness, as they gave themselves over to primitive forces that guided them further and further into that wild, feverish darkness.

Wait. Wait. Not yet, her body screamed, wanting to hold on to the pleasure. But her climax came, earth-shattering in its intensity.

The moment she cried out, Joe hammered into her and found his own release. Groaning and shivering, he held her fiercely and possessively, as if he would never let her go.

While the sexual aftershocks rippled through them, Andi curled around him and laid her head on his shoulder. He wrapped her in his arms and spread soft kisses from temple to jaw.

Joe did not want to let her go. He longed to keep her in his arms until dawn, their bodies still joined, their naked flesh slick with perspiration. He worked his fingers through her hair and cupped her head with his hand.

"I want this moment to last forever," she said.

"Mmm." He closed his eyes, savoring the feel of this special woman. Being with her this way had been a homecoming for his soul. Nothing in his life had ever felt so right.

She murmured his name against his neck. He shivered. His arms tightened around her. And then he realized that she had fallen asleep. Carefully, so as not to disturb her, he flung his arm over the seat and felt around in the back until his hand encountered the jacket she had discarded yesterday. He wrapped the black fabric around her hips, covering her nakedness and protecting her from the nighttime chill. They were in the middle of nowhere, parked on a dirt path. It was highly unlikely anyone would come up on them, so he felt safe enough to close his eyes and rest.

The ringing telephone woke Joe. He discovered Andi draped around him, her body soft and warm against his. She lifted her eyelids and smiled at him. He gave her a tender, hasty kiss, then reached for his phone. He fumbled at his side, where the waistband of his jeans lay folded back, and straightened his belt enough to pull the plastic holder from under his hip. When he lifted the phone to his ear, Andi eased off his lap. The black jacket stenciled with white-and-tan prancing horses that he had laid around her backside hours ago fell to the floor.

Joe grinned when he noted the look of embarrassment on her face when she realized she was naked except for her open bra and the unbuttoned shirt that covered only her back. She scrambled to pick up her panties and jeans, while Joe flipped open his phone.

"Ornelas, here." Joe glanced through the windshield and saw the first tentative rays of morning sunlight spreading across the sky. A rosy pink blush to the east.

"It took you so long to answer that I was beginning to think something was wrong," J.T. said.

"Andi and I were asleep." Joe yawned, emphasizing that he still wasn't fully awake. "We pulled off the road around two this morning. We were both exhausted."

"You only slept about three hours," J.T. told him. "It's just a little after five now."

"Why are you calling?"

"Information."

Clamping the phone between his shoulder and his ear, Joe lifted his hips and pulled up his jeans, then zipped and snapped them. "What sort of information?" His gaze met Andi's. Her eyes widened questioningly.

"Bill Cummings called about five minutes ago. He found a couple—a man and wife—who gave the boys a lift."

"What?"

"Yeah. Mr. and Mrs. Sosi. It seems they'd been to visit the woman's mother in Black Rock and just happened along about the time the boys reached the intersection. They took the boys with them about twenty-five miles and dropped them near Tsas-ka Creek. One of the boys told the Sosis that they had family nearby."

"How did Bill get this information?"

"Seems Mr. Sosi called his local police department," J.T. said. "After he and his wife got home last night, he noticed some blood in the back seat. Seems he couldn't sleep much for worrying about it, so he made a phone call before daylight this morning."

"Damn! That means the police are on their way to Tsas-ka Creek right now."

"Yeah, they'll be heading out soon, but maybe you and Andi can get there before they do and keep things from getting out of hand. Tell me where you are, and I'll tell you how to get from there to Tsas-ka Creek."

Joe gave J.T. his location. J.T. let out a long, low whistle. "What's that for?" Joe asked.

"Luck. Just damn good luck, that's all. You're not ten miles away. Stay on the same road you're on now and it'll take you to Cha-gee Road. The Sosis let the boys out about a mile onto Cha-gee. The creek runs along the side of the road for several miles. And there's a small settlement a few miles north."

Joe turned to Andi, who was putting on her shoes. "Get buckled up. We're leaving." Then he said to J.T., "I'll get in touch the minute we know anything."

"Hey, wait up."

"What?"

"Next time you see Bill Cummings, you might want to thank him," J.T. said. "He didn't have to call and share this information with us. You've got a twenty-minute head start while the police form a tracking party. Bill said to tell you that it was a favor. For old times' sake."

"Yeah, I'll be sure to thank him."

Joe closed the phone and returned it to the belt holder, then started the engine, turned the SUV around and headed toward the road.

"What's going on?" Andi asked.

"The police are headed to Tsas-ka Creek, about ten miles north of here," Joe explained. "The boys hitched a ride to there yesterday, so there's a chance they're still somewhere close by."

Andi groaned. "We have to get to the boys first. If we

don't, I'm not sure what Russ will do. He hates the police. He's liable to start shooting the minute they show up.''

"Hang on. I'm going to see just how fast this Expedition will go.''

Russ turned the wooden spit on which he was roasting the rabbit he had caught in a snare that morning. The last thing he had wanted to do was build a fire and possibly alert someone of their whereabouts. But he'd tried everything else to get Eddie warm and nothing seemed to help. He'd even taken off his jacket a few hours ago, despite the predawn cold, and had wrapped it around his best friend. And Eddie needed food. They hadn't eaten in a couple of days.

"This should help," Russ said. "The rabbit will be ready to eat any minute now. With some food in your belly, you'll get better. You'll see.''

Eddie offered him a weak smile, but he couldn't seem to stop shivering. Russ leaned down, placed his arm around Eddie and pulled him closer to the fire. Although Eddie said he was freezing and his body was racked with chills, he felt hot to the touch. Russ rubbed his hands up and down his friend's arms, then zipped his jacket.

He had to figure out a way to get some help for Eddie. He should have made him stay with the couple who'd picked them up yesterday. They could have taken him to a doctor. But Eddie had nixed the idea—they were in this together, he'd said. Russ had agreed and dragged Eddie along with him. Now, look what had happened.

Russ wondered if the bullet wound had gotten infected. He'd cleaned his pocket knife with fire before he dug the bullet out of Eddie's shoulder, and for a while he'd thought things would be okay. But with each passing day, Eddie grew weaker and his fever climbed. And the last time Russ had taken a look at Eddie's shoulder, it was swollen and badly discolored.

Russ knelt beside Eddie and gently grasped his uninjured shoulder. "Look, you need help. You need a doctor."

"I'll b-be all—all right." Eddie's teeth chattered as he trembled uncontrollably.

"No, you won't be all right. Not without a doctor. So, I'm going to leave you here, and when I get to a phone somewhere I'll call your folks and tell them where you are."

Eddie reached out and clutched Russ's shirtfront, but he was so weak that he couldn't hold on. "Don't leave me. I'll be okay. I promise. Just give me a drink of water and then I'll sleep some more."

What the hell was he going to do? Russ wondered. How could he leave Eddie when his friend had pleaded with him not to? But how could he stay when he couldn't do anything to help Eddie? He had finally realized that if Eddie didn't get help soon, he might die.

Joe inspected the area thoroughly for any signs that someone had recently passed this way. Andi watched him, occasionally searching the ground herself, wondering if she'd be able to spot any clues. Joe stopped so suddenly that she almost ran into his back. She watched with curiosity as he knelt and inspected a flat rock partially buried in the earth.

"Have you found something?" she asked.

"Looks like dried blood on this rock," he said.

"Does that mean—"

"It means dried blood and nothing more. It could have come from an animal."

Joe made his way toward a grove of bushes and rickety

pines. Andi had the oddest sensation that the boys were close. But how could she possibly know? Just another of her odd premonitions?

"More dried blood." Joe once again knelt and examined several dark spots dotting the scrub grass. "And look there—the limbs on that bush have been broken. An animal didn't do that. It would have had too much sense to stumble through."

"Russ and Eddie came this way," Andi said. "I just know it."

"From what I can tell, I'd say that one of them was practically dragging the other." Joe rose to his feet, then surveyed the surrounding area. "I believe that from here the boys would have gone down that gully and continued following the creek." He pointed in that direction with the rifle he held in his hand. "That way they would have water whenever they needed it, and cliff overhangs would offer some protection from the elements. They had to find a safe place to sleep last night. Maybe a cave."

"What time is it?" Andi knew that the twenty-minute head start they had, thanks to Bill Cummings' warning, would mean nothing if they didn't reach the boys before the search party arrived on the scene.

Joe told her the time, then brushed his hand across her cheek. "We'll find them. One of them is badly hurt and they're scared, but as a result they've been careless and left a clear path."

Russ tried his best to get Eddie to eat something, but his friend refused. "Come on, eat just a few bites. You need something in your stomach."

"Sorry, bu-but I—I can't."

Russ squeezed Eddie's hand reassuringly. "It's all right. You can eat later."

Eddie closed his eyes as another series of tremors racked his body. Russ knew that he couldn't wait much longer. He had to do something, and soon. Glancing into the flames of their campfire, Russ realized that they needed more wood. He had to keep the fire alive in order to help Eddie stay warm.

"Hey, I'm going to get some more wood," Russ said. "I'll be back in a few minutes."

Eddie lifted his eyelids and nodded. Russ offered him a tentative smile, then turned and all but ran out of the cave. He'd gather the wood, build up the fire, and then tell Eddie that he was going to leave him, find a phone and call to get him some help. Even if Eddie put up a fuss, Russ had to do what was right. Just because he chose to stay on the run didn't mean Eddie had to die proving his friendship. Besides, what good would it do Eddie if he escaped the law and the killer just to die from an infection?

Within five minutes, after gathering enough sticks to replenish the fire, Russ headed back to the cave. That's when he saw them. Two people making their way along the creek, not far from the cave where Eddie waited helplessly. Since he'd lost the rifle on their mad dash out of the uranium mine the other day, the only weapon he had was his knife. Not much protection from a gun, and he noticed that the bigger guy was carrying a rifle. Russ crept closer to the shallow creek bed, hiding as best he could in the growth of paloverde trees and prickly pears. He barely concealed a gasp when he recognized the two trackers. Andi. And Joe Ornelas!

How could she have teamed up with that bastard? Didn't she remember what he'd done to their father? Ornelas couldn't be trusted. Their father had found that out the hard way. Ornelas had no doubt done a snow job on

Andi, which wouldn't have been too difficult. There had been a time when she'd been crazy about the guy. Joe Ornelas might have fooled his sister, but he didn't fool Russ.

At least, with them showing up this way, one major problem was solved. They were heading straight toward the cave. They would find Eddie and get him the medical attention he needed. And with them distracted by finding Eddie and realizing his condition, Russ would have time to escape. He didn't know where he'd go, but he could figure that out later. Right now, he just needed to get away as fast as he could. No way was he going to give himself up to Joe Ornelas. He's just as soon surrender to the police than put his fate in that son of a bitch's hands.

Andi followed Joe, rock-hopping across the stream. Water splattered their feet and ankles, dampening their shoes and jeans. As she breathed in some fresh air, Andi smelled a peculiar, rather tangy odor, and mentioned it to Joe.

"It's the scent of fermenting sycamore and cottonwood leaves," he explained.

"Oh." His knowledge of nature never ceased to amaze her.

They stopped on the far side of the creek, as Joe searched for signs of a trail. Off in the distance a coyote howled, its mournful cry blending strangely with the sound of flowing water.

"There—" Joe pointed "—see the footprints dried in the mud."

"Yes. Yes, I see them."

They picked up the pace as they followed the obvious signs, Andi only steps behind Joe.

"This trail is leading right to that cave." Joe broke into a run.

"Wait," she cried. "If Russ has a gun or a knife—"

Joe didn't slow down. Andi's heartbeat ran wild at the thought that her brother might be armed and wouldn't think twice about defending himself. She ran as fast as she could and caught up with Joe just as he reached the entrance to the cave. She grabbed his arm. He halted, turned and glared at her.

"Please, let me go in first," she said. "If Russ sees me first, I can talk to him and explain why you're with me and tell him that he can trust you."

"Do you believe he can trust me?" Joe asked.

"He can, can't he?"

"Yes." Joe stepped aside and allowed her to approach the entrance first. "Call out to him and see what happens."

"Russ? Russ, it's me, Andi. Are you in there? I'm coming in to talk to you."

Joe gripped her shoulder. "Be careful."

"Russ won't hurt me."

She took a deep breath, squared her shoulders and walked into the dark, cool cave. For a couple of seconds the blackness blinded her, but shortly her vision returned, and she saw a small fire burning a good twenty feet away.

"Russ?"

Silence.

"Russ, it's me, Andi," she repeated.

She heard a soft moan, like that of a hurt child.

"Russ, please answer me."

"Andi…"

When she heard the weak voice, her heart lodged in her throat. It didn't sound like Russ's voice, but if he were wounded, sick, hurt…?

She made her way toward the fire. There, huddled at the back of the cave was a boy. Eddie Whitehorn! She rushed to him, knelt beside his shivering form and ran her hand over his perspiring brow. He was burning up with fever.

"Oh, Eddie." She scanned the cave's interior and saw no sign of Russ. Where was her brother? "Eddie, where's Russ?"

"Gone."

"Joe!" Andi screamed. "Come in here. I've found Eddie."

With rifle in hand, Joe made his way into the cave and over to her side within seconds.

"Russ isn't here," she said. "And Eddie's burning up with fever. He must be the one who got shot."

Hovering over his nephew, Joe shook his head. "We've got to get him to a hospital as quick as we can." He handed Andi the rifle and then lifted Eddie into his arms. Eddie groaned. "Sorry if I hurt you." He glanced over his shoulder at Andi. "Did he say where Russ is?"

"He just said 'gone.'"

Joe nodded. "Put out that fire, will you?"

"Sure."

Andi broke up the fire and let the remains of the roasted rabbit fall into the ashes. Then she headed out of the cave right behind Joe. Just as they neared the creek, four Tribal Police Trackers appeared, rifles in hand, the barrels pointed at Joe, Andi and Eddie.

"Drop the rifle," Joe told Andi. "And put your hands behind your head. We need to show them that we're not any danger to them."

Trembling, her hands unsteady, Andi dropped the rifle, crossed her hands behind her head and said a silent prayer.

Chapter 12

Eddie was sent by helicopter to the nearest hospital, which was in Gallup, and Joe and Andi faced an intensive interrogation by the Tribal Police. After more than two hours of answering questions, Andi had grown tired and irritable. Joe could sense her unease, and her increasing belligerence was apparent in her replies.

"I have no idea where my brother is," Andi said. "I've told you over and over again that when we got to the cave, Russ was gone. We never saw him."

"Well, it seems odd that without anyone's help, Russ Lapahie has disappeared again," Captain Kinlicheenie said.

"Believe me, Captain, we want to find Russ as much as the police do." Joe wanted to get the hell out of the police station and check on Eddie's condition. He was almost to the point of telling Captain Kinlicheenie to either arrest Andi and him, or let them go.

"I don't suppose I need to tell you that if you learn

anything about Lapahie's whereabouts, you're to notify us." The captain focused his gaze on Joe.

"No, sir, you don't need to remind us," Joe assured him.

Reluctantly the captain said, "All right then, you're both free to go."

The minute they stepped out onto the street, Andi glanced up at the high-noon sun. When Joe grasped her arm, she jerked away from him, but he ignored her hostility, chalking it up to residual anger toward the local authorities.

"I want to get to Gallup as soon as possible," Joe told her.

"I know you're worried about Eddie," Andi said. "But, at least, he's safe now. Russ is still out there. I can't just give up. I have to try to find him."

"You can't go wandering off by yourself. It's too dangerous."

"I'll find someone to help me—maybe one of J.T.'s ranch hands. Or I could see if Aaron Tuvi—"

Joe grabbed her arm again and held fast when she struggled. "Get in the damn car. I'll call J.T. to check on Eddie, then I'll go with you to track down Russ." He wasn't about to let her go traipsing off into dangerous territory without him. Anything could happen to her.

Andi stared at him with round eyes and mouth agape. "You'll actually go with me?"

He tugged her toward the SUV, then opened the passenger door and lifted her up into the seat. She smiled at him, and that smile alone made his decision to help her worthwhile.

When he got in, slammed the door and inserted the key into the ignition, Andi laid her hand atop his on the steer-

ing wheel. "Thank you. This proves to me that you care
what happens to Russ."

"Of course, I care. But I want you to know that I'm
doing this as much for you as for him."

"Yes, I know."

She squeezed his hand. The moment she released her
hold, he started the engine, backed up the Expedition and
headed toward Black Rock. Joe realized there was a
chance that they might be followed, so he kept a sharp
lookout for any surveillance. Five miles out of town, with
no sign of a tail, Joe pulled the SUV off the road.

"What's wrong?" Andi asked.

"Nothing," he told her. "I just want to check the Expedition over and make sure Captain Kinlicheenie didn't
have one of his men plant a tracking devise on us."

When he finished his inspection and found the vehicle
clean, they continued their journey to Black Rock. At the
trading post, Joe bought some provisions, just in case their
search lasted overnight, then drove them straight to Tsas-
ka Creek. With the area having been trampled by half a
dozen police trackers, Joe figured that any signs of Russ's
departure would have led the police to him. Or they'd
have inadvertently destroyed any trail the boy might have
left. It didn't take him long to discover that the latter was
true.

This was pretty much a wilderness area, and unsea-
soned trackers might go off in a dozen different directions.
Being a Navajo policeman didn't necessarily make a man
a good tracker, and since Russ had escaped the search
party, Joe surmised that either the boy had outsmarted
Kinlicheenie's men or all his trackers were novices. Besides, with canyons, gullies and caves throughout the region, it wouldn't be difficult for Russ to hide out for days.
Since the local authorities didn't have the manpower to

mount an extensive search, it was possible for Russ to continue escaping. All he had to do was keep running, stay one step ahead of them, until he was sure they'd given up.

Joe was surprised that the Arizona Highway Patrol hadn't gotten involved in the search. But then, the state authorities often allowed the Navajo to handle their own domestic problems. And Joe got the impression that Captain Kinlicheenie was the type who would resent any interference from outsiders.

"Where we go from here will be nothing but an educated guess on my part," Joe told her. "There's been so much traffic around here the past few hours that if Russ did leave a trail, it's gone now."

Andi slumped down on a small boulder and wiped the perspiration from her forehead. "I have faith in your educated guess. As a matter of fact, I have a great deal of faith in you. So you lead the way."

Joe's heart swelled with pride at Andi's statement. He valued her trust as the precious thing it was. He would do nothing to break that trust. If fate was giving him a second chance to prove himself—to prove his loyalty to Andi— then he planned to be worthy of her faith in him.

"My guess is that Russ stayed near the creek," Joe said. "He might even have gotten into the creek, since along here it's only ankle deep. If I wanted to delude my trackers, I'd probably use that method."

"So, what do we do—follow the creek?"

"Yes. Until we find some sort of evidence or any sign that someone walked out of the stream."

Once again Joe led the way. They kept to the creek side for a good three miles, and then Joe halted. Footprints, just beginning to dry in the sun. Fresh—only hours old, he surmised. Without questioning him, Andi followed as he made his way from the creek, following the trail that someone had been in too big a hurry to disguise. Joe climbed down into a saguaro-filled crevice, then turned to assist Andi. The trail picked up again; the terrain was rocky in places, but eventually evened out, and a narrow wash appeared between boulders. The limestone walls embedded with rose-quartz glistened in the sunlight.

"Where can he be going?" Andi grabbed Joe's arm, stopping his march.

"Need a rest?" he asked, seeing plainly that she did. She was a real trouper, a brave soldier, hiking through the wilderness for hours without one complaint.

"I need just a minute to catch my breath." She bent double and sucked in huge gulps of air, then stood straight again and looked at Joe. "What can Russ be thinking, running off into the middle of nowhere? Anything could happen to him out here."

As if on cue, an animal cry rang out in the stillness. Andi jumped, then clutched Joe's arm. He placed her behind him and moved in a circle, scanning the area for sight of the big cat. The mountain lion, know by some as a cougar or a panther, possessed an unmistakable cry. Once you heard it, you never forgot it.

"What was that?" Andi stood on tiptoe and peered over Joe's shoulder.

"Mountain lion." He pointed the rifle toward the hill to their left. "He's not going to bother us if we don't bother him."

"How can you be so sure?"

"These lions seldom kill humans. Maybe one per decade," he assured her. "They prefer calves."

"That's good to know."

"Are you aware of the fact that we Navajo consider mountain lions messengers from the gods?"

"You're kidding."

"We have been told that these messengers bring healing herbs to humans, and the gall of the lion instills courage."

"Well, I suppose it's better that we eat him than for him to eat us."

Andi laughed, and Joe wished that he could ensure her laughter would not soon turn to tears. He had not told her that the signs grew fresher, which meant their prey was close. Unless something went wrong, they would probably catch up to Russ within the next ten minutes. Joe guessed that the boy was tiring, perhaps had even taken time to stop and rest once he believed he was no longer being tracked.

The clouds swirled overhead, dark and foreboding, overlaying the blue sky with a gray wash. The sun blinked from behind the swelling storm clouds and the scent of rain hung heavy in the air.

"If it starts raining, we'll have to seek out some shelter," Joe said. "Our best bet will be to find some sort of overhang along those cliffs. Now, no more talking. I don't think we're far behind Russ, and if he hears us approaching he'll bolt and run."

"Oh!" She couldn't restrain the startled gasp. "I'll be quiet."

Ten minutes later they found him, resting near the ledge of a sandstone wall comprised of angled slabs. Russ's body was partially shaded by the ponderosa pines on the nearby hillside. The moment Joe and Andi approached, Russ shot straight up and, without looking at them, started to run.

"Russ!"

He slowed, but didn't stop.

"Russ, please, don't run," Andi called. "We'll just have to follow you."

Joe eased away from Andi so that a good ten feet separated them. He wanted Russ to concentrate on his sister and not on him.

Russ stopped and turned slowly to face his captors. "Why did you have to come after me?"

"You need to come home," Andi said. "We can help you. We'll prove to the police that you and Eddie—"

"Did you find Eddie?"

"We found him in the cave where you'd left him," Joe said, his tone harsh.

"I didn't leave him," Russ said. "I went out for more wood to build up the fire, and then I planned to leave and find a phone to call for help. I knew he needed a doctor real bad."

"Why didn't you come back?" Andi moved forward, but when Russ edged backward, she stopped dead still.

"I saw you two and knew you'd find Eddie." Russ's dark eyes darted back and forth as his gaze tried to keep both Andi and Joe in sight.

"The police were right behind us," Andi told him. "They could have—"

"I outsmarted them."

"You've outsmarted yourself," Joe said. "Running makes you look guilty, and by trying to elude the police you put your life and Eddie's at risk."

"Yeah, I figured you wouldn't understand." Russ all but snarled at Joe, then focused on Andi. "Why did you hook up with him? Don't you know that you can't trust him?"

"Russ, you're wrong. We can trust Joe. He wants to help you."

Russ glowered at his sister. "Yeah, sure we can trust him. The same way our father trusted him."

"You can't keep running." Andi held out her hands, a gesture for him to come to her. He ignored her plea. "You don't have any food or provisions of any kind, do you? And you have nowhere to go. Come back with us and tell the police what happened the night Bobby Yazzi was killed."

"I can't. They'd never believe me. You know how much trouble I've been in in the past couple of years. Everybody knows I'm a bad seed. Besides, I've got nobody who'll back up my story."

Joe thought that Russ suddenly looked like a small boy instead of the strapping sixteen-year-old he really was. He was no doubt hungry, tired and scared. And fear seemed to control his thoughts and actions.

"Eddie can back up your story," Andi said.

"Eddie didn't see what happened that night at Bobby's," Russ all but cried. His shoulders slumped in defeat.

"Eddie wasn't with you when Bobby Yazzi was murdered?" Joe asked. "And you've dragged him across New Mexico and half of Arizona with a bullet wound in his shoulder!"

"Yeah, blame it all on me," Russ shouted. "See—" he turned to Andi "—I told you, didn't I? He thinks I'm guilty. He blames me for everything. And the police will be just like him. I'm not going back to be railroaded on a murder charge." He clenched his fists and lifted them toward heaven in an angry protest. "I did not kill Bobby Yazzi!"

"I believe you," Andi said. "I never thought you killed anyone."

"But Joe believes I'm guilty, that I'm to blame, and so do the police."

Andi whipped around and looked right at Joe. He tried to avoid a direct confrontation with her, but knew he had no choice but to accept whatever she tossed his way.

"Tell him that you know he didn't kill Bobby Yazzi, and tell him that you don't blame him for—"

"I wouldn't believe him," Russ said. "So he can just save his breath."

"Well, whether you would believe me or not isn't the point." Joe took a tentative step toward Russ. "Right now, you're coming with us, and when we get back to civilization we can work things out. Between you and me. And between you and the law."

"You must be deaf, Ornelas." Russ started backing away. "I'm not going anywhere with you."

"Yes, you are." Joe lifted his rifle and aimed it directly at Russ.

Andi gasped. "No, Joe, you wouldn't!"

"Yeah, he would," Russ said. "He'd kill me in a heartbeat. He killed our father, didn't he?"

"No, Russ, he didn't kill our father. Our father killed himself."

"Man, Ornelas has done a number on you. You're taking his side over mine, aren't you."

"I am on your side," she tried to explain. "You're my brother. I love you and I want what's best for you. And so does Joe."

"I'm not going back." Russ stood his ground, glaring at Joe. "If you want to take me back, you're going to have to shoot me."

"No!" Andi cried.

Hell, how had things come to this? Joe asked himself. No way was he going to shoot that boy. How could a person be so damn stubborn? Russ was thinking irrationally. But nothing he or Andi could say would change Russ's mind about going back with them. Joe figured he had a chance of overpowering Russ, but the trick would be to catch him. The boy was nearly twenty years younger than he, and if he remembered correctly, Eddie had once mentioned that Russ ran track at school.

"Go ahead, Ornelas. Shoot me." Russ puffed out his chest, then stuffed his hand in his pocket and pulled out a knife. "You might as well kill me, because I'll kill myself before I'll go back with you."

"No, Russ, no!" Andi screamed.

Joe lowered the rifle. Trembling, Russ released a long, deep breath. Then, with an apologetic glance at his sister, he turned and ran as if the devil were chasing him. Within moments, he had disappeared completely in the wilderness once more.

Andi rushed toward Joe and flung her arms around him. Joe pulled her close, then gazed at her as he lifted his hand, tucked his knuckles under her chin and tilted her face to his. Tears trickled down her cheeks.

"We had to let him go," Andi said. "If he had...I really believe he would have killed himself before he would have gone back with us." She clung to Joe, then whispered, "Thank you for letting him leave. I know that decision wasn't easy for you."

In that one moment, Joe knew that at long last he was once again a hero in Andi's eyes.

They arrived in Gallup later that afternoon and went straight to Rehoboth McKinley Christian Hospital on Red Rock Drive. The multistory white building with wide, earthy-red horizontal stripes had a definite Southwestern appearance. Andi kept pace with Joe as he hurried down the hallway toward the surgery waiting area.

The minute Kate saw her brother, she sprang to her feet and rushed into his arms. Andi nodded to Ed Whitehorn and J.T., who both stood in the corner talking quietly. Joanna waved from her sitting position on the sofa. Andi offered her a weak smile.

"How's Eddie?" Joe asked.

"He is in surgery," Kate said. "Oh, Joe, gangrene had set in. Dr. Shull says there is a chance Eddie will lose his arm."

"Oh, no." After the unintentional outburst, Andi covered her mouth with her fist.

"If that happens, we will deal with it," Joe said. "But until it is a fact, we will hope for the best. We must be grateful that Eddie is alive."

"He could still die." Kate clung to Joe as she wept quietly.

Andi walked over and sat with Joanna, but all the while she watched as Joe comforted his sister. Kind. Loving. A strong and caring man. During those moments, she saw in Joe the man she had first fallen in love with so many years ago.

"How are you doing?" Joanna asked.

"I've been better," Andi replied honestly.

"Any word on Russ?"

Andi nodded. "Joe and I found him."

"That's wonderful news."

"Not so wonderful. He wouldn't come back with us. Joe would have had to take him by force, maybe even shoot him."

Joanna patted Andi's arm in a consoling gesture. "So, I take it that y'all let Russ go."

"There wasn't much else we could do. I was so proud

of Joe." Andi clenched her teeth in an effort to hold at bay the threatening tears.

"He would never deliberately do anything to hurt you or Russ," Joanna said. "You must know that. Joe is a good man."

"Yes. Yes, he is. I just wish that Russ could trust him."

Joanna draped her arm around Andi's shoulder. "When this mess is all straightened out, Russ will have a chance to get to know Joe again. Once he realizes that Joe isn't his enemy and never has been, then—"

"But we can't be sure that we'll ever get things straightened out." Andi crossed her arms over her waist and cupped her elbows. "If the police find Russ and he tries to resist, then they might..." Andi drew a deep breath. "And if Eddie were to die...or if he loses his arm, Joe will never forgive Russ. He blames Russ for getting Eddie into trouble and then dragging Eddie with him when he ran away."

"Eddie could have said no at any time," Joanna reminded her. "Besides, both boys were seen running from Bobby Yazzi's apartment, which means they were both witnesses to—"

"No, you're wrong. Russ said that Eddie wasn't inside the apartment with him when Bobby Yazzi was murdered."

"Oh. Then when Russ is caught, Eddie can't corroborate Russ's statement, can he?"

Andi leaned over, braced her elbows on her thighs and her face in her hands. "It's all so unfair. I know in my heart that Russ and Eddie are innocent. But they're paying such a terribly high price for having been in the wrong place at the wrong time."

"Think positive thoughts," Joanna said. "Now isn't the time to give up hope—"

"I'm looking for the Whitehorn family," a female voice said.

Andi jerked her head up and stared at the middle-aged nurse standing in the doorway. Joanna grasped Andi's arm, and Andi helped her pregnant friend to stand.

"Yes, I am Mrs. Whitehorn," Kate identified herself, all the while holding on to Joe's hand.

"Eddie is out of surgery," the nurse said. "He's in recovery. Dr. Shull will be out to see you shortly."

"Please, can you tell us if…" Ed Whitehorn came forward, J.T. at his side. "Is my son going to live?"

"Eddie came through surgery just fine," the nurse assured them. "And he didn't lose his arm. But that's all I can tell you. Dr. Shull can answer your questions."

A collective sigh of relief filled the waiting room. Kate hugged Joe, then went to her husband and clasped his hands in hers. Kate and Ed smiled at each other. Tears trickled down Kate's cheeks. A fine mist covered Ed's eyes. J.T. wrapped his arm around Joanna's shoulder. Joe turned to Andi, who opened her arms and reached out to him. He accepted the comfort of her embrace, his big body relaxing as she laid her head against his chest and hugged him to her.

By the time Dr. Shull entered the waiting room, everyone had released some of their emotional tension with tears and hugs and words of comfort and hope. Ed and Kate approached the doctor, hand in hand.

"Eddie's recovering nicely. We were able to repair his shoulder, but we had to remove a section of the infected area. With medication, the rest of the infection should clear shortly. There's a slight chance that Eddie might lose some mobility in that arm, but only time will tell. We'll be moving him into the surgical ICU shortly."

"When can we see him?" Kate asked.

"In a couple of hours," the doctor replied. "Immediate family only, for the first twenty-four hours."

Joe and J.T. followed the doctor out into the corridor. Andi excused herself, closed the door behind her and waited several feet away, but close enough to hear the entire conversation.

"Doctor, how soon will Eddie be able to talk to the police?" J.T. asked. "Captain Cummings, with the Navajo Tribal Police, was by here earlier, and he has a man waiting to stand guard over Eddie." J.T. gestured with his head to the right side of the waiting area.

Andi was surprised that this was the first time she had noticed the uniformed policeman.

"I won't allow anyone to disturb or upset Eddie. I can assure you of that, Mr. Blackwood. In twenty-four hours, I'll assess Eddie's condition and let the police know when they can question him."

Russ checked his pocket for change. He had four quarters. Enough for four phone calls. He had to get in touch with Jewel. Maybe this time she wouldn't hang up on him. And he wanted to call the hospital and get a report on Eddie. He figured they'd taken him to Rehoboth McKinley. But first, he had to get a cola and maybe some crackers. He studied the cola machine in front of the garage and sighed with relief when he saw that the machine took dollar bills. Thank goodness, he still had the two dollars Eddie had given him. His buddy had almost forgotten that he kept a couple of dollars stuck inside his shoe, for emergencies. Russ's stomach growled. Yeah, he was hungry. Hungrier than he'd ever been in his life.

Before inserting a dollar into the cola machine, he glanced up and down the road. No one was in sight. Everyone had closed up shop and gone home. Even the trading post had closed for the evening. Maybe he'd been a fool to come back to Black Rock. But then, he figured nobody, least of all the police, would expect him to back-track.

The machine took his dollar on the second try, spit out a quarter change and dumped a frosty can into the bottom slot. Russ retrieved his quarter, picked up the can and popped the lid. He gulped down the dark carbonated beverage as if it were water—cold, sweet, delicious. When he finished half the cola, he eyed the machine that held candy, crackers and cookies. He used another dollar to buy two packs of peanut butter crackers. Taking his food with him, he walked behind the garage, out of sight of any passing vehicles, and slumped down on the ground. He ripped open the cellophane paper covering the food and gobbled both packs of crackers. After washing the food down with the remainder of his drink, he crushed the can in his hand. He slipped around the building, checked out the surrounding area, and decided it was safe to make his way to the pay telephone outside the trading post. He tossed the empty can into a trash basket along-side the gas pumps, then made a mad dash across the desolate street. Ever mindful that someone could spot him at any time and notify the law, Russ kept one eye out for any sign of human life.

He picked up the telephone receiver, dropped in a quarter and sighed when he heard a dial tone. He contacted an operator who dialed the hospital for him, and Rehoboth McKinley's switchboard transferred him to Information. He enquired about Eddie.

"Ed Whitehorn, Jr.'s condition is critical," the woman's voice said.

"What does that mean? Has he had surgery? Is he going to live?"

"If you'd like the number for the SICU waiting room, I can give it to you and you can speak to someone in the Whitehorn family."

"No, thanks." Russ hung up. He couldn't talk to anyone in Eddie's family. They probably all hated him and, just as Joe Ornelas did, blamed him for Eddie's condition.

Scanning the area again, scared that his luck was going to run out any minute now, Russ lifted the receiver again. After dropping in another quarter, he dialed Jewel Begay's number. With each ring, his heart nearly pumped out of his chest. Jewel was his one hope.

"Hello?" The voice was male. Either her father or her older brother.

"May I speak to Jewel?"

"Just a minute." Definitely the brother. He hadn't asked Russ to identify himself.

Russ waited. *Please, let her talk to me. Please.*

"Hello."

"Jewel, it's Russ. Please, don't hang up."

"I'm sorry, but you must have the wrong Jewel. I don't know anyone named Jim Gatewood."

The dial tone hummed ominously in Russ's ear.

Chapter 13

Andi flipped on the light switch as she entered her house, then dropped her keys on the table in the small entry hall. Her place was only a few miles from the hospital, which made it convenient for them to rush back to the hospital at a moment's notice. Staying here together was the only logical choice since Joe's home was a good hour or more away. Joe closed the door and locked the deadbolt, then took a look around, glancing from the living room on the left to the dining room on the right.

"Come on in," Andi said, inviting him with a welcoming sweep of her hand. "Make yourself at home."

He followed her into the living room. The walls were covered with a warm, honey-colored pine, as was the floor. A large handwoven Navajo rug spread out under the glass and black wrought-iron coffee table. At the far side of the room, two large windows flanked a massive rock fireplace. A huge green leather chair and ottoman sat before the pine armoire entertainment center, and a wood-enframed sofa rested in front of the fireplace.

"Nice place you have here," he said.

"Thanks. It's probably bigger than I need, but I like the roominess."

"Your arts and crafts store must be doing pretty well for you to afford a place like this, or did you use—"

"I used money from my trust fund," she admitted. "After all, the money came from my mother's father, so it's not only legally mine, but mine via heredity, too."

"I didn't mean to sound judgmental," Joe told her.

"Yeah, I know." She shrugged. "I promise that from now on, I won't take everything you say the wrong way."

The corners of his mouth lifted into a relieved smile. "I'm hungry. How about you?"

"Starved," she admitted. "I'm not sure what we'll find in my refrigerator, but I think there might be salad and sandwich fixings."

"You don't happen to have any beer, do you?"

She shook her head. "Sorry. I have some chardonnay and a bottle of tequila. But no beer."

"Tequila, huh? You must still like margaritas."

"Guilty as charged."

Joe came up behind Andi and curved his hands over her shoulders. "Maybe decaf coffee or tea would be better for us at this time of night."

"I'll fix us some coffee, and you can help me pull together some sandwiches and a couple of salads," Andi said. "But then I'm going to take a nice, long hot bath and clean off all this grime. I feel as if I haven't bathed in a week."

"If you want to take a bath first, I can put on the coffee and fix us something to eat. I've become pretty handy in the kitchen since I've lived alone for so many years."

"Oh, Joe, that would be great." She pointed toward the dining room across the hall. "Just go through there and you'll find the kitchen."

"I'll find it okay. You take your bath, and I'll serve you dinner on a tray in your bedroom. How does that sound?"

"Sounds like heaven."

Playfully swatting her behind, Joe sent her down the hallway. Within minutes of going upstairs, Andi shed her dirty clothes, turned on the water faucets and submerged her body in the big garden tub beneath the four-foot square stained-glass window. She laid her head on the cushioned rest attached to the tub, then reached out for a bottle sitting on the ledge. After pouring several capfuls of the liquid into the running water, a bubbly foam began to appear, and grew thicker and higher with each passing moment.

Andi's thoughts flashed from one concern to another. From worry about Eddie Whitehorn to fear for her brother. Where *was* Russ? He knew the police would continue to look for him, that he would be hunted down like an escaped animal. If only she could have persuaded him to come back with her. She felt as if she had somehow failed him. And thus failed her father, too.

But what more could she do? Even now, while the police continued to search, J.T.'s ranch hands did, too, along with the two Dundee agents, Hunter and Wolfe. She prayed that someone—even the police—would find Russ before another hit man tracked him down and killed him.

She had phoned Doli from the hospital and brought her up to date on everything that had happened. Her stepmother had become understandably distraught when she learned that Russ was still on the run. Andi had tactfully refrained from mentioning Russ's threat to kill himself.

She wanted to believe that Russ wouldn't actually have taken his own life, but as desperate as he was, he might have acted out of irrational fear.

Poor Doli had enough compassion for the Whitehorns to express her sympathy for what Joe's family was going through, although she still disapproved of Andi's alliance with Joe.

"If you had not been with Joe Ornelas, Russ would have returned home with you," Doli had said.

"I don't think he would have. Russ is too frightened to trust anyone. Even me."

Andi grabbed a bottle of shampoo, poured a quarter-size amount into the palm of her hand and lathered her hair. She slid farther down into the tub until she was practically covered with water, only her face visible above the froth of bubbles.

She had no idea what was going to happen tomorrow. All she could do was hope and pray for the best. If it were within her power to save her brother from any and all harm, she would do it—in a heartbeat.

And if she could perform a miracle and vanquish all the obstacles in the path that led to a future with Joe, she would do that, too.

Joe had found the kitchen easily and, after scrubbing his hands with antibacterial soap, he'd gone right to work putting on a carafe of decaffeinated coffee and searching the contents of Andi's side-by-side refrigerator for sandwich makings.

He was impressed with the kitchen. Heck, he was duly impressed with Andi's house. But what had he expected—that she would be living in that tiny apartment she'd rented when she first arrived in Gallup five-and-a-half years ago? After all, why shouldn't Andi enjoy the wealth she had inherited from her maternal grandfather?

You couldn't have given her anything this fancy. He thought about his modest four-room house and how proud he'd been to be able to afford a place of his own. Of course, his finances had improved a great deal since he'd left the Tribal Police force and joined the ranks of Dundee agents, whose yearly salaries were in the six-figure bracket.

Now isn't the time to start enumerating all the differences between you and Andi, he told himself. There had been enough differences to discourage him from pursuing a relationship with her years ago, but he had forged ahead then because he hadn't been able to stop himself. He'd fallen hard for Andrea Stephens. He had dated a lot of women before he met Andi and quite a few since, but no other woman had ever affected him the way she did.

As the coffee brewed, Joe slapped slices of ham and turkey onto wheat bread and loaded the sandwiches down with tomatoes, lettuce and pickles. He liked dills; Andi liked bread-and-butter. After rummaging through her cupboards, he found a large serving tray, which he filled with the contents of their midnight snack. Glancing at the wall clock, he revised the time—their eleven-fifteen snack. He eyed the wall phone. Kate and Ed had promised that if there was any change for the worse in Eddie's condition, they would call immediately. Joe had told his sister that he wanted to stay at the hospital, but she had insisted that he go home with Andi and get some much-needed rest.

"You've done more than enough in bringing Eddie back to us," Kate had said. "You're still recovering from a gunshot wound. You go with Andi. Eat. Sleep. Come back in the morning."

"I will call you if we need you," Ed had vowed. "We

have your cellular phone number, and Andi's number, also.''

Andi's home was on the outskirts of Gallup, a fairly quick drive back to the hospital. He hoped that Eddie spent an uneventful night. The boy had been through so much these past few days. His whole life had been turned upside down. And once he woke up and the doctor gave the police permission to question him, Eddie would have to confront the authorities on his own, without Russ. Andi's little brother was still running scared, out there alone and vulnerable. If ever two boys needed some divine intervention in their lives, Eddie and Russ did.

Joe tossed a couple of cloth napkins on the food tray, then searched the cabinets for dessert. He found an unopened box of chocolate mint cookies—Andi's favorite. He dumped half a dozen onto a small plate and added it to the already crowded tray.

Carefully balancing the tray, he made his way down the hallway and up the stairs, then started searching for Andi's room. There were four doors. Two were closed. One was a bathroom. The fourth door, the one closest to him, stood wide open, and light poured from within. As he approached, he heard the sound of splashing water. At the thought of Andi totally naked, Joe almost dropped the tray.

Get hold of yourself, man! It wasn't as if he'd never seen a naked woman before—he just hadn't seen Andi completely nude.

He entered her private domain. He had thought the room would be completely feminine, perhaps with a few ruffles and a bit of lace here and there. He'd been wrong. At least, partially wrong. Although the wooden rocker in the corner boasted flower-print cushions with matching narrow ruffles around the edges, the rest of the room pos-

sessed a distinctively Southwestern flavor. From the black
iron bed, with half-moon headboard and footboard, to the
Navajo rug on the floor, the decor projected an aura of
earthiness and tranquillity.

Joe placed the food tray on a black metal table situated
between an overstuffed plaid armchair and an antique settee piled high with pillows, each covered in a different
Native American print. On the walls were paintings that
he instantly recognized as the work of Joanna Blackwood.
One exquisite bronze statue held a place of honor on the
mantel; a proud Navajo astride a magnificent stallion.
J.T.'s brother-in-law, Alex, was no doubt the sculptor.

The door to the adjoining bathroom was half open. Joe
hesitated, his body urging him to take one good look at
Andi and then dive into the tub with her. But his mind
cautioned him that he would be wise to wait for an invitation. After all, he had no idea if he'd be welcome.

While he stood near the bathroom door, aroused and
undecided as to what action he should take, he heard
movement in the bathroom and caught just a glimpse of
Andi's backside as she emerged from the tub. Before he'd
had time to fully appreciate her long, slender waist, the
curve of her hips or the sleekness of her legs, a flash of
white terry cloth suddenly whirled around her, obscuring
her delicious body. He forced himself momentarily to
glance away, but couldn't stop himself from taking another look. Suddenly the door opened all the way and
Andi stared at him, wide-eyed, mouth open on a startled
gasp.

"I didn't hear you come in." She clutched the lapels
of her robe together and tightened the belt around her
waist.

She was clean and fresh, her hair wet, her skin flushed
from the warm bath water. The red silk robe barely

reached her knees and hung open in front, revealing a length of tan flesh just above mid-thigh.

After clearing his throat, Joe nodded to the tray he'd placed on the table. "I brought dinner for us."

"Oh, Joe, thank you." She hurried toward the meal and quickly surveyed every item. "It looks delicious. Please, sit down and let's eat."

Joe eyed the chair and the settee. "I'm still pretty dirty," he said. "I don't want to mess up anything."

She whipped a handwoven blanket off the back of the settee and arranged it over the chair. "There. Now, sit."

He obeyed her command. "This is a nice room."

"I'm glad you like it. I decorated it and the entire house myself." She lifted the coffee mug from the tray. "I wanted this to be a place that felt like home. I wanted this house to make me feel as if it truly belonged to me. My parent's home...my mother's home always seemed so austere. It was perfect. Nothing ever out of place and every room filled with priceless antiques and things little girls weren't supposed to touch. I wanted my house to be child-friendly, so that when I have children someday... Well, you get the idea."

He nodded, then picked up his sandwich and took a huge bite. Andi had built this house with the future in mind. She had planned it and decorated it for a husband and the children they would one day bring into the world. Who would that husband be? Joe wondered. What lucky man would share Andi's life and give her the children she wanted?

There would be no way he could stay in New Mexico and watch her marry another man, see her happy without him. But now that she had been his—truly his—how could he ever leave her? Passion alone was not a good basis for a lasting marriage, and he and Andi both deserved a lifetime commitment. Would it be possible for them to work through all their differences? Could they find a common ground on which to build a future? And was that what he truly wanted—to spend the rest of his life back on the reservation with Andi?

As long as Russ hates you, Andi and you can never have a permanent relationship, an inner voice reminded him. Joe would never ask her to choose between her brother and him. Perhaps he'd done just that—asked her to choose—when he had expected her to stand by him and understand why he had arrested her father. Had he been asking her to choose between Russell and him?

You shouldn't have run away. You should have stayed and given her time to accept Russell's suicide and the part you played in his death. If you had stayed, she might have forgiven you years ago.

"You're awfully quiet," Andi said as she reached for a chocolate mint cookie.

"Just busy eating." And as if to demonstrate, he finished off his sandwich and downed the last drops of coffee.

"I can carry the tray back to the kitchen, if you'd like to take a shower. There's a huge walk-in shower in the other bathroom."

"Thanks. A shower is just what I need."

Andi rose from the settee. "I'll get you some towels and a washcloth." She went into the bathroom and returned with the items—big, fluffy yellow towels and matching washcloth. "There's a one-size robe hanging on the hook behind the door in the bathroom. I bought it for guests...female guests, so it may be a bit small for you."

"I'll make do." He glanced down at his grungy shirt and jeans. "I'll need to wash these tonight. Otherwise, I'll have to go home and get a change of clothes."

"No problem. Just toss your things out into the hall, and I'll put them on to wash while I clean up the dishes."

"Which bedroom do you want me to take?" he asked. "I noticed two closed doors up here and assumed they were bedrooms."

"Oh, yes. Use the room to the right of the bathroom. The other room doesn't have any furniture in it."

Joe stood, took the towels from her and shuffled his feet as he waited, not exactly sure for what. "Well, I'd better get that shower and then turn in. I want to go back to the hospital first thing in the morning."

"Right." Andi smiled at him, an anticipatory look in her eyes, as if she, too, were waiting.

"I'll toss my dirty clothes out into the hall."

"Yes. Fine. I'll put them in the washer."

Joe started backing out of the room, his steps awkward. As he neared the door, his heels clumsily encountered a round pot that held a tall cactus. He grinned at Andi, then, sidestepping the pot, backed into the hall.

"See you in the morning," he said.

"Good night."

He lumbered down the hall and into the bathroom, all the while calling himself an idiot. Why hadn't he just told Andi that he wanted to spend the night in her bed? The worst that could happen was she'd kick him out.

After placing his phone on the windowsill, he quickly divested himself of his clothing, from shirt and jeans to socks and briefs. He tossed the items out into the hallway, closed the door, and then stepped into the large shower. He eased the bandage from his side and took a good look at the healing wound. He threw the slightly soiled bandage across the room and into the wastepaper basket near the sink. He shut the glass door, turned on the water and shivered when the cold mist hit his naked body. Maybe that's just what he needed—a cold shower.

Andi latched the door on the dishwasher, then went into the laundry room and dumped Joe's clothes into the washing machine. He was upstairs right now in her guest bathroom. Big, beautiful and naked. The thought of what Joe's body must look like totally unclothed sent shivers of desire along her nerve endings. She could be in the shower with him right this minute, scrubbing his back or lathering his... Heat rose inside her, flushing her face and warming her skin.

When he'd asked her which bedroom to use, why hadn't she said "mine"? That's where she wanted him, wasn't it? In her bed, in her arms, all night long. She had only tasted a sample of the delicious pleasure of being Joe's lover. She wanted more. A banquet. Hours of lovemaking, when she could thoroughly explore his body and give him the chance to explore hers.

If Joe wanted her, why hadn't he told her that he did? Surely he knew that one word from him and she would be his. Was he afraid that she would pressure him, try to wrangle a commitment out of him? Was that why he hadn't instigated something intimate between them tonight? Maybe Joe didn't want to consider the possibility of a future with her.

Andi opened the back door and walked out onto her patio. The cool night air chilled her. She looked up at the large full moon, the same yellow-white moon that had shone down on Joe and her in the wee hours of the morning when they had made love in her SUV. Like a magical orb of light, it shimmered up there in the heavens. Romantic. Hypnotizing. Bewitching.

Wrapping her arms across her chest, she breathed in the

sweet, dry air. Desert air. The scent of a summer night wafted on the breeze. She closed her eyes and imagined Joe there with her. Behind her, enclosing her within his embrace. Kissing her cheek, her neck, her breast. Whispering earthy, seductive words into her ear.

Joe dried off hurriedly, ran his fingers through his hair and grabbed the robe off the door hook. When he slipped on the blue robe, he saw immediately that it was a tight fit across his shoulders and hit him above the knees. But what did it matter? No one would see him in the feminine garment. After picking up his boots and cell phone, he opened the bathroom door and scanned the hall, then dashed toward the guest bedroom. He flipped the light switch, and two short, squat bedside lamps came on, illuminating the room with a soft creamy glow. He took inventory hurriedly. The room was smaller than Andi's, but had been decorated in a similar Southwestern style. A pine daybed spanned a nook on the left wall and was flanked by two pine nightstands topped with bookshelves that contained books and an assortment of small Native American craft items.

The daybed looked awfully small, but he supposed once he removed the plethora of pillows, he might find a bed large enough to accommodate a man of his size. He dumped his boots in the corner, laid his phone on the nightstand to his right and immediately set to work clearing the bed. When he stripped back the spread, he found cool tan sheets awaiting him.

After discarding the robe, he lay on the bed and covered himself up to his waist. He crossed his arms under his head and stared up at the ceiling. Hell, he'd forgotten to turn off the lamps. He reached the one above his head quite easily, but had to sit up and scoot to the end of the bed to turn off the other one. Returning to his former position, he tried to relax. Moonlight streamed through the windows. He hadn't pulled down the shades. And he wasn't going to. His eyes would adjust to the light. It shouldn't be that difficult. He was tired and sleepy and... Hell, what he was was horny. Maybe he *should* have taken that cold shower.

Try not to think about Andi, he told himself. That might help. And whatever you do, don't think about what happened between the two of you this morning. Yeah, sure. Easier said than done. The minute he closed his eyes, an image of Andi flashed through his mind. A naked Andi, straddling his hips, riding him, crying out his name.

At first he thought he had imagined the sound of the door opening and of footsteps padding across the wooden floor. And when he opened his eyes and saw Andi standing beside the daybed, he knew he had to be dreaming.

"Joe?"

He shot straight up, the sheet dropping to his hips. "Andi? What's wrong?"

"You're in here and I'm in yonder," she told him. "That's what's wrong."

"Are you sure you want—"

"Yes, I'm sure." She held out her hand. "Come to my room and sleep with me. Please, Joe. Please, come with me. I need you to hold me. I need you to—"

Before the next word came from her mouth, he was out of bed and standing before her totally naked, the moonlight outlining his bold silhouette. The sight of him almost took her breath away. He slid his hands beneath her robe and eased the garment down her shoulders. It pooled about her feet in a silky red circle.

When she held open her arms to him, he scooped her up and carried her out of the guest room and down the hall to her own semi-dark bedroom. Moonlight filtered through the sheer cream curtains. He deposited her in the middle of her bed, then came down over her. When he grabbed first one wrist and then the other, trapping them with one of his hands, she stared up at him questioningly.

"You're going to lie there and cooperate." His voice was deep and dark and sensuously dangerous. "And I am going to do whatever I want to do. But you aren't going to touch me. Not yet."

"But, Joe," she whimpered, suddenly realizing his intention.

His mouth took hers in a slow, sweet tasting. Not hurrying. Not forcing. Seducing with gentle pleasure. Bracing himself on one elbow, he aligned his thighs on either side of hers, allowing the ridge of his shaft to intimately rub against her mound. She sighed, and he swallowed the sound as his tongue entered her mouth and moved about inside with languid ease.

Andi squirmed, wanting more, wishing that he would be less gentle. But he would not be rushed. His lips made a journey south, inch by slow, torturous inch, until he licked a ring around first one and then her other nipple, but didn't touch the puckered tip.

"Joe, please..."

He nudged her over onto her belly, her hands beneath her. He eased his hands free, then straddled her. When she lifted her head, he pushed her face down and nipped her neck with a stinging love-bite. She moaned and shuddered. He moved from her neck to her shoulders and down her spine, sparing no part of her from his ravaging mouth. When he nibbled the soft flesh on her buttocks, she cried out as desire flooded through her. Before she had a chance to catch her breath, he parted her thighs and painted a moist trail from inner thigh to knee and on to ankle. And then he began the upward climb on the other leg. When he returned to her hips, he slipped his hand between her legs and sought out her hidden kernel. She bucked against his hand when he stroked her, then lifted her hips as she keened softly with frenzied need.

"You like this, don't you?"

"Yes," she replied, breathless with longing.

Joe eased her over onto her back, freeing her hands, but when she reached for him, he slid downward until his head rested at the juncture between her legs. She gripped his shoulders. He reached up and ran his palms over her breasts. She sucked in her breath.

"Joe? What—"

He flicked both nipples at the same time. She gasped. He took each between a thumb and forefinger and began a delicious torment. Wiggling her hips, inviting him without realizing it, Andi moaned. He spread her thighs and nuzzled her intimately.

"Oh, no, don't." She groaned.

"You're mine," he told her. "My woman. Mine to do with as I will. And what I want is to love you until you can't bear any more pleasure."

His mouth and tongue teased and taunted, tasting, licking, laving and loving, until Andi was mindless with the pleasure he had promised. Every fiber of her being came to full alert, aware of the building pressure that Joe forced tighter and tighter until she burst with sensation. Wild and uncontrollable, the shock waves pulsated throughout her body.

While she cried with satisfaction, Joe rose up and over her, then lifted her hips and entered her. One hard, swift thrust. Embedding himself deeply and securely. She had taken all of him, and loved the fullness of having him buried within her.

Setting the pace, he began with slow, deep plunges. Quickly catching on to the tempo, she joined him, their undulations perfectly matched. But as the pressure built anew, Joe increased the speed and fierceness of his jabs until he hammered into her. Her second climax hit with the force of a tidal wave, washing her adrift in pure sensation. She knew nothing. Saw nothing. Heard nothing. She only felt Joe inside her, around her, a part of her now and forever.

While she lingered in those timeless moments of complete satiation, Joe jetted his release into her and groaned as his body shuddered with fulfillment.

He rolled over and onto the bed, tugging her until she fit snugly against him. She clung to him, wanting to whisper that she loved him. But he had said nothing about love, so instead she murmured his name. *Joseph.* And when she did, he tucked his fist under her chin and lifted her face for a tender, loving kiss.

Chapter 14

When they walked into Rehoboth McKinley Christian Hospital the next morning, Andi felt as if the whole world could tell, just by looking at her, that she was Joseph Ornelas's woman. Wasn't it obvious that she was no longer the person she had been only a few days ago? She certainly didn't feel like the same woman. And she did not think the same. About Joe. About the past. And definitely about the future. Joe might not be ready to make a commitment, but in her heart she was already committed. Totally. Completely.

Her first loyalty was to Joe, and she sensed that his was to her. In the past neither of them had given their all to the relationship, which had been tested in its beginning stages. She had failed Joe as surely as he had failed her. But now they had a second chance, and she had no intention of wasting this priceless opportunity.

Kate Whitehorn met them, a warm smile on her face and a hug for Joe and for Andi. "He rested through the night, and this morning he is awake but not completely alert.''

"This is good,'' Joe told her. "He will be his old self soon.''

Kate's smile flickered, but she forced it in place. "Yes, this is good. And all that matters is that he is alive and will recover.''

"How is his arm?'' Joe asked, and Andi realized as did Joe that something wasn't quite right with Kate.

Kate's smile melted away, leaving a somber expression on her face. "He has no feeling in his arm and he cannot move it. He can't even wriggle his fingers.''

Joe took a deep breath. Andi laid her hand on Kate's shoulder. A palpitating silence lingered for several minutes. Alive with unspoken words, the stillness grew heavy and cumbersome.

"This will pass.'' Joe finally broke the silence. "It will take time, but he will regain use of his arm.''

"I hope you're right.'' Kate grasped Andi's hand. "Is there no word on Russ?''

"No,'' Andi replied.

"This endless waiting must be torment for Doli,'' Kate said. "I must call her and speak with her today.''

"That's terribly kind of you.'' Andi hugged Kate, genuine appreciation in the gesture.

Joe glanced around, scanning the waiting area. "Where is Ed?''

"He has gone to the cafeteria for breakfast,'' Kate said. "He insisted that I eat before he did.''

Joe glanced toward the door to the Surgical Intensive Care Unit. "May I go in and see Eddie?''

"Yes, of course, you may see him. Soon. But now he is sleeping again.'' Kate patted Joe's arm. "Why don't you and Andi go to see Joanna before she delivers her baby?''

"What?" Andi and Joe spoke simultaneously.

"You did not know?" Kate laughed. "I did not think to call you, and I'm sure J.T. is much too nervous to think of making phone calls. They drove all the way home last night and had to come right back to Gallup this morning."

"She's not due for another few weeks," Andi said. "I hope everything is all right."

"Yes, J.T. told me that the doctor believes she and the baby are both fine," Kate replied. "Babies come when they are ready to be born. My three certainly did." A wistful look appeared in Kate's dark eyes, and her gaze settled on the SICU door. "Eddie was supposed to be born in May, but he wasn't ready until early June. He was such a big, fat baby. And so healthy."

"He's going to be all right," Andi said. "He will have doctors and nurses and family to make sure that everything possible will be done for him."

Kate nodded. "There is a policeman standing guard outside Eddie's door," she said.

"That's as much for his protection as it is anything else," Joe explained.

Kate focused her gaze on Joe. "Bill Cummings wants to question him the minute Dr. Shull gives his permission."

"Has Eddie said anything about Bobby Yazzi's murder?" Joe asked.

"No, all he has said is that he is sorry for worrying us. And he asked about Russ."

Andi touched Joe's arm, and he responded immediately, warmth and concern in his expression. "I think I'll go check on Joanna," Andi said. "They won't let me in to see Eddie, anyway, since I'm not family."

"I will go with you," Joe told her. "I would like to speak with J.T. I'm sure he is nervous, waiting for Joanna to give birth. At a time like this, a man is helpless to ease his woman's pain. I can only imagine how difficult that is for J.T."

As it would be for you, Andi thought. Joe was a man who loved with the same dedication and passion he brought to everything in his life. This trait, Joe and J.T. shared.

At 3:18 in the afternoon, Joanna Blackwood gave birth to her fourth child, a second daughter whom she and J.T. named Mary Helene in honor of their mothers. The newborn had eyes as black as J.T.'s and a fluff of dark hair, but her tiny face was a replica of her beautiful mother's. While Andi and Joe were gushing and gooing over the new Miss Blackwood and congratulating the happy parents, Ed Whitehorn appeared in the doorway of Joanna's room.

Joe excused himself and met Ed in the hallway. Andi said her goodbyes and quickly followed.

"Dr. Shull is allowing Captain Cummings and a police officer from here in Gallup to question Eddie," Ed told them. "They are on their way to the hospital now. We want you to be with us—" he looked directly at Joe "—when they question him."

"I'll go with you now," Joe said. "Eddie's family will be at his side when the police arrive. And I will call Tom Nelson. He is the lawyer that J.T. has arranged to represent Eddie."

"I can wait here," Andi suggested.

"No, you come with me," Joe told her. "Whatever Eddie has to say will directly affect Russ. You represent the Lapahie family. You must be present."

* * *

Andi could tell just by looking at him that Eddie White-horn was scared half out of his mind, despite the fact that his parents stood on one side of his bed, she and Joe on the other, and the doctor just a few feet away. Tom Nelson, who resided in Albuquerque, was a quarter Navajo, a quarter Zuni and half white. J.T. had told them that Nelson was an excellent criminal lawyer. When Ed had mentioned the cost of paying such a man, Joe had dismissed Ed's concerns, assuring Ed he would pick up the bill.

"Since I've known Eddie all his life, Captain Dashee has agreed to let me do the questioning," Bill Cummings said.

"We appreciate this." Ed nodded first to Captain Cummings, a short and stocky man whose neat, military-cut hair make his round face appear fat. And then Ed nodded again, silently thanking the Gallup police department's chief, Captain Dashee, a thin man with a shock of white hair and a hawk nose.

"All we want is to find out what happened the night Bobby Yazzi was murdered," Bill told Eddie. "Take your time. Tell us everything you remember about that night."

Eddie's big brown eyes darted back and forth from his parents to Joe. Joe reached down and patted Eddie's pale cheek. The boy sighed and lifted his good arm, holding out his hand, which Joe clasped tightly.

"Russ and I—" Eddie began.

"Just for the record, you're referring to Russell Lapahie, Jr., whenever you say Russ. Is that right?" Captain Cummings asked.

Eddie nodded, then began again. "Russ and I had a double date that night."

"With whom?" Bill asked.

Eddie glanced at Tom Nelson. "I'm not going to say. Russ and I agreed to keep the girls out of this. We don't want the real killer to know who the girls are and go after them."

"Did the girls see who shot Bobby?" Bill asked.

"I'm not going to say anything about the girls," Eddie replied. "I don't have to, do I, Mr. Nelson?"

"No, Eddie, you don't. Not today," Tom replied.

Eddie looked directly at Captain Cummings. "But I'll tell you what happened with Russ and me that night."

Joe glanced at Bill Cummings, hoping to convey that he wanted Bill to go easy on Eddie and not push him—not right now—about the identity of the two girls.

"All right," Bill said. "Tell us about what happened."

Good man, Joe thought. When this mess was all cleared up, he owed Bill Cummings a debt of gratitude for more than one good deed.

"We...well, actually, Russ wanted some beer, but because we were all sixteen, Russ said the only place to get beer was from Bobby Yazzi. Everybody knew that Bobby sold beer to underage drinkers."

"Were you aware that Bobby Yazzi dealt in illegal drugs, also?" Bill asked.

"Yes, sir." Eddie gulped. He squeezed Joe's hand. "But we weren't going there for anything like that. Not even marijuana. We just wanted some beer."

"We believe you, son," Bill assured Eddie. "Go on. Tell us what happened when the four of you arrived at Bobby's apartment."

"Well, we were in Je—a car that belonged to one of the girls. Russ and I don't either one have a car or a truck. When we got there, Russ went into Bobby's apartment to get the beer."

"Are you saying that you weren't in Bobby's apartment that night?" Bill asked.

"Yes, sir. I mean, no, I didn't go in with Russ, but...well, I—I followed him. I thought he might need me."

Joe and Andi shared a quick glance—meaningful and filled with understanding. Eddie and Russ were best friends, loyal to a fault. Andi knew Joe believed as she did—that if the situation had been reversed, Russ would have gone into that apartment to help Eddie.

"I heard what sounded like a car backfiring a few times. Only it wasn't. It was gunshots. Several gunshots." Eddie paused, inhaled deeply and then exhaled. "When I got to the door of Bobby's apartment, it was wide open. I called out to Russ and asked him what was going on, and he came flying out of the apartment. I looked inside— and that's when I saw the body. Bobby Yazzi's body."

"Was Bobby dead?" Bill asked.

"Yes, sir, as far as I know he was. He sure looked dead."

"What happened then?" Bill took a couple of tentative steps toward the foot of Eddie's bed.

"Somebody started shooting at us, and we ran. When we got outside we realized that the girls had driven off and left us. I know they were scared out of their minds. But with them gone, Russ and I had no way to leave, except on foot. The guy who shot at us was coming after us. We just knew he was. Russ had seen the guy's face. He could identify him."

"Eddie, did Russ have a gun?"

"No! Russ has a rifle at home, the same as I do, but he didn't have a gun with him that night. I swear he didn't."

"Okay. Okay." Bill's voice lowered to a soft, soothing

tone. A look of pure puzzlement crossed his face. "Tell me this, son—why didn't you and Russ wait for the police to arrive?"

"We panicked. Plain and simple. Russ had just seen Bobby murdered, and the guy who did it was after us. We ran and kept on running. Russ said nobody would believe us, especially not him since he's been in so much trouble the past couple of years. And people saw us running away from Bobby's apartment."

"Eddie, did you ever see the shooter? Can you identify him?"

"No, sir. I never saw the man's face."

"If you couldn't identify the shooter, why did you run when Russ ran? Did you think the shooter believed you saw him?"

"Yeah, I guess I did. I'm not sure. Neither Russ nor I was thinking straight that night."

"After you and Russ ran way from Bobby's apartment, did you two steal Mr. Lovato's truck?" Bill asked.

"Eddie, you don't have to answer that question," Tom Nelson informed him.

Eddie nodded and kept quiet.

"Do you know where Russ is?" Bill asked, not pursuing the question about the stolen truck.

"No, sir, I don't."

"I think that's enough for now, don't you?" Joe released Eddie's hand and walked toward Bill Cummings.

Bill glanced over his shoulder at Dr. Shull. "What do you say, doctor, can we continue?"

"I think Mr. Ornelas is right," Dr. Shull said. "You have all the information Eddie seems able to give you about the night in question. Any further interrogation can surely wait until tomorrow."

Bill nodded. "Very well." Bill walked over and shook

hands with Eddie. "You get well, young man. And if you feel up to it, I'll be back tomorrow with a few more questions."

When the two police captains started to depart, Eddie called, "Captain Cummings?"

Bill turned. "Yes?"

"When the police find Russ, please, don't hurt him."

Joe sipped on lukewarm coffee as he sat in the waiting area alone. He had persuaded Kate and Ed to go to Andi's house to bathe and eat before coming back to stay another night at the hospital. He and Andi had spent the day at Rehoboth McKinley, dividing most of their time between visits with Eddie, who had remained quiet and withdrawn after the police interrogation, and Joanna Blackwood's maternal domain, which was overflowing with floral arrangements, balloons and stuffed animals. J.T. alone had bought out the local supply of pink roses.

Joe was glad that his family and J.T.'s had become close over the years and that Kate felt comfortable leaving Summer and Joey with Elena and Alex, who with Rita Gonzales's help were looking after the three older Blackwood children. While his family needed to concentrate all their time and energy on Eddie, J.T. and Joanna were celebrating a welcome addition to their growing brood.

Joe couldn't erase from his mind the look on Andi's face when Joanna had allowed her to hold Mary Helene. She had beamed with maternal bliss. It was at that moment he realized not only that Andi wanted to be a mother, but that she was meant to be one.

"Mr. Ornelas?" A pretty young nurse stuck her head just inside the waiting room.

"Yes?" Joe met her gaze.

"Your nephew would like to see you."

"I thought he was asleep for the night."

"No, sir. He's awake and seems quite agitated. He asked me to come out here and get you."

"Thanks. I'll be right there."

Joe dumped the foam cup in the garbage on his way out the door, then followed the nurse into the SICU and straight to Eddie's door. He nodded in greeting to the uniformed police officer standing watch. The man returned the amicable gesture.

Joe eased the door open and walked into Eddie's room. For just a second, Joe saw Eddie as he had looked five years ago, as a boy of eleven. Small. Skinny. All bony arms and legs. And a big smile. The young man who lay in the hospital bed was no longer small, and although he was lean, he was no longer thin. And his carefree smile seemed to have vanished forever.

"Did you want to see me?" Joe approached the bed.

"Yes, I must talk to you…" Eddie swallowed hard. "I didn't tell the police everything. I left out parts. I—I want to tell you the truth. Then maybe you can help Russ."

Joe held his breath, entertaining a certain amount of healthy fear about what Eddie was going to tell him. He pulled up a chair by the bed, sat and focused his complete attention on his nephew.

"I'm listening."

"Well, everything I told Captain Cummings was true," Eddie said. "It's just that I didn't tell him that when Russ got out of the car, Jewel went with him."

"Jewel?"

"Jewel Begay. Russ's date."

"Jewel Begay went into Bobby Yazzi's apartment with Russ?"

Eddie nodded.

"Did she see who killed Bobby?" Joe asked.

"Yeah. She and Russ both saw the man kill Bobby."

"Then Jewel can back up Russ's story, can't she?"

"She could," Eddie said. "But she won't."

"What do you mean, she won't?"

"Russ tried to call her a few times, and she always hung up on him. He doesn't think she'll admit to being there and seeing anything because she's scared of the guy who shot Bobby. And without Jewel to tell the police that somebody else killed Bobby, Russ is convinced they'll arrest him for murder and he'll wind up spending the rest of his life in jail."

"Damn!" Joe dropped his hands between his knees and stared down at the floor. "You're going to have to tell Bill Cummings about Jewel Begay."

"No, Uncle Joe, I can't. I promised Russ that we'd protect Jewel. He said if the police question her, then the guy who shot Bobby will find out and he might kill her."

Joe sat up, braced his palms on his thighs and blew out a long, exasperated huff. "Do you know who killed Bobby Yazzi?"

"I told you, I didn't see the guy's face. I wasn't—"

"Do you know who he was? Did Russ tell you?"

"Yes."

"Then how about telling me?"

Eddie bit down on his bottom lip. "LeCroy Lanza. He's a—"

"I know who he is," Joe said. "J.T. has a ton of information on that son of a bitch."

"He does?" Eddie's eyes widened.

"Yeah. Lanza's name came up. Seems more than one person knows there was a connection between Bobby Yazzi and Lanza."

"He's a real bad guy, Uncle Joe. Russ says that he

won't stop until we're both dead. He's not going to let us live to testify against him.''

"You're safe, Eddie. There's a police officer outside your door twenty-four hours a day, and a Dundee agent will arrive soon to help protect you. But the best way to keep you and Russ both safe from now on is to put LeCroy Lanza behind bars where he belongs.''

"I know you're right. I tried to convince Russ that—" Eddie stopped and stared at Joe, a look of deep concern on his face. "Don't blame Russ for what happened. It wasn't any more his fault than it was mine. I know we shouldn't have run away, but sometimes you run even when you know you shouldn't. You understand, don't you, Uncle Joe?''

"Yeah, I understand.'' He had run away five years ago, and deep down inside he had known that leaving was the wrong thing to do, that he should have had the courage to stay on the reservation. "And I know Russ is your friend and that a lot of his problems are because he lost his father. Believe me, Eddie, I want to help Russ just as much as you do.''

"You really do, don't you? I mean, you care about what happens to Russ.''

"We have to figure out a way to get Russ to safety and bring LeCroy Lanza to justice. But first, we have to fill Bill Cummings in on all the details you left out of your statement earlier today.'' Joe patted Eddie on his uninjured shoulder. "I'm going to give Tom Nelson a call and tell him what you just told me. We'll want him here when you talk to Bill again.''

Andi met Joe at the front door. Weariness hung heavily on his broad shoulders. She took his hand in hers and led him up the stairs to her bedroom.

"How did it go?" she asked.

"Good," he replied as he flopped down on the overstuffed plaid chair. "Eddie told Bill everything. He'll rest better now that he's gotten everything off his chest. Afterward, Bill and J.T. and I met with Captain Dashee, and representatives of the New Mexico State Police and Arizona and Utah highway patrols, as well as Sawyer McNamara from the FBI and Vic Noble from the DEA."

"Good grief, Joe, why are all those different law enforcement agencies involved?"

"Because we're dealing with a very dangerous man, and everybody wants a little piece of him." Joe motioned for Andi to come to him. "This is considered a Navajo crime, committed on the reservation. And Bobby Yazzi was Navajo. Since the reservation spans areas in all three states, all three states are involved. And we're dealing with three murders, the death of a hit man and the likelihood that everything that's happened is drug related, so the FBI and the DEA both have a horse in this race."

Andi went to Joe, and when he grabbed her on either side of her waist and dragged her onto his lap, she draped her arm around his neck and laid her head on his shoulder. "Now that I know for sure Russ saw this man—this LeCroy Lanza—commit murder, I'm even more afraid for him. Joe, we have to do something to—"

"We agreed on a plan," Joe told her. "It was a joint decision, and when it comes together, there will be so many law enforcement people there that nothing bad will happen to Russ."

Andi lifted her head and looked directly into Joe's eyes. "What do you mean, nothing bad will happen to Russ? What sort of plan did y'all agree on? And just who is the *we* that made the decision?"

"*We* is all the different men I told you about. We put

our heads together and devised a plan to bring Russ out in the open, to bring him right to us. We have to do this. It could be the only way to save his life.''

Andi swallowed, nervousness obvious in the simple movement. "Whatever it is that y'all planned, will it put Russ in danger?''

"He's already in danger. And if Lanza finds him…" Be honest with her, Joe told himself. Be totally honest. "Yeah, the plan puts Russ right in the middle of all the action, which will mean danger.''

"I don't like the sound of this already," she said. "I want to know everything. And don't leave out one little detail.''

Joe nodded. "I'll give you the condensed version first, and then I'll answer any questions you have. Will that be all right?''

"I guess so.''

"Arrangements are going to be made with Jewel Begay. Eddie told us that Russ tried to contact her several times, but she always hangs up on him. Well, the next time he calls her—" Joe held up his hand "—and before you ask, yes, we believe he will contact her again soon— Jewel will tell him that she will back up his story about Lanza killing Bobby, but that she wants to meet and talk with him first. She'll set up this meeting for the Navajo Nation Fair.''

"That begins Wednesday, doesn't it?''

"Yes.''

"What if Jewel won't cooperate?''

"I think if we handle things just right, she'll be more than glad to cooperate.''

"What if Russ doesn't call—''

"He'll call. He believes getting Jewel to back up his

story is his only hope. And when he does call and they
arrange to meet, our plan will move forward.''

"I want to be there," Andi told him. "When Russ
meets Jewel and the police arrest him. Oh, Joe don't you
see that he'll be less likely to bolt and try to run if I'm
there. All I want is to help ensure his safety. If he runs,
they might shoot him.''

"No. No way. I don't want to have to worry about Russ
and you. Since Russ doesn't trust me, then J.T. is going
to handle things. But I'll be there, in the background, to
ensure nothing happens to Russ.''

"I'm going to be there and you can't stop me. I promise
I'll stay out of the way and not cause any trouble. But I
need to be there.''

"What the hell am I going to do with you, woman?''

Andi smiled wickedly. "You're going to let me have
my way. Tonight and at the fair.''

"I am?''

"Yes, you are.''

"And if I let you have your way tonight, just what do
you intend to do?''

She unbuttoned his shirt. "I intend to help you relax.''
She unbuckled his belt. "You've had a long day, and what
you need is a shower.'' She unzipped his jeans. "And a
comfortable bed.'' She slid out of his lap and onto the
floor at his feet, then proceeded to remove his boots and
socks. "And a massage.''

"You're right," he said. "I *am* going to let you have
your way.''

Chapter 15

*T*he gun fired. Andi screamed. Joe slammed his body into Russ, knocking him out of harm's way. The bullet hit Joe in the back. Andi screamed again. People swarmed all around her, like flies around an animal carcass. She tried to fight her way through the crowd, struggling to reach Joe. Desperately needing to help him.

"Get out of my way," she pleaded. "Let me through. Joe needs me!"

Joe needs me… Joe needs me… Joe needs me….

Andi woke with a start, tears streaming down her face and her body trembling with anger and fear. Her gaze focused on the man who held her shoulders and shook her gently.

"Joe!" She rose from her reclining position and threw her arms around his neck. "Oh, thank God, it was just a nightmare." With her mind still partially in that hellish dream state, she clung to Joe with all her might.

"It's all right, Andrea, I'm here." Joe pressed his lips

against her right temple, his breath warm on her face. "You're safe and I'm safe."

"But it was so real," she said. "I can't believe that it was nothing more than a bad dream. I'm awake, but I feel as if what I saw and what I felt really happened." She pulled back, then grasped his face, her hands cupping his cheeks. "He shot you. Oh, Joe, he shot you in the back."

Joe rubbed her neck, her shoulders and down her spine, his touch caressing, circling, soothing her. "Nobody shot me. I'm fine."

"I know." She sighed deeply. "I know it was only a nightmare, but it was—"

"You're worried about Russ and about what will happen at the fair when he meets Jewel," Joe told her. "All those worries stirred up your subconscious mind and created that bad dream. And that's all it was, just a dream."

"No! No, it was more than a dream." She tightened her hold on his face as she gazed into his eyes. "Don't you see—it was a premonition. I have them all the time. Odd feelings. Strange worries when something bad is about to happen." She released his face and clutched his shoulders. "But this is the first time I've ever dreamed about what is going to happen."

"Andi, listen to yourself," Joe said. "You're talking nonsense."

"It's not nonsense." She dug her fingers into his flesh. "You know that premonitions are possible, that visions can be real."

"For a *yataalii*, yes, but not for—"

"You can't go to the fair. Do you hear me? If you go to the fair and try to protect Russ, you'll get shot...in the back."

"You're getting all upset for nothing."

Joe took her in his arms and caressed her, slowly and

sensuously. She shivered as pleasure mixed with the fear that had been tormenting her. He kissed her neck and nuzzled her shoulder. She sighed. While he delved his hands beneath the sheet to fondle her naked hips, he lowered his head until his mouth could reach her breast.

Realizing that he was trying to use seduction to take her mind off her nightmare, Andi forked her fingers through Joe's hair and clutched the back of his head. "I won't forget the dream," she told him. "I know it was a premonition. You can't go to the fair. You must let—"

He sucked hard on her breast. She gasped as the sensations spiraled from her nipple to the very depths of her femininity.

"Let's talk about the dream later," he murmured as he moved to her other breast to give it equal attention.

"Mmm." She knew she was fighting a losing battle at the moment, she could not resist Joe's touch. But the war was yet to be won. After the loving, reality would return, and then she would make him listen to her and take her premonition as a real warning.

Joe whipped back the covers, exposing their naked bodies. The moment she ran her hand over his chest, he dipped his fingers between her feminine folds and found her hot and wet and ready. She closed her thighs to capture his hand, and when she did, he cupped her hip with his other hand and lifted her, nudging her until she rolled over on top of him.

She pushed herself into a sitting position, straddling him. His sex pulsed against her, big and hard and demanding. She leaned forward, offering him her breasts, and rubbed herself intimately over his arousal. He clutched her hips and repositioned her just enough to seek entrance into her body. She happily accommodated him, sliding over his erection and opening herself for his up-

ward thrust. She settled around him, moaning with pleasure at the fullness he created within her. Large, hot and
throbbing. She ached with wanting.

Joe waited. She understood that he was giving her the
power to set the rhythm, to be the one in control. Like
round ripe globes, her breasts dangled over his mouth, and
he quickly took advantage of their nearness. While she
sat astride him, loving the feel of him buried deep inside
her, he began a tender assault on her breasts. Suckling
greedily at one breast, he massaged the other nipple with
his thumb and forefinger.

Her femininity clenched tightly as quivers of arousal
spread throughout her body, tapping along her nerve endings, tightening her muscles and melting her bones. While
pleasure rippled through her, encouraging her to seek
more, to demand all that was possible, Andi moved. Up
and down. Up and down. She found her pressure point
and rode it hard against Joe's erection.

He continued the attention to her breasts, his mouth
moving with frenzied lust from one nipple to the other as
he stroked her hips. Andi's body tightened around Joe's
shaft, clasping him securely as the first waves of her climax washed over her. Then and only then did Joe join in
the sexual movements. While she came apart in his arms,
he intensified his thrusts until completion claimed her in
a maelstrom of spasms. She cried out, gasping for air,
thrilling from the indescribable pleasure. Her release trig-
gered his, and Joe's big hands bit into the flesh of her
hips and held her in place for the final series of fast, hard,
repetitive lunges. He went dead still, groaning deep in his
throat, and then trembled from head to toe.

They clung to each other as the aftershocks of fulfillment flowed over them and slowly diminished, leaving
them relaxed and sated. Andi's body meshed with Joe's

as she lay atop him, her breathing slow and steady, her heartbeat matching his to perfection.

Suddenly Joe's cell phone rang. He grumbled. Andi slipped to his side, allowing him to rise from the bed and search for his jeans. He found them where he'd left them the night before—tossed across the settee.

He snatched the phone out of its holder and flipped it open. "Ornelas, here."

"Joe, this is David Wolfe. Hunter and I have just arrived in Gallup and have taken a motel room. Do you want us to go straight to the hospital or meet you somewhere else?"

"No, I want you to go to Rehoboth McKinley right now," Joe said. "I've already cleared things with the local authorities. They're expecting you and Hunter. All you have to do is show them your identification. I want one of you with Eddie at all times. Break up the twenty-four hours any way you like."

"Do we have clearance to stay in the room with your nephew?"

"Yes, even when a doctor or a member of the medical staff is with him. Dr. Shull understands that you two are professionals who will in no way interfere with Eddie's medical treatment."

"Then I'll see you at the hospital later today," Wolfe said.

"Yeah. I'll be stopping by soon. Thanks, Wolfe. I'm glad you and Hunter are here to keep an eye on Eddie."

Joe closed his phone and tossed it on top of his wrinkled jeans, then went back to the bed and sat on the edge. Andi sat up, wrapped her arms around his waist and laid her head on his naked back.

"I take it that the Dundee agents have arrived in Gallup."

"Yeah, now I won't have to worry about Eddie's safety. No way anybody's going to get to him except through Hunter and Wolfe. And believe me, that isn't going to happen."

"I wish Russ were half as safe." Andi sighed.

Joe turned, lifted her into his arms and placed her on his lap. "We're going to make sure Russ is safe, too. My top priority is to bring your brother home and get him out of this mess he's in."

She hugged Joe. "We're so lucky to have you to look out for us, to care about Russ. I love you for being the kind of man you are."

He kissed her forehead. "You have no idea how much your opinion matters to me."

"I didn't. Not before. But I think I do now."

Jewel paced the floor in her bedroom. She felt trapped. Would she ever be free again? It had been bad enough before, when she had lived in fear that Russ or Eddie would show up on her doorstep and Bobby Yazzi's killer would be right behind them. But now—now that the police knew the truth, that she had witnessed Bobby's murder, that she could identify LeCroy Lanza—her fear had grown.

And since Lieutenant Benny Gishi had moved in with her family yesterday, posing as a relative, she had no sanctuary even in her own home. When the police officer had come to her parents and told them all about the night she had been with Russ Lapahie and Eddie Whitehorn, her mother had wept and her father had barely controlled his rage. But they had agreed with Lieutenant Gishi that the only way to keep their daughter safe was to help bring Russ in so that he and Jewel could testify against LeCroy Lanza and put him behind bars for the rest of his life.

Once Russ was in custody, a warrant could be issued for Lanza's arrest.

She hadn't wanted to take part in the ruse that was planned to bring Russ out into the open but when her father had said she would cooperate, she'd known she had no choice. They had been waiting more than twenty-four hours for Russ to call again. Every time the phone rang she nearly jumped out of her skin. She wasn't sure how good an actress she was. Would she be able to convince Russ that she was willing to meet him? Or would he immediately sense that she was part of a grand scheme to trap him?

A soft knock sounded on her door. She breathed deeply and said, "Come in."

Her brother Leo entered carrying a tray of food. "You haven't eaten anything all day," he said. "You're worrying Mama. Try to eat just a little something. It will make you feel better."

"I don't think I can eat a bite." She eyed the stew and the slice of cake, and knew if she ate anything, she would throw up.

"Russ will call again, and you'll set up a date to meet him at the fair. When this Lanza guy shows up, the police will capture him." Leo placed the tray on her bed, then took her hands in his. "You're going to be okay, little sister. What you're doing is a brave thing, and your family is very proud of you."

"I'm so scared. I'm afraid to sleep. I keep having these dreams about the night Bobby was killed. Sometimes Bobby turns into Russ and sometimes he turns into me. But every time, LeCroy Lanza is laughing as he kills us."

Leo squeezed her hands. "Lanza will not be laughing when the police arrest him."

The phone in the living room rang. Jewel tensed. Leo

gripped her hands even tighter. She whimpered. Almost immediately her father appeared in the doorway.

"Someone wishes to speak to you," Dan Begay said.

"Is it—"

Her father nodded. "It is a young man."

Like a condemned prisonor taking that last walk from her cell to the place of execution, Jewel left her bedroom and shambled across the floor as if she had leg irons attached to her ankles. With a trembling hand, she picked up the receiver from where her father had placed it on the table.

"Hello?"

"Jewel, don't hang up. Damn it, don't hang up!"

"Russ, are you all right?"

She heard a whoosh of air and knew he had released a pent-up breath.

"I'm alive. But I've run out of money and I'm sleeping in a shack and I haven't eaten since yesterday."

"I'm sorry that I hung up on you before, but I was afraid to talk to you."

"I understand," he said. "Look, Jewel, have you heard anything about Eddie?"

"Oh. Yes, yes, I have. He's going to be all right. He's still in the hospital, but they say he's in stable condition."

"That's great. I sure messed up bad and nearly got my best friend killed."

"Russ, I know that you need for me to tell the police about what happened at Bobby's that night, about how—"

"Will you do it, Jewel? Will you really go to the police and tell them?"

"I—I might." She had to make this sound convincing, had to make sure Russ believed her. "Before I agree to go to the police, I want to see you. I want to talk to you."

"Yeah. Sure. You name the place. But it has to be somewhere I think is safe for me to show up."

"I've been thinking about that and I have the perfect solution." Jewel clutched the phone until her knuckles ached from the tension. "The Navajo Nation Fair is going on in Window Rock this week. You know how crowded it will be. No one would notice us meeting in a crowd that large."

"Good idea. When will you be there?"

"My whole family is attending this year," she said. "My parents, Leo and I will leave for Window Rock in the morning. If you can meet me at the entrance to the arts and crafts building around noon, we can find someplace to go and talk. Just the two of us."

"I'll meet you. And Jewel..."

"Yes?"

"Do you think you could bring me some food?" Russ laughed, and the sound was so hollow and sad that Jewel almost burst into tears.

"I—" she swallowed her tears "—I'll bring you some mutton and fry bread."

"With roasted green chilies. I'll dream about it tonight."

"Russ?"

"Yeah?"

"Be very careful."

"Thanks, Jewel. I'll see you tomorrow."

"Okay. Yes. I'll meet you tomorrow. At noon."

"I will be there." Russ paused, his breathing hard, as if he were trying to build up the nerve to say something. "Jewel, you wouldn't betray me, would you?"

"Oh!" she gasped. *I must say the right thing,* she told herself. *If I screw up...* "I promise that I am on your side. I will prove it to you tomorrow."

The dial tone hummed in her ear. She replaced the receiver and turned to Lieutenant Gishi. "Everything is set. He's going to meet me at the entrance to the arts and crafts building at noon tomorrow."

When the word came in from the Tribal Police that Russ had contacted Jewel and everything was set for noon tomorrow, Andi had become a hyperactive demon. She couldn't sit still, couldn't calm down, couldn't be pacified in any way. Finally Joe gave up and suggested they drive out to Blackwood Ranch for a visit. Going to see the new baby was the only thing Joe hadn't tried—it was a last resort. But he figured that if anything or anyone could take Andi's mind off the uncertain outcome of tomorrow's events, holding Mary Helene and playing with the other children might do the trick.

Watching Andi now as she cuddled Mary Helene in her arms, Joe knew he'd done the right thing. The stress had begun to take a toll on Andi and on him. He had promised her that nothing bad would happen to Russ. He had every intention of keeping that vow, even if it meant laying his own life on the line. Once again he was a hero in Andi's eyes. She trusted him. He would rather die than ever lose her trust and have her look at him with anger and disdain.

"I hate to break up this cuddle-fest," Joanna said. "But it's feeding time for my little girl."

Andi kissed Mary Helene on the forehead, then handed her over to her mother and stood. "You're so lucky. You have everything that's important. A husband who worships you and four fantastic children."

Joanna glanced in Joe's direction, then looked at Andi and smiled. "You'll have everything that I do one of these days. You just wait and see."

Joe looked away and caught J.T. staring right at him.

He knew something was up, but J.T. didn't want to speak in front of the ladies.

"I could use a walk after that big dinner Rita fixed for us," Joe said. "How about it, J.T., want to go with me?"

"Yeah, I think I will." Before he left, J.T. wrapped his arm around Joanna, leaned over and planted a kiss on his daughter's cheek. "We'll be just outside if you need us."

Joe had to avert his eyes. The look of love that passed between J.T. and Joanna was such an intensely private thing that he felt embarrassed and yet privileged to have witnessed it. Joe's gaze lifted and immediately connected with Andi's. His gut tightened. Was it love he saw in her eyes, or simply an illusion because love was what he wanted to see? Being around J.T. and Joanna certainly had a way of making a man think about what he did and didn't want for himself in the future.

Do I want a wife and children? he asked himself. And the answer came to him immediately—a resounding *yes*. But could Andi be that wife, the mother of those children?

J.T. nodded toward the foyer. "Ready?"

"Yeah."

The two men went outside. The September night air had a bit of a nip to it. J.T. stuffed his hands into the pockets of his jeans and leaned against the wrought-iron gate that separated the small private yard from the outer grounds.

"You realize that everything has to go down perfectly for us to pull this off tomorrow without a hitch," J.T. said.

"What are you trying to say to me?"

"We all agree that you shouldn't go to the fair tomorrow," J.T. said.

"Who's we?"

"Bill Cummings and Sawyer McNamara from the FBI. We know you aren't Russ's favorite person, so—"

"I'm going to be there," Joe said. "I'll stay out of the way, but if anything goes wrong, I'm coming in. I promised Andi that I'd make sure nothing bad happens to her brother. Surely, you understand how I feel."

"I understand that you're taking a risk by even being there. What if something does go wrong and you can't stop it? You've got an honest-to-God second chance with Andi, but if you're there tomorrow and things go badly, she might blame you. Are you willing to take that risk?"

"I've promised her that I'll protect Russ. How can I keep that promise if I'm not there, taking responsibility for safeguarding his life?"

"Let me take that responsibility," J.T. said. "I've already asked Wolfe to be on hand to help me out, so there's no need—"

"I'm going to the fair tomorrow with Andi. I don't like her being there, but she wants to go and I've accepted the fact that I can't stop her," Joe said. "Right before noon, I'll get out of the way and let you take over. But I'll be close by."

J.T. grunted. "You and Andi should stay away and let us handle things."

"I can't do that," Joe admitted. "And neither can Andi."

LeCroy Lanza nursed the glass of whiskey, then lifted the tumbler to his lips and downed the last drops of the hundred-proof. He wouldn't be drinking any more tonight. He didn't want to wake with a hangover in the morning. Tomorrow his head had to be clear and his hand steady. He had a big job to do—eliminate the only two witnesses to Bobby Yazzi's murder.

One of his loyal informants had called him with the news. There had been a girl with Russ Lapahie that night, just as LeCroy had first thought. Eddie Whitehorn hadn't witnessed the murder.

LeCroy chuckled. Jewel Begay was going to meet up with Russ tomorrow at the Navajo Tribal Fair in Window Rock. The setting was perfect. He could easily slide in unnoticed, find the two teenagers and dispose of them with two quick and easy shots. Then he could blend into the crowd and simply disappear.

Things just happened sometimes, coming together perfectly. Like him finding out about the teenager lovers' rendezvous tomorrow. Hell, if Leo Begay hadn't told a trusted friend about his sister's predicament and that friend hadn't told some other people, then word wouldn't have reached LeCroy.

Of course, there was always the off chance that the whole thing was a setup. A trap. He'd have to be extra careful. And being smarter than the lawmen in these parts would serve him well. He could always send in someone else to do the actual killing, but he preferred handling this job himself, just as he'd done with Bobby. However, it wouldn't hurt to have a little backup—a couple of men to distract the crowds and any law enforcement that might be on hand.

Whatever came down tomorrow at noon, LeCroy knew one thing for certain—Russ Lapahie and Jewel Begay were going to die.

Chapter 16

Andi and Joe blended into the crowd at the Navajo Nation Fair. They had dressed so as to not draw undue attention by either being too "over the top" or by looking like outsiders. Joe had on jeans, a plaid western shirt with silver snaps, his well-worn boots and a small, nondescript headband. He'd also put on his silver-and-turquoise necklace. Andi had chosen a rust-red blouse and tiered print skirt in varying hues of the same rich color. Around her neck she had placed a necklace of turquoise with orange, spiny oyster shell and coral beads. A pair of small turquoise-and-silver earrings dangled from her ears. Joe had wished the bracelet she'd returned to him weren't at his house. He would have liked to see his great-grandfather's jewelry around her wrist once again.

Joe knew Andi was nervous. Hell, he was rattled, and they had only just arrived. By the time noon rolled around, he figured Andi would be on the verge of screaming and he'd be ready to rip off heads if anything went wrong. *Nothing can go wrong!* an inner voice demanded.

The powwow drums undulated between a lulling murmur and a demanding throb. Men and women performed ritual dances to the drums' constant rhythm. Joe and Andi stopped briefly to watch the group of Navajo men as they pounded a four-foot-wide kettledrum. Listening to the beat, Joe thought how very primitive the sound was as it blended with the music of shot-filled, tin-can gourds. Others joined the dancers, each one in turn yelping, whirling and yelping again.

"Do you know where the lawmen have been stationed?" Andi whispered as she leaned close to Joe so he could hear her over the festival din.

"They'll be all over, mixing and mingling in the crowd, just as we're doing," he told her. "And already there are several people in place near the arts and crafts building."

"Odd isn't it, that my shop actually has a display table in that building?" Andi said. "One of my employees, Barbara Redhorse, has been a godsend by taking over the shop's business for me ever since Russ and Eddie got mixed up in this mess."

"Do you want to go over to the building now?" he asked, cupping Andi's elbow to guide her.

"No, I'd rather not. Not yet."

Joe nodded.

He led her along a row of concessions, which the Navajo call "Mutton Row," where vendors served a variety of Native delicacies.

"Would you like something to eat?" Joe asked.

"Lord, no. If I tasted a bite, I'd throw up. My stomach is tied in thousands of knots right now."

Joe and Andi took a tour of the fair, from carnival rides to games of skill and chance, all the while waiting for high noon to arrive. Joe noted the presence of men he recognized, each one blending into the huge crowd. During the week of the fair, as many as 200,000 people took part in the festivities. Every motel in Window Rock and Gallup was filled to capacity. This was the largest all-Indian fair in the country. In the past the fair had been less commercialized, but then, nothing ever stayed the same. Joe sighed. Like the rest of the world, the Navajos were changing with the times. While fiercely holding on to the past, they were adapting to the present.

Joe made eye contact with FBI agent Sawyer McNamara, who looked like a typical cowboy in his boots and Stetson. And when Joe caught a glimpse of DEA agent Vic Noble, he almost did a double take. The guy could easily have passed for a Navajo. Joe couldn't help wondering if some Native American blood flowed through his veins, too.

"What time is it?" Andi asked.

Joe checked his watch. "Eleven-fifteen."

"Oh, God, forty-five more minutes of this," she murmured. "I think I'll go crazy before then."

Joe clasped her hand and hurried her along the midway, weaving them in and out among the shoppers perusing the silver and turquoise jewelry. Andi glanced at the hand-crafted items, obviously trying to act interested, but Joe could tell that this ploy had not taken her mind off Russ and the upcoming showdown.

Once away from the midway, they stopped to rest under a shade tree and to watch the parade of mostly Native Americans, many dressed in vivid costumes. Navajos. Zunis. Hopis, Apaches and even Comanches. Suddenly Andi grabbed Joe's arm as her gaze traveled to the tall man wearing a black eye patch who meandered through the crowd a good thirty feet away. "J.T. is here," Andi said.

"Hmm." Joe looked up at the sky. Bright blue and clear. Only thin, milky white clouds were scattered across the horizon. And the sun was high, almost directly overhead. "Let's walk," he said.

"Where to?"

"How about over there?" He pointed to a steel-shell pavilion.

Andi chuckled. "Don't tell me that you want to go take a look at the entries in the canned food competition."

"Sure, why not?"

Before they reached the pavilion, Joe saw David Wolfe. J.T. had asked Wolfe to be here today, to act as backup. The man was the best marksman Joe had ever known. Despite the warmth of the day, Wolfe wore a jacket. Lightweight tan leather with fringe. The jacket concealed his weapon. And although the man had to be hot, not even one dot of perspiration was visible on his face. Joe mentally shrugged. It was as if Wolfe weren't quite human, as if he didn't suffer from the same physical weaknesses as other men.

"When is Jewel Begay supposed to get here?" Andi asked.

Joe drew his attention away from Wolfe. "Jewel and her family are already here. They arrived shortly before we did."

"I can only imagine what that poor girl is going through right now."

"She's doing a brave thing today."

"Everyone is here and in place, right?" Andi asked.

"Right."

"The only person who hasn't shown up, as far as we know, is Russ."

"He could be here already but no one has spotted him yet."

Joe grabbed her hand and pulled her along to where people were dancing to a low, soft drumming and chanting rhythm. He linked their arms together and led her into the circle dance, two-stepping sideways. She moved with him, keeping time to the music and allowing the beat to become a part of her. All around them people danced. Young and old alike. Husbands and wives. Fathers and daughters. Old men. Teenagers. Everyone participating. Most talked to their partners as they danced. But Joe and Andi remained silent for the duration, each allowing the music to flow through them and, even if only temporarily, remove them from reality.

LeCroy Lanza adjusted the wire-frame glasses and checked the hem of the ground-length dress he wore. He wanted to make sure the skirt wasn't so long that it would trip him up, if it became necessary for him to run. His costume was ingenious, if he did say so himself. In this getup, neither Russ Lapahie nor Jewel Begay was likely to recognize him. Not even when he killed them. Would their last thoughts be *Why did that woman shoot me?*

He had brought along a couple of his men, solely as backup. If this meeting between Russ and Jewel turned out to be some sort of trap, then he might have to leave the killing to his subordinates. And if somehow the teenage sweethearts escaped death, he had a contingency plan. He didn't want to leave the country, so departing the good old U.S.A. would be a last resort. Whatever happened, he had no intention of spending even one day in jail for Bobby Yazzi's murder.

Russ had always loved attending the Navajo Nation Fair. Last year Eddie had taken home a blue ribbon for his prize sheep in the 4-H contest. And they'd both run off laughing after Russ had stolen a kiss from one of the Miss Navajo contestants. How could things have changed so much in a year? How could things have gone so wrong? Eddie should be here today, having fun and acting like a teenager instead of lying in a hospital bed, recuperating from a bullet wound. *And if it weren't for my stupidity, he would be,* Russ reminded himself.

Russ tried his best to mingle with the crowd and act as if he were just one more Navajo enjoying himself at the fair. He checked his watch: eleven forty-five. That gave him fifteen minutes to keep a low profile before he met up with Jewel. Suddenly, in his peripheral vision, he caught a glimpse of a tall man wearing a tan Stetson and a black eye patch. He turned around just enough for a second glance. J.T. Blackwood! Damn, he couldn't let J.T. see him. And if J.T. was here, then Joanna and the kids were probably somewhere close by. Any one of them, even the twins, would recognize him. Russ hurried in the other direction, weaving his way through the thicket of happy, laughing people.

He could go to the arts and crafts building now, he told himself. The place would be crowded. Yeah, but some of the men in that crowd just might be police. He couldn't let them catch him before he talked to Jewel. He had to make sure she would back up his story before he decided what to do.

Joe left Andi at precisely five minutes before twelve, after cautioning her to stay exactly where he left her. Close enough to see what was happening, but far enough to be out of harm's way. She promised him that she would stay put, and he had no choice but to take her at her word. Joe glanced right and left, seeking confirmation that everyone was in place. That everything was as it should be. Wolfe stood with his arms across his chest, one hand inside his jacket. In the distance Joe saw one of the plain-clothes police officers give another the signal. *Russ La-pahie has been spotted.*

Joe exchanged a brief glance with Jewel Begay. The petite brunette stood stiff as a marble statue, fear etched on every feature of her pretty little face. Joe passed her without a word and stepped inside the arts and crafts building, then turned so that he could watch for Russ's approach.

The minutes pounded inside his head with each beat of his heart. He checked the time again. Straight up noon. An operation like this never occurred on the minute, he reminded himself. Russ might not show at the arts and crafts building for another ten or fifteen minutes. The boy could be scanning the area, making sure Jewel wasn't being watched. Joe hoped that no one gave himself away and alerted Russ. If Russ took much longer, there was every chance Jewel would come apart completely. Joe could tell just by looking at her that she was on the verge of an emotional collapse.

Russ saw her standing alone in front of the arts and crafts building. She looked so pretty in her blue dress. She had plaited her hair into one long braid, which hung over her shoulder. Her gaze kept moving, looking right and left and then straight ahead again. She was looking for him, waiting impatiently. He sensed her fear and understood it only too well. He was scared stiff himself. *Remember to tell her how brave she is,* an inner voice reminded him. *And let her know how much her doing the right thing means to you. You'll owe her for the rest of your life for having the courage to tell the truth.*

Russ waited for a few minutes, watching the crowd,

taking special note of everyone who went in or came out of the building where Jewel waited. He didn't see anyone he knew or anyone who looked suspicious. A group of young kids chased one another. One of them accidently ran into Jewel. She cried out and jumped as if she'd been shot. A tall, ugly woman, wearing a purple Navajo dress, an abundance of turquoise jewelry, a pair of gold-rimmed glasses and a trading-post style hat, gave the boys a disapproving glare and shooed them away. Then she smiled at Jewel before disappearing inside the building.

Two women, one holding a baby on her hip, passed right beside Russ. They chatted away in Saad, talking about their husbands. A white guy in a fringed leather jacket stood only a couple of feet from Russ, his attention focused on the crowd. A spectator, no doubt, here to watch the Indians in their Native habitat. Another guy stopped a few feet away from Jewel, leaned back against the wall and pulled out a pack of cigarettes. He looked like he was waiting for someone, too. A girlfriend maybe or... But before Russ had a chance to finish the thought, the guy waved at somebody in the crowd and rushed off to join her.

Russ walked toward the arts and crafts building. Jewel saw him. She started to lift her hand, but didn't. Her gaze locked with his, and he followed that linked stare, each step taking him closer and closer to the one person who could give him back his life.

As he watched Russ approaching, Joe eased toward the doorway, making sure he could see but not be seen. He stood less than ten feet behind Jewel. With the girl's back to him, he had a perfect view of Russ's face. A combination of fear and happiness comprised the boy's expression as he drew near.

A flash of purple swept past Joe as a tall Navajo woman walked out of the building. Joe thought she had to be the ugliest woman he'd ever seen and one of the biggest. She looked more like a man in drag. For a couple of seconds her body blocked Joe's view. An odd sensation hit him in the pit of his stomach. Something was wrong. But what? A flash of metal glistened in the sunlight. Joe's gaze traveled quickly to the big woman's hand—holding a gun! Realization hit him, like a ton of bricks falling out of the sky.

Damn! Damn! How could he have been so blind? The woman was too tall. Too ugly. Her movements unfeminine. She walked like a man because...she *was* a man.

Joe motioned to the lawmen placed strategically inside the building, then he eased outside and prepared to attack. Everything happened all at once. The pseudo-woman was right behind Jewel. Joe's first instinct was to call out a warning, but who would be alerted by his cry?

As he raced out of the building, Joe heard Russ speak to Jewel. "Hi. Thanks for coming."

"I'm sorry it took me so long to agree to help you," Jewel said.

The person in the purple dress bumped into Jewel, and when Jewel turned to see who was behind her, the man-in-disguise pressed himself against her back. Only because Joe was so close was he able to see that the man held a knife in one hand and a pistol in the other. The knife, which could be seen only from a certain angle, was pointed downward directly at Jewel's lower back. The gun barrel glistened as the man tried to hide it in the folds of the massive purple garment.

Jewel's face lost all color. Her eyes grew large and glazed over with sheer terror. Her lips parted on an indrawn breath. Her mouth rounded in a silent cry. Drums boom-boomed. The drone of laughter and conversation filled the air. The yelp of dancers echoed in the distance. People milled all around them. Innocent fair-goers had no idea they were in danger.

With only a couple of feet between them, Russ froze to the spot, directly in front of Jewel and the purple-clad angel of death. No doubt, Russ had somehow recognized Lanza. Moving as casually as possible, Joe walked around to the side of the threesome. When he did, he saw Jewel's lips moving. She was mouthing the word *run* to Russ. Joe realized that Lanza didn't realize he'd been spotted, that he didn't know anyone other than Jewel and Russ were aware of who he was or that *he* wasn't a *she*.

Sunlight reflected off metal as the man lifted his arm. A wide silver bracelet circled his wrist. And a 9-mm Sig Sauer pointed directly at Russ. Three things happened simultaneously. Andi came out of nowhere, placing herself in the line of fire as she ran toward Russ. The purple-clad man shoved a knife into Jewel's back and stepped around her fallen body to grab Russ. And a bevy of small children carrying balloons came between Wolfe and his target.

Russ and his abductor disappeared into the crowd.

Joe motioned to the lawmen directly behind him, and two officers immediately rushed to check on Jewel. Joe grabbed Andi's arm and dragged her through the throng, then shoved her toward Wolfe. "Take care of her."

"I can handle things for you," Wolfe said.

"Yeah, I know you can, but it is something I need to do."

Wolfe nodded.

Andi realized that she had inadvertently jeopardized Russ's life and Jewel's. She had acted on instinct because she hadn't been sure that anyone else saw what was happening—that the tall Navajo woman was no woman and that *he* had a gun in his hand.

Andi started to follow Joe, but Wolfe held her wrist. She stared into the coldest green eyes she'd ever seen. A shiver of fear raced up her spine. "Please. I have to go with him."

Wolfe nodded, and together they followed Joe through the crowd but didn't catch up with him. Andi suspected that Wolfe deliberately kept her a safe distance behind. She caught a glimpse of J.T.; then Bill Cummings appeared at J.T.'s side. She sensed more than she noticed a hum of activity, and she understood that the lawmen gathered at the fair were on the move.

And then she heard the awful sounds. Gunfire. People screaming.

Joe figured that the gunfire was between some of Lanza's goons and the law. A distraction to draw attention away from Lanza and Russ. Ignoring the uproar the gunfire caused, Joe kept them in view—Russ and the person he felt in his gut had to be LeCroy Lanza. Once or twice he lost them in the crowd, but then caught sight of them again as they hurried through the chaotic masses.

As frightened people ran helter-skelter, some screaming, Joe stayed the coarse, keeping a discrete distance behind his prey. He followed them to the parking area. Lanza led Russ in and out between the parked vehicles. Did the guy know he was being followed? Joe didn't think so. Lanza acted as if he thought he'd gotten away safely.

Silent as a panther, Joe crept up on his quarry. His heart roared inside his head when, looking up from his crouched position, he saw Lanza's reflection in the rearview mirror. The guy shoved Russ up against the side of the truck and lifted the gun. Bile rose in Joe's throat. The bastard was going to shoot Russ in the head.

He had one chance to stop Lanza and save Russ. He had to act fast and shoot straight. He was almost as good a marksman as Wolfe. He prayed that would be good enough.

The truck's windows were rolled down, leaving no glass to obstruct the bullet's projection. With lightning speed, Joe jumped up, aimed and fired. A look of pure shock crossed Lanza's face. Blood trickled from the hole between his eyes. His hand gripping the pistol lifted straight up into the air, and the 9-mm fired into the sky. Then Lanza slumped over and disappeared behind the truck.

Joe raced to the other side of the old pickup. Lanza lay on the ground, his sightless eyes seeming to stare straight up. Russ stood by the truck, shivering. His gaze met Joe's.

"Are you all right?" Joe asked.

"Yeah."

Joe approached Russ, uncertain how the boy would react to him. But when he placed his hand on Russ's shoulder, Andi's little brother looked at him with a quivering smile on his lips.

"Man, I thought I was dead," Russ said. "I saw Andi before Lanza caught me. And I thought I saw you, but I wasn't sure. I didn't know what was going to happen." Russ stopped, clutched Joe's arm and groaned. "How's Jewel? He knifed her, didn't he?"

"I'm sure Jewel is on her way to the hospital right now."

Suddenly Joe and Russ were surrounded by representatives of various law enforcement agencies. Wolfe released his hold on Andi, who ran toward her brother. She grabbed him and hugged him, and then kissed him on both cheeks.

"What the hell's going on here?" Russ pulled free of his sister's hold and glanced around at the army of lawmen surrounding the parking area.

"We'll explain everything later," Joe said. "For now, the police are going to want a statement. After you're finished up at the police station, then we'll go to the hospital and check on Jewel."

Russ turned to Andi. "Joe saved my life."

"Yes, I know."

"I thought I couldn't trust him." Russ held out his hand to Joe. "Thank you for helping me. I owe you my life."

"You don't owe me a thing," Joe said. "I owed your father."

"Yeah, I understand." Russ clamped his hands together, obviously trying to stop them from shaking. "I guess your debt to him has been paid in full."

Andi slipped one arm around Russ's waist and then grasped Joe's hand, drew him to her and wrapped her other arm around his waist. The three of them, side by side, walked toward the waiting lawmen.

Two weeks later, Joanna and J.T. Blackwood hosted a barbeque to celebrate the release of two patients from the hospital. Eddie and Jewel held the place of honor at the day's festivities. Three families were united by a common emotion—thankfulness. The Lapahies. The Whitehorns. The Begays. Each had come close to losing a child. After Mr. Lavato refused to press charges against the boys for "borrowing" his truck, the police agreed they had no reason to prosecute Russ or Eddie or Jewel.

Andi and Joe watched the younger children playing in the pool, and the older ones laughing and talking. Had it not been for the cooperation and hard work of so many people, this perfect day could not have happened, Andi thought. But the person most responsible for her happiness was Joe Ornelas, who had not only saved her brother's life, but had announced only a few minutes ago that he planned to remain in New Mexico, on the reservation. She understood, even if no one else did, that Joe was staying not just for himself and perhaps even for her, but for Russ and Eddie. The boys needed someone to look up to in their lives, a role model to show them what a modern Navajo warrior should be.

Russ left the other kids and came over to where Andi and Joe were sitting. He nodded to Joe, who returned the gesture.

"I want to talk to you," Russ said.

"Sure. Here or in private?" Joe asked.

"Here's fine." Russ smiled at Andi and then looked back at Joe. "I just thought you should know that if you and Andi want to get back together...you know, get married or something, then it's okay with me."

Andi's mouth fell open. Joe chuckled. Russ grinned, then turned and went back to his friends.

"Joe, I don't—" Andi said.

He shot to his feet, grabbed her hand and said, "Russ might not have needed any privacy for what he had to say, but I do."

"What?"

He led her into the house and down the hall, all but dragging her in his haste. He pulled her into the nearest room, which just happened to be a powder room. After flipping on the overhead light, he closed the door, then eased her up against the wall and kissed her. He took her breath away. She shoved on his chest until he stopped kissing her. He gazed into her eyes, a soft smile curving his lips.

"Andrea Stephens, in case you don't already know it, I thought it was about time that I told you I love you."

"You do?"

"Yes, I do. Very much."

"I love you, too," she said.

"That's what I was hoping you would say." He delved into his vest pocket and brought out the silver-and-turquoise bracelet that she had returned to him only a few short weeks ago. "I want you to have this." He clasped the wide band around her wrist.

She fingered the bracelet. Joe stuck two fingers down into his shirt pocket and came up with a ring. Andi stared at the shimmering, square-cut topaz surrounded by small diamonds.

"I bought this in Albuquerque yesterday," he said. "The minute I saw it, the golden stone reminded me of your eyes."

"Joe, it's beautiful."

"Not half as beautiful as your eyes." He lifted her hand and slipped the ring on the third finger of her left hand. "Andi, will you marry me?"

"Oh, Joe." Tears clouded her vision. She flung her arms around him and cried, "Yes, yes, a thousand times yes."

He kissed her again. Hard and hot, but quick. "Let's go out there and announce our engagement today. And then you and Joanna had better get started on planning a wedding. I don't want to wait to make you my wife. Do you think you two can pull something together in a couple of weeks?"

"A couple of weeks?" She snuggled up against him, her arms around his neck. "I think that can definitely be arranged."

Epilogue

The new Navajo Tribal Police captain, Joseph Ornelas, posed for a picture with his wife and their two children, eight-year-old Seth and five-year-old Dinah. At twenty, Joe's niece, Summer Whitehorn, had become quite an accomplished photographer and she loved to practice, using family and friends as her subjects. Andi had arranged this family event to celebrate Joe's promotion. She was so proud of her husband. In the ten years since he had returned to New Mexico, their lives had become more enriched with each passing year. And with the births of their children, their marriage had only strengthened.

Kate brought out a tray of fresh fruit and added it to the table already overflowing with food. Joanna Blackwood poured iced tea into tall glasses, and Doli Lapahie placed a bouquet of fresh flowers in the center of the banquet.

"I do hope Eddie doesn't forget about the party," Kate said. "I called him this morning to remind him, but the boy lives and breathes those horses."

"'Those horses' are making a lot of money for Joe and Eddie," Andi reminded her sister-in-law. "Breeding thoroughbreds is a lucrative business. And Eddie is doing a fine job of running the O&W Ranch."

Five years ago, when Eddie graduated from college, Joe had invested in Eddie's idea for a horse ranch, and under Eddie's management the venture had been a huge success.

"Mama, I'm hungry," Dinah said. "When are we going to eat?"

Andi looked down at her daughter and, as she did every time she gazed into Dinah's black eyes, saw Joe staring back at her. "Eddie is running a little late today. As soon as he gets here, we'll eat."

"When will that be?"

"Soon, my darling."

Joanna lifted a strawberry from the fruit tray and handed it to Dinah. "Nibble on this. If Eddie and— If Eddie doesn't get here soon, we'll go ahead and start without him."

Andi had been having one of her odd feelings all morning, and just now she had picked up on Joanna's slip of the tongue. Who else was Joanna expecting? The Blackwood clan was here, as were the Whitehorns, minus Eddie. The Ornelas family was all accounted for. And Doli was here, too. Excitement tightened Andi's stomach. Could it be? she wondered. Yes, of course, that was it!

As if her thinking about them conjured them up, the front door opened and in walked Eddie Whitehorn. At his side was Lieutenant Russ Lapahie, U.S.N. They hadn't seen Russ in over a year and they hadn't heard a word from him since he had returned from his last assignment as a Navy SEAL.

Doli gasped and began crying. Russ made a beeline to his mother. After hugging her and wiping away her tears, he turned and grabbed Andi, lifted her off her feet and whirled her around.

The minute Russ put her down, Andi pointed her finger at Joe's nephew. "Eddie Whitehorn, you knew Russ was coming home, didn't you?" Then she eyed Joanna. "And so did you and J.T."

"I drove to the airport to pick him up," Eddie said. "He's going to be home two whole weeks."

Joe walked over and held out his hand to Russ, who immediately accepted his brother-in-law's greeting. "You're looking fit these days, Lieutenant," Joe said.

"So are you, Captain."

"Son, we're proud of you. I hope you know that."

"Thanks, Joe. I guess when you first married Andi, you had your work cut out with me, didn't you? But by example, you showed me what a man should be." Then he grinned and embraced the man who had become like a second father to him.

Later, Eddie and Russ mingled with the others. Andi looked on and thought, another good day in an altogether happy life. Today was special for two reasons: Joe's promotion, of course, but also Russ's homecoming. She had been opposed to Russ joining the service after college and greatly opposed to him becoming a SEAL. But Joe had pointed out that her brother had a right to live his own life and that the wild, adventurous streak in Russ would be channeled into productive work in the special forces. He seldom came home, and occasionally Andi felt as if they had lost him to that wide world outside the reservation. But in her heart, she knew that someday he would come home for good.

By late afternoon, with all the youngsters piled into J.T.'s SUV and Eddie's truck, half their guests were headed out to the O&W Ranch to ride horses and pet the new colts. Joe and Andi plopped down on the sofa in the den and put their feet up on the coffee table.

"Quite a day, wasn't it?" Joe said.

"One of life's perfect days," she told him.

He draped his arm around her shoulder, and she cuddled close. After the day's excitement, the house was eerily silent.

"We have a couple of hours before we have to leave for the ranch to pick up Seth and Dinah." Joe nuzzled her neck. "Do you have any suggestions on how we can spend those two hours?"

"Well, you could help me do some laundry, or we could watch a movie on TV, or—"

Joe kissed her. She giggled. He swallowed the sound as he intensified the kiss. When he finally let her come up for air, she gasped.

"Any other suggestions, Mrs. Ornelas?" he asked.

"Well, I can think of a project upstairs in our bedroom that will require both of us to accomplish it. And I'm sure we can get it done in two hours."

Joe stood, swept her into his arms and headed toward the stairs. Andi laughed, her heart overflowing with happiness.

Her life with Joe was just as she had dreamed it would be when she first came to the reservation. Perfect.

* * * * *

Look for Whitelaw's Wedding
the next exciting book in Beverly Barton's series,
THE PROTECTORS,
available in May from
Silhouette Intimate Moments.

INTIMATE MOMENTS™

presents a riveting 12-book continuity series:

A Year of loving dangerously

Where passion rules and nothing is what it seems...

When dishonor threatens a top-secret agency, the brave
men and women of SPEAR are prepared to risk it all as they
put their lives—and their hearts—on the line.

Available April 2001:

THE WAY WE WED
by Pat Warren

They had married in secret, two undercover agents with nothing to
lose—except maybe the love of a lifetime. For though Jeff Kirby tried to
keep Tish Buckner by his side, tragedy tore the newlyweds apart. Now
Tish's life hung in the balance, and Jeff was hoping against hope that he
and Tish would get a second chance at the life they'd once dreamed of.
For this time, the determined M.D. wouldn't let his woman get away!

July 2000: MISSION: IRRESISTIBLE by Sharon Sala #1016
August: UNDERCOVER BRIDE by Kylie Brant #1022
September: NIGHT OF NO RETURN by Eileen Wilks #1028
October: HER SECRET WEAPON by Beverly Barton #1034
November: HERO AT LARGE by Robyn Amos #1040
December: STRANGERS WHEN WE MARRIED by Carla Cassidy #1046
January 2001: THE SPY WHO LOVED HIM by Merline Lovelace #1052
February: SOMEONE TO WATCH OVER HER by Margaret Watson #1058
March: THE ENEMY'S DAUGHTER by Linda Turner #1064
April: THE WAY WE WED by Pat Warren #1070
May: CINDERELLA'S SECRET AGENT by Ingrid Weaver #1076
June: FAMILIAR STRANGER by Sharon Sala #1082

*Available only from Silhouette Intimate Moments
at your favorite retail outlet.*

Where love comes alive™

Visit Silhouette at www.eHarlequin.com   SIMAYOLD11

LINDSAY McKENNA

continues her most popular series with a
brand-new, longer-length book.

And it's the story you've been waiting for....

Morgan's Mercenaries:
Heart of Stone

They had met before. Battled before. And
Captain Maya Stevenson had never again
wanted to lay eyes on Major Dane York—
the man who once tried to destroy
her military career! But on their latest
mission together, Maya discovered that beneath
the fury in Dane's eyes lay a raging passion. Now she
struggled against dangerous desire, as Dane's command
over her seemed greater still. For this time, he laid claim
to her heart....

Only from Lindsay McKenna and Silhouette Books!

"When it comes to action and romance,
nobody does it better than Ms. McKenna."
—*Romantic Times Magazine*

Available in March at your favorite retail outlet.